Dragon Fire

ᴬ Tiger Lily's Café® Mystery

By Kathleen Thompson

Kathleen Thompson

Dragon Fire

Volume 12

ᴬ Tiger Lily's Café® Mystery

By Kathleen Thompson

ISBN-13: 978-1-7320166-1-3

ISBN-10: 1-7320166-1-5

© Registration # TX 8-707-146

Library of Congress Control Number: 2019901933

Kathleen Thompson

A List of Tiger Lily's Café® Mystery Series Books:

This cozy mystery series has everything you seek: an eclectic cast of characters, a mystery or two, and diligent detectives on duty. The detectives just happen to be feline.

Tiger Lily's Café is set in a Midwestern town nestled into the coast of a Great Lake. The setting itself acts as a character, bringing the reader into the sights, sounds and smells of the small resort community of Chelsea.

Read the series in order, or read any book alone. While characters grown and change, each volume stands alone with a clear beginning and a clear end.

- Turtle Soup (2014)
- Boo! (2015)
- Phishing (2015)
- Holiday (2016)
- A Rock And A Hard Place (2016)
- Splash (2016)
- Chasing A Butterfly (2017)
- Pumpkin Squash (2017)
- Snowblind (2017)
- Hearts On Fire (2018)
- Morel Of The Story (2018)
- Dragon Fire (2019)
- Beach Bunnies (2020)
- Shipwreck (2020)

Kathleen Thompson

Kathleen Thompson

Cast of Characters

Humans

Annie Mack, with the help of her "kids" and a talented staff, owns and manages a bed and breakfast, a cafe and other businesses on the south side of The Avenue. She has lived in Chelsea for only a few years, but her ancestral roots to the town date to the Civil War era.

Annie's SASHET Rainbow: (sa SHAY) a model that assigns color to each core feeling. **S**adness is blue; **A**nger red; **S**care green; **H**appiness yellow; **E**xcitement orange; and **T**enderness purple.

For more information, visit Liberation Psychotherapy: www.libpsych.com/articles/sashet/sashet.html.

Austin and Angela live in another state. They are the parents of Chris and have not been supportive of his career in the Coast Guard or his choice of a woman. Annie.

Ben and JoJo are college students. They work part-time all over town, including most of Annie's businesses.

Boone is the person to call if you need anything: mowing, snow removal, landscaping, maintenance, preventative maintenance, and just about anything else. He is married to **Harriet (Hilly)**, who provides business cleaning services. His sons **Daryl** and **Donny** work for him. Their roots are in rural Appalachia, and they are so much more than people think.

Brian and Janet Thomas own the Chateau Simon Winery in rural Chelsea. Their biggest competition is the Blue Bottle Winery. Jesus and Minnie are their silent partners.

Candice is the head waitress at Mo's Tap. A native of Chelsea, her long, thick, dark hair is the envy of most women who meet her. She is married to George.

Carlos is the manager and baker at Mr. Bean's Confectionary. He is a citizen of the US but was originally from Mexico. He supports his mother and younger sisters, who still live there. He is married to Isabel.

Cheryl inherited The Marina from her parents. It's a small deep water marina with basic amenities. Cheryl is married to Ray. She has known Annie since they were children.

Chris is Annie's special friend. They have committed to a permanent relationship that doesn't necessarily include marriage. He is the Officer in Charge of the Coast Guard Station. His stress relieving hobby is art. His watercolors and sketches – in charcoal, pencil and pastel – are sold for charity.

Clara owns the flower and gift shop, Bloomin' Crazy. She is a citizen of the US, originally from Haiti, and has an ebullient personality. She keeps The Avenue decorated with fresh and silk flowers year-round.

Daniela is a former professional baker from Mexico. She has been a mother figure to Isabel, who is married to Carlos. She and her adult daughters, **Rosa** and **Valeria**, now live in Chelsea

Diana is the chief instructor at L'Socks' Virasana (Veer AHS ana). She is Mem's daughter. Diana left home right after high school and did not speak to her mother until her return ten years later. Their relationship, while tenuous, continues to grow stronger.

Felicity is the chef at Tiger Lily's Café. She is young, perky and extremely talented in the kitchen. She manages the Café, the upstairs catering facility and outside catering operations.

Frank owns an antique shop, Antiques On Main. He and Mem are in a relationship.

Gema owns Gema's Creations. She makes and sells unique jewelry pieces from a space in the front corner of Antiques On Main.

George is the bartender and manager of Mo's Tap. He is a top-notch bartender and can be counted on to keep confidences. He is a volunteer with the local Coast Guard and is married to Candice.

Georgia is the head cook at Mo's Tap. Her father, **Fred Calendar**, comes to town on occasion to see her and her daughter Frederica **(Little Fred)**.

Geraldine has turned a corner and is no longer a thorn in Annie's side. She has developed community spirit. Somehow. It's a mystery…. **Everett** is her on-again-off-again husband.

Ginger is the daughter of Pete, the Chief of Police, and Janet. She works part-time at L'Socks' Virasana. Because she moved to town as a teen (when her father retired from the Marine Corps), and because she is one of the few African American teens in town, she sometimes feels like an outsider.

Greg is a progressive realtor in Chelsea. His goal is to get the right property to the right owner, always moving Chelsea forward.

Gwen is Annie's accountant. A motherly figure, her financial acumen is hidden from all but those lucky enough to have her in their corner.

Hank is a former member of the Town Council. He opposes Annie in every way.

Harry is the regular driver for the rental company used almost exclusively by folks on The Avenue.

Henrie manages the KaliKo Inn in an elegant manner. He does not invite confidences and speaks little about himself. Always formal in tone, people have difficulty pegging his accent. Is it French? Cameroon? Rwandan?

Holly and Jolly, twins, own DoubleGood, an electronics and hardware store. Holly lives in a wheelchair. Natives of Chelsea, they used to hate the names given them by their parents. Now, they enjoy the novelty of it.

Ian is a childhood friend of George. He coordinates local sporting and community events. He is light-hearted and fancy-free, especially for a loan officer at a local bank.

Isabel is married to Carlos. She is attending classes to become a citizen. She works in the kitchen at Mo's Tap.

Janet is Pete's wife. She spent twenty years as a Marine officer's wife. She traveled the world and is now living in Chelsea. She is an outsider, not having grown up here like Pete. She is the ultimate community volunteer.

Jeff Bennett is a Special Agent with the FBI. He visits on occasion to help with local investigations.

Jennifer and Marie, sisters and nurse practitioners, own The Drug Store and The Clinic. Folks call the sisters before calling nine-one-one. Chelsea natives, they know everyone. And their secrets.

Jenny is an attorney who focuses on family law. She enjoys taking on cases that will right an injustice. She is always ready to engage in battle with those who don't believe a woman, much less a woman of color, can dance with the big boys.

Jerry learned how to make candy in a minimum security federal prison. He was not an employee. Jerry works hard to overcome his shyness, particularly around women.

Jet is from Puerto Rico. He moved in with Holly and Jolly, taking up residence with Holly. He works at Sassy P's Wine & Cheese.

Jerry is the candy maker at Mr. Bean's Confectionary. He learned how to make candy in a minimum security federal prison. He was not an employee.

Jesus manages Sassy P's Wine & Cheese and also selects the wines. His family, famous vintners in the Napa Valley, owned, farmed and made wine for generations before California became a part of the United States.

Joan is a member of the Town Council. She opposes Hank in every way. Clara's pet name for her is "Joan of Chelsea."

Juanita is a reporter for the local newspaper. As every reporter on every small town paper, she also sells ads, develops and places the ads, does photography and…reports.

Justin is a former bully boy who now works for Boone. Justin is making a break from his former bad partners and misplaced energy. He attends community college part-time.

Laila owns Babar Foods. A traditional Pakistani, she is raising her children without the assistance of a husband. Her children are **James**, **Ava** and **Carl**, who lives with Autism.

Maggie is the animal control officer from Marsh Haven, the county seat.

Marco is a police officer in Chelsea. He is "second in command" because he was the only officer that didn't go off-kilter during a hostage situation. Marco prides himself on being one-hundred-percent-Italian-American.

Martha used to own a bed and breakfast. The cottage was renovated to add an apartment suite, now occupied by Georgia and Little Fred. Martha is retired and enjoys spending time at the Inn.

Mem owns the health food store and cyber café, CyberHealth. Her wisdom is reassuring to everyone, including her daughter, Diana. She teaches the safe use of social media to all ages and has equipment and technology that is helpful to the small-town police department.

Minnie chooses perfect cheeses to accompany the rotating wine selections at Sassy P's Wine & Cheese. She comes from several generations of cheese makers in Wisconsin.

Nancy and Sam are Annie's mother and step-father. They have been married since Annie was a child. They moved to Chelsea to be closer to Annie.

Pete is a native of Chelsea. He retired from the Marine Corps and is now the Chief of Police. Like Annie, his ancestors arrived in the Civil War era. His, however, came up via the Underground Railroad. He and his wife Janet have three children, the eldest of whom is Ginger. Clarice and Tamara are in high school and junior high.

Ramon is Clara's boyfriend. A Jamaican by ancestry, he plays saxophone with a jazz fusion band called Bergamasco (after the breed of his dog). He and Clara work hard to maintain their mostly long-distance relationship.

Ray owns and operates The Escape, a yacht fashioned into a cruiser for fishing, diving and pleasure. He is married to Cheryl; Chris is his best friend.

Tank is the Chief of the local fire department. He grew up in Chelsea and knows everyone in town.

Teresa came to this community to serve. She pastors a small church, Soul's Harbor, and pastors the community through her outreach.

Terrence and Jerald Timmer-Schmidt are recent arrivals to Chelsea. Terrence is a heart surgeon; Jerald is a psychiatrist. They opened a medical office building in town.

Trudie is the barista at Tiger Lily's Café. She is from Jamaica and ended up in Chelsea when a former boyfriend dumped her at the campground. Felicity saved her, and they have been the best of friends ever since.

WQVX Channel Two. "The Lake Region's good news station." The "ace onsite reporter" is **Dan Tapper**. **Felix** does weather.

Annie's Cats

Annie has seven cats. Most people would call them "rescue kitties." From Annie's perspective, each of them rescued her.

Tiger Lily is a beautiful tabby cat with soft green eyes. She is the titular manager of Tiger Lily's Café, the main gathering place for Chelsea. She is generally calm and logical.

Little Socks is a bright-eyed black cat with white socks. She has a commanding personality and is small and sneaky enough to serve as a cat burglar. She spends time at the yoga studio, L'Socks' Virasana (Veer AHS ana).

Kali, Ko and Mo are litter mates. They shared a secret language as kittens; Kali and Ko now speak "cat," but Mo still speaks "secret." Kali and Ko can be found at the KaliKo Inn, a lakeside bed and breakfast. Mo spends time at Mo's Tap, an upscale blues bar.

Sassy Pants is aptly named; it's difficult to keep this little girl's attention. She is overly sensitive and will react out of emotion instead of reason. She entertains at Sassy P's Wine & Cheese.

Mr. Bean is the baby of the family and is mostly gray with traces of tiger. He has two speeds: fast and love me.

Other Companions

Brown Mousie lives in the long building and roams from the Café to the Wine & Cheese shop. He stays primarily at Sassy P's.

Claire is a blue point Himalayan cat whose human is Frank. She's beautiful and loves people. She is stand-offish with other cats.

Cyril is an English setter whose human is Pete, the Chief of Police. Cyril is friendly and calm. He is an excellent hunter.

Daryll is a multi-colored tabby cat with an air of perpetual confusion. His original human was the manager of the state park. Following his untimely death, Daryll was rescued by Tiger Lily and eventually went to live with Martha.

Fiamma is a Bergamasco. Dreadlocks cover her face. In fact, her entire body is covered with a combination of long dreadlocks and mats of hair. She is an outrageous flirt. Her human is Ramon.

Honey Bear is a large, golden, long-haired mutt of a cat who believes it is his perfect right to be anywhere. Other cats hate him. His human is Annie's mother, Nancy.

Jock is a Portuguese water dog whose human is Ray, the captain of The Escape. Jock is spirited and affectionate; he loves children.

Moriah is a dilute calico cat with long hair and a lioness mane. She is "fluffy" all over, with a sexy little waddle. Clara is her fur-ever human.

Oscar McMurphy was a stray, named Scaredy Cat by Annie's cats. Despite the name, she is a girl who now lives with Holly and Jolly. She claims Holly as her very own. She is often in and out of the Inn and other places on The Avenue with her brother, Simon Finnegan.

Simon Finnegan was a stray, named Fat Cat by Annie's cats, who now lives with Holly and Jolly. He claims Jolly to be his mom. He is often in and out of the Inn and other places on The Avenue with his sister, Oscar McMurphy.

Simon is a famous local winery cat. He lives at Chateau Simon Winery. His humans are Brian and Janet Thomas. He is a tuxedo cat with a wicked white stripe from his nose to the middle of his eyes.

Sis is a dark gray giant schnauzer. Tiger Lily rescued her during a snow storm. Together, the kids introduced her to Chris, who is now her human.

Speckles is a tortoise shell cat, named for her orange speckles. She belongs to Georgia and is Little Fred's chief nanny.

Tillie came to live on The Avenue with her dreadful family from England. She is a Jack Russell Terrier and now lives with Carlos and Isabel above the Confectionary. She has free run of The Avenue, including the Inn. She is small enough to squeeze in and out of the cat doors.

Guests at the Inn

Don and Suellen have come to town to get married on The Escape. They will be joined by their friends from Marsh Haven, **Percy and Sarah**.

Kara has come to town to visit Candice and George.

Wyatt has come for the week. He's from Veterans' Affairs at the State Capital and hope to provide services for the homeless veterans in Chelsea.

Guests for the Ultimate Scavenger Hunt

Contenders staying in the Carriage House

- **Bill & Kristen**
- **Chet & Justine**
- **Damien & Tasha**
- **Thad & Treena**
- **Tim & Barbara**

Moderators staying in the Inn

- **Bonita**
- **Rich**

Homeless Veterans

- **Ben** (Army) served in the Gulf War, Desert Storm. He has no visible injuries, but he jumps at the smallest sounds.
- **Farrell** (Army) served in the Gulf War, Desert Storm. He escaped without an arm and one eye. His face is scarred with third degree burns.
- **Gene** (Army) served in Afghanistan. He wants to get off the street.

- **Harper** (Army) served in the Gulf War, Desert Storm. He suffers from leg and back injuries.
- **Malcolm** (Army) served in the Gulf War, Desert Storm. He has a nose for drugs.
- **Perry** (Marine Corps) served in Afghanistan. He has a nose for booze and can find a stray bottle or can anywhere.
- **Tempo** (Army) served in the Gulf War, Desert Storm. Tempo is not his given name. He can't stop moving; he is always in rhythm to something in his head.

1

Tiger Lily pressed her nose against the window pane. Her siblings and their friends from the neighborhood surrounded her at the back of the Café. They watched Pete and the Chief of the Fire Department across the street. They conferred by their cars, red lights still flashing. Cyril paced back and forth, agitated. He glanced at the cats in the window from time to time to shake his head. On every third turn, he let out a mournful howl.

On this cool June morning, the Café was more crowded than usual. Locals and tourists shared what they knew and started rumors with what they didn't know.

From the table facing The Avenue, she heard two men. They were older, apparently hard of hearing, and definitely missing a screw or two.

"There was a fire at the old marina."

"I heard it was that upscale condo place."

"No, the marina. There was something about a boat."

"No, it was an abandoned building."

"At the marina."

"No, the condo place."

"What building is abandoned over there? Did you drive by?"

"No. I heard it from Joe who said he could see it."

"From where? Joe lives on the southeast side of town."

"He, well, I thought he said he saw it. He might have said Tully saw it."

"That makes sense. Tully lives over there."

"By the condos."

"No, by the marina."

Tiger Lily turned her ear to the table straight behind her. Two women this time.

"Did you hear? The Marina burned to the ground!"

"The Marina? I didn't see anything going on down there."

"Well, that's what they just said over there. The Marina!"

"Poor Cheryl! She grew up there! What will she do now?"

Even Tiger Lily knew the marina in question wasn't "The Marina." It was the old junky place she had heard about. Oh, well. She tuned her ears to another table. Four women added their knowledge to the pile.

"They suspect arson."

"Arson? You don't say. Who did it?"

"I heard it was one of those homeless men living out there."

"Out where?"

"At the old marina. Sometimes they crawl into one of those old boats to sleep."

"You don't say. Homeless men? In Chelsea?"

"It's a problem. That's for sure."

"We need to do something about that. Before they come into town and start sleeping in the street."

"And setting fires."

"Raping women."

"Leaving their trash."

"Why would they start a fire?"

"Maybe they needed to keep warm."

"It's June. Why would they need a fire?"

"Who knows? With homeless folks, you never know what you're getting into."

Tiger Lily huffed to herself and concentrated on a table further back in the room. Loud voices this time. A man and a woman.

"They found a body."

"Who?"

"Don't know. It was burned."

"That bad? Can't tell who it was?"

"Don't know if it's a man or a woman, but probably a man."

"Who said?"

"I heard it at Mr. Bean's."

"You went to Mr. Bean's? Whatcha doin' eatin' breakfast here for?"

"I didn't eat there. Just went in for gossip. Saw that old guy that used to be on the Town Council in there, Hank's his name, and asked him what he knew."

"And he said there was a body?"

"Yep. Burned beyond all recognition."

Tiger Lily had heard enough. She concentrated on Cyril. He stood still now and faced the Café. Apparently he was going to try to convince Pete to come in. If Pete came in, they'd get the straight scoop.

A motion caught the corner of her eye. Boone and Pastor Teresa had come out of the church, Soul's Harbor, and walked toward Pete. Boone said something, turned and pointed to the Café. Pete nodded, and Boone turned with Teresa to walk in the direction of the Café.

Tiger Lily watched as they walked past the windows to the door, entered, looked for an empty table, and spied one. It was in the back of the room, near the window. Near her.

Tiger Lily turned to her siblings and friends, *"Spread out. Get what real news you can. I'll need someone to stay here with me. I'll bet Boone and Pastor Teresa know something."*

Moriah said, *"I'll go sit with my mom. She hears everything."*

Little Socks nodded. *"I'll go with you. She always gets good stuff."*

Mo didn't answer, but he turned to follow them. He liked being near Moriah's mom, Clara. Moriah, low to the ground, light-colored and rotund – she called herself "fluffy" – well, she was "fluffy" also – was the Jeff to Clara's Mutt. Clara was a tall Haitian beauty, whose long black hair was nearly always pulled tight to her head. A bright red flower generally adorned her hair behind the left ear.

Clara always gave Mo marvelous full body pets, from the top of his head to the tip of his tail. Frankly, he didn't care if he heard gossip or not, if he could get that.

Kali and Ko, unaccountably away from the Inn, said at the same time, *"I'm going to sit with Trudie." "I'm going behind the coffee counter."*

Tiger Lily sighed. *"Okay. You might hear something good there."*

Mr. Bean and Tillie looked at one another and raced to the hostess stand. Mr. Bean could jump to the top; Tillie would be forced to stand at the foot of it. They could hear gossip as people walked in.

Sassy Pants said, *"I stay wit you here."*

"That's good, Sassy. I can use your help. What about you guys? Where will you go?"

She had turned to look at their neighbors from across the street, Simon Finnegan and Oscar McMurphy. Simon Finnegan looked at his sister before answering. *"We'll go into the back room. The Café's full today, and those tables are being used. Maybe we'll hear something."*

"Maybe someone will drop food on the floor."

Tiger Lily nodded. As they turned to go, she saw Sassy Pants, already on top of the table, getting a "stummy" from Pastor Teresa. She jumped to a cat ledge on the table and hissed, *"Not on top of the table. Get onto a ledge."*

"Me get stummy first. Den I get down. Not yet."

Tiger Lily hissed one more time then gave up. Pete was on his way in, and Cyril was headed in their direction.

Now they would hear what really happened.

Tiger Lily had awakened in the middle of the night. The alarms woke her first, and the smell of the fire kept her awake. The soft June air had gone rancid in seconds. Annie and Henrie had gone through the Inn, closing the windows to try to keep the smell away.

Tiger Lily realized the humans couldn't tell. Not from the distance of the fire, at least. But she could. She smelled burning flesh. The humans wouldn't know until the gossip started to roll in.

From their third floor windows, Tiger Lily and her siblings watched the flames over the trees. The flames looked like a dragon. Dragon fire, she thought. Evil. Devouring everything in its path.

Little Socks had cried, *"Oh, no! Sis will get burned up!"*

Mr. Bean stopped her. *"No. Mommy just called Chris. It's not them. She said it's further up the coast."*

Relieved, they calmed a bit and continued to watch the flames.

Sassy Pants asked, *"What's dat smell?"*

"It's something alive. Or something that used to be alive," answered Tiger Lily.

"Like a cat?"

"Bigger than a cat. Probably bigger than a dog. Probably a human."

"But not Chris?"

Tiger Lily looked at Mr. Bean, who shook his head. She answered, *"Not Chris. Mommy said he's okay. And Sis is okay, too. It's nobody we know."*

Silently, she prayed she had told the truth.

This was Chelsea, a small resort town on the sunset side of a Great Lake. The summer had barely gotten started, and now a fire – a killing fire – had come to visit.

Tiger Lily and her siblings lived on Sunset Avenue – known as The Avenue to the locals – and were proud to be the best cat detectives in the area. They had an office on the main floor of the Inn. It was a table covered with a cloth that reached the floor. A sign on the wall read, "Detective Agency. Felines & Canines On Duty 24/7. Inquire Within."

The KaliKo Inn was the most prominent bed and breakfast in the community. It sat at the end of The Avenue on an expanse of lawn and white sand and was named for Kali and Ko. They were big girls, dilute calicos, who rarely ventured outside their home. They were very good hostesses. They greeted each guest, tested the truffles left on the beds at night, sniffed each piece of luggage, and left love hairs all over the place.

Their litter mate, Mo, spent his daytime hours at another business owned by their mommy. It was a blues bar, Mo's Tap. Mo was a luscious long-haired gray who had never learned to speak beyond the kitten language he shared with Kali and Ko. He still spoke in trills and purrs and relied on Kali and Ko to translate. Oh, and Sassy Pants. Sassy Pants didn't understand his trills, but she could read minds.

Sassy Pants, the mind reader, was an enigma. Her sometimes vacant eyes and her loose relationship with grammar led to an impression that she wasn't all there. Tiger Lily had explained it to the rest of them. Sassy Pants had been rescued when she was older than most, and her language skills were a little behind. That didn't hamper her abilities of perception. Sassy Pants was a smart little girl underneath her ADHD appearance. She helped to manage Sassy P's Wine & Cheese.

Mr. Bean, the youngest of the group, was a strong gray cat. His leg muscles, especially those in his hind legs, gave him the appearance of a young panther. He danced in the windows of Mr. Bean's Confectionary all day, luring tourists and locals in to get the best baked goods and sweets in the region.

He was helped by Tillie, a Jack Russell Terrier who lived upstairs with the baker and his wife. Tillie was small enough to take advantage of the cat doors that were all over The Avenue. Every business had an exterior cat door to allow the neighborhood felines access. The businesses owned by their mommy, Annie, had interior cat doors as well.

Little Socks, the smallest of the group, a tuxedo, and the alpha, claimed the yoga studio, Lil Socks' Virasana, as her home-away-from-home. She spent the days sleeping in the windows. On rare occasions, she would participate in a yoga class, generally to show off her signature move, the Lessiver Mon Derriere. For those who can't handle a foreign language, the phrase translates to the Wash My Behind. It was a move few humans could duplicate.

Little Socks, while the alpha of most, was careful to never, never, ever try to alpha Tiger Lily.

Tiger Lily was the unquestioned matriarch of the group. She presided at Tiger Lily's Café during the day, the best place in town to see people and hear about everything going on in town.

This family of cats, with their across-the-street neighbors, Simon Finnegan, Oscar McMurphy and Moriah, made up the detective agency. And Uncle Honey Bear. They had to include the haughty, long-haired orange cat who belonged to Annie's mother. On occasion, when their human brought them to The Avenue, Speckles and Daryll, nanny kitties, helped as well.

The feline detectives often used the assistance of local canines. Tillie helped often, as she was in and out of all the local businesses. Cyril, the English Setter who called the Chief of Police his human, and Jock, a Portuguese water dog who worked with his human on a yacht-for-hire, were extraordinarily good help. They were large, intelligent and loved by everyone. Except bad folks. Bad folks didn't care much for them.

The most recent canine addition was Sis, a dark gray giant schnauzer. The cats rescued Sis from a snow storm – and from a bad human – and helped her find a fur-ever home. Her new human, Chris, just happened to be their mommy's best friend in the whole world. Her really best friend. Her special friend.

Today at the Café, they were minus some of their help. They would have to clue them in later. For now, Tiger Lily determined to find out all she could about the dragon fire and the human it had consumed.

2

The Chief of Police, Pete grew up in Chelsea, entered the Marine Corps and retired from the military police. He returned to Chelsea with his family and was a prominent fixture in the community. His presence, large and confident, generally exuded calm to those around him.

Today, the Café buzzed as he walked through, some calling out to him as he passed, "What can you tell us?" "Pete, what happened?" "Who died, Pete?"

As he walked through, he patted the air with his hands and shook his head as if to say, "Not now," or, "Later."

He wove through the tables and chairs with Cyril at his heels until he reached the table with Pastor Teresa and Boone. Pastor Teresa ministered to this tourist community from her church, Soul's Harbor, much as a hospital chaplain ministers to any number of faiths. Leading Christian in her sermons and preaching, she could minister in every faith to which she had been presented.

Boone, a transplant from the Appalachian area, sometimes lapsed into the affected drawl of that area. Not because it was his language of choice, but because it was what people around him expected. In reality, he was a highly educated man who happened to be very good with his hands. He kept most of Chelsea in good repair and managed their landscaping and snow removal as well.

Today, he was too distressed to think about doctoring his speech pattern. He dived into the conversation missing only a few consonants.

"I think I know who it is, Pete. I've been tryin' to help several guys out there. Vets. Homeless vets. They've come here for the summer. They'll move on to someplace warmer in the winter, but a group of 'em, well, they've kind of taken up residence in a few of those abandoned boats."

"And you know the victim?"

"I think so, yes. Teresa and I went out there this mornin', and we found all of 'em but one. The missin' one is a guy named Malcolm Williamson. I don't know where he's from, but he was in the Army. Served in the Gulf War, Desert Storm."

"Gulf War. So he'd be about fifty? Thereabouts?"

"I reckon."

"When you were looking for him, did you happen to ask if the other guys saw anything?"

Teresa looked at Boone before returning Pete's gaze. She said, "They said they didn't know how it happened, but I think they might be scared."

"Scared how? Or should I ask, scared of what? Who?"

"I don't know, Pete," she said. "It just seemed to me that they knew something."

Boone said, "It might have been a homeless thing. You know, you're out there on the street and you don't want folks askin' questions."

"It could have been that," said Teresa, "but it could have been more than that."

Pete accepted the cup of coffee delivered by the server and nodded his assent that she give Cyril a treat. "If you have a few more of those, he's been working hard all night."

Sarah, a long-time server at the Café, said, "I'll bring a dish of something and some water."

"Thanks, Sarah."

Pete looked back to his friends. "I didn't see anyone out there, not the entire time I was there. During the fire, after the fire, while the body was found, while it was removed. Just where are these vets staying? And when were you there?"

Boone looked at the table and chuckled a bit. "It's a homeless thing, Pete. I knew if they were anywhere, they'd be where no one could see 'em. That's where we went. They were up on that dune back behind the marina, the one that has all the scrub weeds. They were layin' up there, watchin' you do what you had to do."

"Do you think they'd talk to me?"

"One might," said Teresa. "One of the younger ones, Gene, might talk. I think he's ready to start living off the street. I offered him that apartment that I have at the church. He didn't say for sure, but I expect him this afternoon."

"What will he do? I mean, besides live with you for a while. What will he do?"

"If he wants to work," said Boone, "I'll give 'im a job. If he wants money to move on or go back home, wherever that is, I'll make sure he gets it."

Pete thought for a minute, then he looked at Teresa. "You understand we don't know who set this fire, right?"

"I do."

"Are you comfortable having this man under your roof, not knowing for sure that he's innocent?"

"I'm sure he's not innocent, Pete. He's been a soldier in an ugly war. He's not innocent. But I don't believe he set that fire. And I don't believe he killed Malcolm, on purpose or otherwise."

"Okay. I'd like to talk to him."

"I'll check with him and let you know if he's willing."

Under the table, Tiger Lily and Sassy Pants kneaded Cyril's back and right haunch while they listened to the humans at the table. When Tiger Lily was certain they had learned everything of interest, she asked Cyril what he knew.

"It was arson," said Cyril. *"Pete isn't sure, but he thinks the guy was dead before the fire started. But he said it was possible whoever started the fire didn't see him, and he got caught somehow. It could have been either."*

"How duz he find out?" asked Sassy Pants.

"The coroner's office will tell him. If he was dead first, his lungs will be clear of smoke. If not, well, anyway, that will tell them."

"Will dey know how he dies?"

"Maybe. If the evidence didn't burn away, or if something is obvious in his bones, or, well, I don't know everything they can check, but they're pretty good at finding out this stuff."

Cyril stood to accept a treat, knocking the two cats to the floor in the process. He grabbed the treat, nodded to Sarah, and in between crunches said, *"Sorry. Hungry. Long night."*

"*It's okay,*" said Tiger Lily. "*I should have asked someone to bring you something.*"

"*How would you do that?*"

Tiger Lily huffed. "*I would have gone to the kitchen and, well, I would have asked.*"

"*Like they would have understood you.*"

Tiger Lily huffed again. She knew he was right. No matter how smart the cats had become, how skilled at ferreting out the who-done-its and the how'd-they-do-its, they would never be able to communicate with most of the humans in the world. The humans weren't smart enough.

Oh, well. No sense worrying about that now. She had real detecting to do.

"*So now Pete thinks it was one of those homeless guys. How will he check out the name Boone gave him?*"

"*He'll probably ask the Army about him. Boone had the name and the war, so they'll probably be able to find him. He'll try to talk to those other homeless guys, too.*"

"*Why hasn't he done that already?*"

"*They weren't out there this morning, and they hide when we drive around out there.*"

"*Why?*"

"*Scared of cops, probably. Who knows? This is going to sound awful, like I'm saying all homeless folks are like this, but several of them have mental issues.*"

"*Wot's dat?*" asked Sassy Pants.

"*It means they aren't all right in the head. Sometimes something doesn't work like it should.*"

"*Like dere eyes go in circles or sumpin'?*"

"*No, more like their eyes might see something that, in another life, they would interpret correctly, but with whatever issue they've got, they see something else.*"

"*Like dey see a fish and dey tink it's a cow?*"

"*Something like that,*" said Cyril. "*Let's say they see a fish swimming in the lake, and they think it's coming to get them.*"

"*Oh,*" said Sassy. "*An' really it's not. Really it's jus' swimmin'.*"

"*Right.*"

"*Okay. So dey sees you and Pete. Wot duz dey see dat izn't real?*"

"*They might see someone with guns drawn, yelling and mean and stuff.*"

"*An' you an' Pete, you izn't like dat.*"

"*Right.*"

By now, Sarah had delivered a plate of diced ham and a bowl of water. Cyril politely knocked a few pieces of ham to the floor for Tiger Lily and Sassy Pants before chowing down.

Just as he finished, Pete stood to go. Cyril said, "*I'll find a way to let you know what we learn. Oh, before I forget, I found a cat.*"

"*A cat?*"

Tiger Lily followed him to the door to learn more, but Pete opened it to let him out. She would have followed, but she recognized the trot. Cyril was desperate to find a place to relieve himself. She would have to ask about it later.

Pete let Cyril out but turned back to the hostess stand before leaving. Annie had watched, and as he stood to leave, she went to the stand, knowing he would speak on his way out.

"Is it bad, Pete?"

"It is. Looks like a homeless vet. Boone gave me a name to check out. The Army might be able to tell me something."

"Is there anything I can do?"

"Yes. Keep an eye on Teresa. She offered her studio apartment to one of them. A younger one. Make sure someone talks to her a few times a day."

"Will do. How about you? Are you doing okay?"

"Yeah. I've seen this kind of death before, you know, in my other life. This is the first one for Tank, though."

Tank, the fire chief, had seen nothing worse than the fires in this community, mostly vacant buildings and small house fires. Until today, he had seen nothing remotely similar to the scene that greeted them at the marina.

"I think he and George are friends. I'll say something to him."

"That'll work. Thanks, Annie. Talk to you soon."

Nestled among the boats at the old marina were a few old cars. One car, a 1959 Ford Edsel, dull rusty blue with dull rusty white fins, was almost buried beneath a pile of old tires and corroded car parts. Most of the windows were broken, pieces of glass long ago carried away by the winds of every season.

A feral mother cat sat in the driver's seat. She had huddled in the car throughout the night, keeping low to the floor and covering her kittens with her body. They were too young to follow her, and she didn't think she could carry them away from the fire, one at a time.

She hoped the man would come to help, but she didn't think he would ever make it out of that boat again. Not after what she had seen. She would just have to stick it out here, try to keep her babies safe.

The fire was several boats away, and the wind took the smoke in the opposite direction. Still, she had to deal with the fear, the flame, the smell, the sirens, the emergency personnel, and that dog. That big dog saw her. He sniffed around the car; he seemed concerned. She knew better. He wanted a snack. She wasn't about to give up one of her children for that.

Now that the fire was out, only the smell lingered. Most of the people were gone, but the men who lived in the boats came back. They walked around. Some cried. She couldn't tell if it was because of the smell or something else. She thought it was probably something else.

One of the men stopped at the car. He looked in, found her, and tossed in some rancid food. He must have found it in a dumpster somewhere. He said, "I know Malcolm used to feed you. I'll try to find stuff. I'll do better next time."

She waited until he was gone, then snatched up the meat – she thought it might be meat – and swallowed it almost whole. She didn't have to taste it so much if she didn't chew. Maybe she could hold it down. Anything was better than nothing. She had mouths to feed. And where was that tom when she needed him? He wasn't good for much, but if she really needed it, he would sometimes bring a mouse. She could use a mouse right now. A fresh one.

Gene stood and looked around. He wanted to do right by the cat Malcolm had befriended, but more than anything, he grieved for Malcolm. He grieved as if he had lost him in battle. When Gene found himself on the street, Malcolm helped. He showed him how to panhandle, how to find day jobs. How to find places to shower and clean his teeth every few days. How to find the best food trash. Where the most forgiving shelters and food kitchens could be found. How to find clothes when the ones on your back were torn to shreds.

What was he going to do now? Without his friend? And even more, what were they all going to do? The boat colony, a group of four derelict boats they had slept in, was gone. A few boats were scattered around, but they were not in as good shape as the ones they had used.

He sighed.

His friends, if they could be called that, were not going to be a help. He would have to help them get on, but what he wanted more than anything was to get out. He wanted to take that pastor up on her offer. A place to stay. A leg up. The possibility of a job, or maybe money to go home. That was a scary thought, but it was better than this.

Gene and one other man were younger than the others. They had both served in Afghanistan, although Perry was a few years older. He had finished his second tour before Gene was deployed.

The others were Gulf War vets. Hardened. Streetwise. On the street for up to two decades, depending on the year they had given up.

Gene wondered again why he had followed them to Chelsea. He heard the men talking about it one night, and he asked if he could tag along. Most of the men had shaken their heads, started to say no, but Malcolm had said, "It'd be a good thing to have a young feller along."

Gene left with them.

Malcolm met a trucker getting ready to deadhead it from Detroit to Chicago. For a few hits of cocaine, he allowed them to ride in the back. He let them off at the access road that headed into Chelsea.

Gene wondered again, why Chelsea? It was a pleasant enough town, but there were few options to find day jobs or panhandle, and even fewer options for shelter.

The older men would huddle on occasion. They didn't allow Gene to hear all of their conversations. They kept Perry out of it, too. Maybe they had issues that only Gulf War vets could understand. Or maybe it was something else.

Gene turned when he heard a shout. Harper walked slowly, painfully toward the group, waving his hand. "I found a place. Back on the highway. Spotted it on our way in last week."

The group gathered around him. Harper continued, "It's over by that box store. Grocery there, too, and a few fast food restaurants. They got good trash, and there's a garage or somethin' that no one's usin' now. I got a door open. It's dry. Not too many rats."

The men looked at one another and nodded agreement. Gene looked at each one. Harper with his leg and back issues. Farrell with one arm and one eye. Face didn't look too good, either. Ben had no visible injuries, but he jumped at the smallest sounds. Tempo, certainly not his given name, but the name by which he was called. He couldn't stop moving, always in rhythm to something in his head. Perry had a nose for booze. If a bottle or can of anything were around, he found it. Malcolm had been the same for drugs.

While their circumstances appeared desperate, they had incomes. They had monthly checks for disability or veterans' assistance. Chelsea, like any other town, had a Post Office and a bank, all they needed to receive and cash their checks. But it didn't have much else. At least, not much that Gene could see.

First things first. He would have gathered his small pile of belongings, but they had burned to a crisp. He turned to help the others walk to their new home. He stopped beside the Edsel on the way.

"I'll try to get food out here. As often as I can."

He didn't care that the cat paid no heed. He needed to do this for Malcolm.

3

Henrie had been at the Inn all day. He and Hilly, Boone's wife, and the person he relied upon to keep the Inn sparkling, had stopped on occasion to text or Skype with others on The Avenue.

The Inn had been full through the weekend, and only circumstance had everyone leaving this morning. As luck would have it, another full house would arrive en masse by Wednesday. Rooms must be cleaned, laundry done, groceries purchased, menus finalized. That it was only Monday mattered not. Guests could call to reserve a room at any minute.

Henrie, the five-star manager of the KaliKo Inn, was nothing if not professional and prepared. Formal and buttoned down, Henrie spoke perfect English, using no contractions. If one heard a grammatical error from him, it was used merely to make a point. The faint French accent was unmistakable. Only those who knew him knew the accent was from his native Cameroon. He was also the town's best keeper of secrets, if secrets needed to be kept, and the best gatherer of gossip.

When the cats began to arrive home for the afternoon, he realized he had neglected the most important duty of the day. It was time for the cats' afternoon snack, and it was not prepared.

He opened a bag of always-on-hand bacon bits. The bagged variety was not as good as freshly cooked, but in a pinch, it would do.

He added a portion of shredded cheese, reached into the cupboard for the stack of cat dishes, and walked into the dining room. A tail disappeared under the detective table.

Henrie leaned down as he picked up one corner of the cloth.

"Ah. Tiger Lily. You brought Kali and Ko home, I see. Am I to expect all of the neighborhood to join you today? There is a fresh crime, after all."

Tiger Lily gazed into Henrie's eyes and blinked one time.

"Please allow an extra minute or two, and I will prepare a bit more."

Henrie stood and thought about it. There was the ham, left over from this morning, and a few pieces of link sausage. That would have to do.

Quickly, he diced and minced, stirred and fluffed, found a few extra cat dishes, and placed a small amount in each one. He counted by name. "Tiger Lily, Little Socks, Kali, Ko, Mo, Sassy Pants, Mr. Bean, probably Tillie, Simon Finnegan, Oscar McMurphy, and that cute new one, Moriah. That should be it for the day."

By the time Henrie returned to the dining room, the detective agency overflowed with furry bodies and whipping tails. He placed dishes on the floor outside the agency and called out, "Snack is served."

He got out of the way just in time. Cats came from under every inch of the tablecloth edge and hurried to find a dish of his or her own. He observed only one spat. Moriah wanted the dish that Sassy Pants reached. Sassy soon found another one.

Hilly got to the dining room just in time. "I see you found something for them. You have a full house today."

"Oh, yes. When a crime is afoot, even if it happened on the other side of town, they all gather. Actually, they have gathered for crimes before humans were aware they occurred. That is the amazing thing."

Hilly laughed. "There must be a jungle telegraph. Well, Henrie, I've got to go. Boone is so upset about this. He was hoping Malcolm would start to work for him. He has hopes for one more, a young one, but this death has gotten to him."

Henrie said, "I hope you take this in the spirit it is intended, Hilly. My prayer is that the death and fire were accidental. Unfortunately, the talk in town would have it otherwise."

"Thanks, Henrie. Unfortunately, I think the otherwise is the way it will be."

The main telephone rang. As he answered, he walked back and forth, trying to keep a step ahead of Mr. Bean, who had taken a liking to talking to whomever was on the other end of the phone.

The caller was a guest. A new guest. Did the Inn have a room for tomorrow?

Henrie sat at the desk to view the reservation program. "Yes, several rooms are available tomorrow night. Most are reserved beginning Wednesday, but one room is available for the foreseeable future. Would you prefer to take that room?"

"Yes, please. Could I stay through the weekend? Maybe until Sunday?"

"Certainly, I will make the reservation."

Henrie took the particulars, moving Mr. Bean from one side of the computer to the other in the process, and fixing errors made by a cat walking on the keyboard.

Finally, call ended, he took Mr. Bean's head in both of his hands, kissed his forehead, and said, "You will be happy to know that Wyatt will be here for several days. You may speak with him then."

By then, Mr. Bean didn't care. The phone was quiet. He jumped down and ran to the detective agency. They were beginning the meeting without him!

Annie sat at the back of the Café with Felicity, the chef and manager, and Trudie, the barista. Felicity was perky, innovative and fearless, great characteristics for a chef in the best eatery in the area. Trudie, her best friend, was, as far as Annie knew, the only Jamaican in the area.

Typically, this time was spent eating left-overs of the day's specials. Today, that wasn't possible. The Café had been far too busy, and the specials, all of them, were long gone. In fact, both women sat in front of their notebooks, making emergency orders for delivery in the morning. They had been – literally – eaten out of house and home. Or business, as the case may be.

Both women were good at multi-tasking and they chatted as they worked. Felicity said, "So, we have homeless vets at that old marina?"

"We do," said Annie.

Trudie said, "Maybe we can do something to help them."

"What?"

"I don't know, but here, look at these." Trudie typed a phrase into a search engine and turned the notebook for Annie to see. "Tiny houses. I've heard that some communities purchase tiny houses for the homeless."

"Really?" Annie scrolled through the pictures of tiny houses, showing the outsides. She clicked on the picture of one of the homes and scrolled through shots of the interior. "Very compact, but it looks like they have everything a person would need."

Felicity said, "I've thought about getting one. Buying a postage stamp piece of land in some vacation spot and putting a tiny house up."

"Really? I wonder. I like the concept, but I can't imagine seven cats inside one. Not for any period of time, at least. Add Chris and a big dog. . .well, I don't want to think about it." Annie looked around. "By the way, where are the cats?"

Trudie said, "They left just as I came this way."

Annie checked her watch. "I should go. I need to talk to George on the way home. Do you need anything from me before I go?"

Felicity waved her away. "Nope. Have a great evening. We'll be out of here shortly."

Annie sat at one of the small tables on the sidewalk for a few minutes, happy to be in the soft air of June. The Café had remained busy all day and she had barely had time to visit with her friends.

She checked and answered some text messages, one in particular from Chris, took a deep breath of summer air and moved on. She stuck her head inside the yoga studio and waved at the manager, Diana, who was in the middle of a class. If Diana needed anything, she would call.

The next storefront was Mo's Tap. Inside, she allowed her eyes to adjust, then walked toward the bar. Candice was behind the bar. Generally, as floor manager, she stayed on the other side of it. George must be busy somewhere.

Candice was, finally, after many ups and downs over the years, married to George. Annie couldn't imagine living and working with the same person day after day after day. They made it work, though. Kudos to them, she thought.

As she sat at the bar, she said, "I promised Pete I'd make a special request of George. Is he around?"

"He is. He's in the kitchen. We were so busy today, he's helping Georgia put in emergency orders for tomorrow."

"The same happened at the Café. It's probably the same up and down The Avenue. Oh, here's George."

And there he was. Handsome George. George, who had broken the heart of many a woman when he married Candice. George, who, just two months ago, handled the Inn and a desperate situation halfway around the world in her absence. He was a rock. And a rock star.

"Hey, boss lady. How are ya?"

"Beat. How about you?"

"The same. We had the rush of a lifetime, and we haven't even hit our busy time of day yet. I think we have enough to get us through the evening, but we may have to close the kitchen early."

"If you do, you do. Hey, the reason I stopped is that I have a request from Pete. It's about Tank."

"Yeah. Tank. I hear it was rough out there last night, well, this morning. I haven't seen him yet."

"Pete thinks it might be a good idea if someone reaches out."

"I can do that. I'll give him a call this evening. Have you heard that group of guys out there are veterans?"

"I have. Trudie wondered about maybe getting some little houses...small houses..."

Candice said, "Tiny houses?"

"Yeah, them."

George nodded. "That might be a good idea, but they have other issues that a house can't fix."

"Like what?"

"Emotional issues, you know, after you've been in combat, exposed to the horrors of war, away from your family. I can't imagine what it's like, what they go through, both there and when they get home."

Annie nodded. "I imagine emotional injuries can be harder to heal than physical injuries."

"That, too. There are physical injuries and there are physical injuries. I mean there are visible injuries and invisible ones. Someone may look whole, but have hidden damage, like chronic fatigue or headaches, sight or hearing loss, lung trouble. There are lots of things."

"It sounds like you have experience."

"I'm a bartender. I hear things."

"I'll bet. Well, I'll leave the two of you to it. Thanks for reaching out to Tank."

Annie took her time walking from Mo's to Mr. Bean's. Once again, she made a few yards last longer than normal. Once again, she breathed in the fresh air, heavy with smells of the lake.

Finally, she had to leave the fresh air to go inside. At least she was greeted with the smell of fresh bread and chocolate.

Carlos, the head baker, was at the counter. He replenished what appeared to be raked-through baked goods, breads, cakes, cookies, muffins and sweet rolls.

"It looks like you were busy today."

"We didn't stop. We had to keep baking, and we ran out of several things. Isabel is putting an emergency food order in now."

"Everyone is doing it. How'd the chocolates hold up?"

Jerry, the candy maker, appeared as if on cue, a tray of truffles in his hands. "We ran out of nearly everything. I just now finished fresh candies."

"What do you have?"

As usual, Annie's mouth began to water at the thought of a new truffle.

"Starting today, and for the rest of the month, we're featuring an Italian white truffle, white chocolate with lemon filling."

"Yum, and…"

Jerry reached under the counter and brought up a small box. "Here are some for you."

"You know me so well."

Carlos gave her a medium-sized pastry bag. "Henrie called and asked me to send these, if we should see you."

"What are they?" she asked, as she opened the bag. The smell was heavenly.

"He told me to use my imagination. I made yeast rolls, like cinnamon, only with raspberries. He's planning a small breakfast for the two of you, to celebrate one day free of guests."

"How sweet of him. I don't know what I would do without him. Without all of you."

"Oh, you'd get by, but it wouldn't be nearly so fun."

"You're right about that. Say, Jerry, you and Teresa are close. Did you know she's going to have one of the vets stay in her apartment?"

"I did. She came in and got bread for this evening and tomorrow morning."

"Will you stay in touch with her?"

"I told her I'd stop in every afternoon after we close here."

"Good. We need a few people to make sure they see her every day."

Annie left with a bag, a box, and a lighter heart. On the few yards to the wine shop, she breathed in the air again. This time, she smelled what might be the first scent of a summer rain. Perhaps it would wash away the ash and soot at the marina. She hoped there were more places for the vets to stay, more than the boats that had gone up in flame. She wasn't familiar with the old place and wished now that she had at least driven through.

Inside the winery, she looked around for Jesus or Minnie. Minnie came out of the office. "Hi. Just making an order. Come on back."

"Did you miss having your girl around today?"

"I did. I hope she enjoyed staying at the Café. Did she do her thing?"

"She did. The customers at the Café are more used to Tiger Lily. She stays on her ledges. But I think they got a kick out of having a cat on top of the tables on occasion. I saw Tiger Lily spar with her a few times, like she was telling her to get down."

"That's never worked here."

"It didn't work there, either. So, you ran out of things? What did you have for lunch?"

"We're doing Italian this week. Jerry told us about his truffles, so we thought a little Northern Italian sounded good to us as well."

"Do you have anything left?"

"Some. We were pretty busy today."

"Save me four – no – five portions of something. Chris and I are having dinner, Mom and Sam are coming, and I'll see if Henrie can join us."

"I'll do better than that. I'll make sure we have enough that everyone can have a little of everything."

Tiger Lily asked for reports, looking first to Mr. Bean and Tillie. *"Did you learn anything?"*

Mr. Bean said, *"Pete said that Pastor Teresa is going to let a man live in her apartment. Pete wants us to keep an eye on her."*

Tillie jumped up, hit her head on a table brace and sat back down. *"Mostly what we heard was questions. Well, until Pete left. But at first, people came in and asked Annie what she knew, and Annie kept saying she didn't know anything."*

"Yeah," said Mr. Bean, *"Mommy wanted to hear what everybody else was saying, but all she got was questions. It was really frustrating."*

Kali and Ko said together, *"It was the same at the coffee bar." "Trudie didn't have time to hear anything. Not while we were there."*

Tiger Lily turned to Simon Finnegan and Oscar McMurphy. Unfortunately, she called them Fat Cat and Scaredy Cat, the names by which they were known before they found a fur-ever home. Their new humans, being sadly ignorant of cat language, provided new names. Proud of the number of syllables now used when they were called, they preferred their companion friends use the human-given names.

Simon Finnegan (Fat Cat) hissed before giving his report. *"Mostly there was just gossip, but there was one table that seemed to know something."*

"Yes," added Oscar McMurphy. *"It was kind of funny. They didn't realize what they were saying."*

Simon Finnegan gave his sister a long glare before taking the story back. *"We don't know their names, but they shop here on The Avenue at least once a week."*

Oscar McMurphy cut in, *"They get their computers from us."* The siblings lived with twin sisters who owned the electronics and hardware store, DoubleGood. *"Sometimes they come in to see if there are new gadgets."*

Simon Finnegan hissed, *"Stop it! This is my story!"*

"Is not!"

"Is too!"

"Oh big baby buggy bumpers. Go ahead then. But don't forget anything."

Tiger Lily sighed and shook her head. *"Really?"*

"Okay," said Simon Finnegan. *"They recognized us, so they dropped food every now and then. And they talked. They sent a drone over the fire."*

"Wot's dat?" asked Sassy Pants.

Simon Finnegan answered, *"It's like a little airplane but it flies like one of those play cars. You know, with someone holding onto a control."*

"Why?"

"Why what?"

"Why did dey sended a flying car an' wot dey send it over?"

"Oh!" cried Oscar McMurphy. *"If my brother knew how to tell a story, you wouldn't be so confused. I'll tell it."* She put her body in front of her brother's and started over. *"These young guys are computer geniuses. They can find out lots of things on the web, and they use gadgets to find out stuff. Like these drones. They put a camera on theirs and fly it over things. When the fire started last night, they sent their drone with a camera and they watched from their computers. They talked about the things they saw."*

Simon Finnegan pushed his sister out of the way and took over. *"They saw Pete and that fire chief, Tank, and lots of firemen. A whole bunch of boats were on fire."*

Oscar McMurphy shouldered her brother out of the way. *"And it looked like it was, what was the word…"*

"Accelerated."

"Yes, accelerated."

"Wot's dat?"

Tiger Lily answered. *"That's like what Cyril was saying. He said it might be arson. That's when someone sets it, and they use something that makes it burn faster."*

"Oh," said Sassy Pants. *"I see."*

Tiger Lily thought it appeared that clearly, she did not, but she let it pass. She turned back to the siblings. *"Thank you. That was an interesting report. I wonder if we might be able to take a look at that?"*

Oscar McMurphy and Simon Finnegan looked at one another. Oscar McMurphy said, *"We'll investigate. Maybe there's a way."*

"Or maybe," said Little Socks, *"there might be a way to get Cyril to get Pete to ask for it."*

"Trill!!!"

Everyone turned to Mo. Kali said, *"He says we can send an email."*

A chorus responded. *"Who to?"* *"Another email?"* *"Good idea!"* *"But who to?!"*

The "who to" questions came from Moriah. She stomped her foot on the cushion, which didn't make a noise and angered her greatly. Finally, she put a petulant look on her face and pushed it nose to nose with Mo.

"Who. To."

Mo backed up an inch or two and said, softly and with a little tremor, *"Trill….."*

Ko said, *"He says we can send it to Pete."*

Sassy Pants said, *"An' he tinks you should be more polite."*

Moriah sat, fluffed her mane and licked a paw. She needed to maintain her fluffy good looks.

Tiger Lily said, *"Let's put that on the back burner. We can try to figure out sending it and what to say later. Let's go on with other reports. Little Socks, you went with Moriah and Mo. What did you learn?"*

Little Socks was happy to take the lead. Mo would take way too much time trilling and needing an interpreter. Moriah was smart, but sometimes she was just too full of herself.

"Clara was trying to listen to everybody, so it was kind of confusing. But she did hear a couple of things that were interesting."

"Trill!"

Kali said, *"He agrees."*

Little Socks closed her eyes and shook her head but continued. *"She talked to that horrible man, Hank. Remember him? He said he sees some homeless guys out there all the time, and he wondered if maybe the dead guy was one of them."*

Sassy Pants said, *"Yeah. Cyril sez dey sees tings dat duzn't exist."*

"What?" asked Little Socks.

"He sez…"

Tiger Lily cut in, *"Cyril said that sometimes homeless people have issues that cause them to, um, misinterpret things. But that doesn't necessarily have anything to do with the dead body. Well, the dead body could be one of them."*

"Well, then," said Little Socks, *"I guess maybe Hank was right."*

Tiger Lily said, *"But my question would be, what's Hank doing out there at that old marina? Oh, well. He's weird."* She turned to Moriah. *"Moriah, did you hear anything else?"*

"Just that the dead body couldn't be identified. They weren't sure who he was. But Hank was pretty sure it was a guy."

Sassy Pants said, *"But why duzn't we tells dem, Tiger Lily? We knows who da guy is."*

Another chorus ensued. *"What?" "Who?" "Why didn't you say so?" "How did you find out?"*

Tiger Lily shushed them. *"Quiet now. I wanted to hear what everyone else found out before giving our report. Like Sassy Pants said, we have a name. It's a probable name, and it's one of those homeless guys, and he's probably a vet."*

Mr. Bean asked, *"Like Dr. Ralph?"*

"No, like a veteran of some army or something."

"Oh. Like Pete and Ray."

"Yeah, like them. But homeless."

"I still duzn't understand why dey duzn't got homes."

"I'll explain that later. For now, let's just give our report. Do you want to give it?"

"*Yeah. I gives it. Da guy, his name Malcolm someting. We duzn't know him. Leastwhys, dat's wot Boone say. Oh, an' Cyril says he sees a cat.*"

Little Socks bent to the cushion and pounded her head a few times. This was too much. "*What does a cat have to do with it?*"

Sassy Pants looked at her feet. Her lip trembled. Tiger Lily stepped up. "*Sassy Pants is right. Cyril found a cat, and we don't know what the importance is. Maybe the cat saw something. We don't know.*"

All eyes turned toward the sound of the front door opening and closing. Mommy was home. "*That's all for now. Everyone think about that email, or some way of getting Pete to look at the camera stuff.*"

4

Annie walked through the dining room, careful not to step on the feet of a few cats and one dog heading out. She knew them all. She had rescued each of them.

Well, in truth, the rescues were a combination of the actions of her cats and her own actions. But however it happened, Oscar McMurphey and Simon Finnegan met their fur-ever humans at the Inn; Tillie met her fur-ever human at the Inn; and Moriah met her fur-ever human right here. At the Inn. They were special, each and every one.

She reached the kitchen, dropped the bag and the box, and sank into a chair at the table. She took the coffee from Henrie's outstretched hand. "What a day. Were you able to keep up?"

"I believe so. Hilly, of course, had the benefit of Boone's information. She knew the name of the victim. Well, perhaps that is hasty, as a proper identification must be made."

Annie opened the box of truffles. "From Jerry. Italian, he says, white chocolate with lemon."

Henrie helped himself. "Delicious. And what did Carlos send?"

"Raspberry yeast rolls. You'd better hide them or I'll eat them before breakfast. Did you hear that Pastor Teresa will have a boarder?"

"I did. I plan to take a meal over every day, perhaps mid-morning, to check in. I offered and she accepted."

"Good plan. Did you hear how many homeless guys are out there, and that they may all be vets?"

"I did. Boone had hopes of putting at least one, perhaps two, to work. I do not know if he thought further than that."

"I wonder if there is something we can do. Maybe, I don't know, have you heard of communities that build small homes for the homeless?"

"Small homes? I believe you mean tiny houses."

"Yeah, them. So you've heard about that?"

"I have. I admit, I did not think of that possibility, but you are correct. That would be something we could do."

"Where would we put them?"

"That would take planning with the Town Council and others, perhaps County government."

"And how would we pay for them?"

"Another issue. We would have to plan for payment up front and payment for utilities and other items for all time."

"Something to think about. George said he's aware of several issues with local vets, both these guys, who may not have been local to begin with, and our neighbors."

"What issues?"

"Emotional difficulty, physical injuries, both seen and unseen. I imagine there are suicidal tendencies. We aren't taking care of the men and women who took care of us."

"Perhaps we should focus our block party efforts this month on veterans' issues."

"Good idea. I'll bring it up at our next meeting. Oh, well. I've spent the entire day on this murder and the fire. What did you do?"

"Cleaned, shopped for groceries, planned menus, took a reservation."

"Oh, who? And when?"

"A man named Wyatt who arrives tomorrow. He will stay, perhaps, through Sunday. One room is available for that length of time. The back room."

"Okay. Why's he coming to town?"

"I do not know. Perhaps I would have asked more questions, but your youngest child, Mr. Bean, has decided he must speak with everyone who calls. I had difficulty managing the phone, the computer and the child at the same time."

Annie laughed. "Good for him. I'm happy he's breaking out of his shell."

"As if he were ever in one. What are your plans for the evening?"

"Mom and Sam are coming over, and, of course, Chris and Sis. Want to join us for dinner?"

"I may do that. Are you eating in or out?"

"Out."

"Where do you plan to go?"

"Sassy P's. Minnie has some Northern Italian something-or-other, and she's going to put something together for us."

"I cannot decline such an offer."

"Great. I'm going upstairs to feed the children and put my feet up for a few. They should be here by six."

George stood at the end of the bar as often as he could, leaving to take care of other customers and take orders from two servers on the floor. Still, he was able to talk to Tank and listen while he unloaded.

"I tell ya, George, I ain't never seen the like."

When Tank said nothing more, hanging his head and gazing into his beer, George prompted him. "I hear it was pretty bad."

"It was. It was…well…it wasn't just the look of 'im. It was the smell. We could smell it before we could get in. Pete told me what it was. He was right."

"How are the rest of the guys taking it?"

"I think okay. Well, how can any of us really be okay? They're takin' it. We stayed around the station for several hours today. You know. Talkin' about it and getting it out of our system. Most of those guys go home to someone. Wives. Well, husbands, too. I kind of think of the gals as guys. Don't think, you know, when I say 'guys' that…"

"I know, Tank. I know what you're saying."

George went quiet, hoping Tank would talk some more. He did.

"I called the state fire marshal's office to get some stuff, you know, info about counseling and things we could get. They're supposed to send someone out tomorrow to talk with us. Help us deal with it better, I guess. It'd be worse if we knew the guy. You know. Well, this morning, we didn't know if we knew him or not, but Pete figured out who it was. Some Army guy. Homeless."

"That's what I heard."

"Bunch of 'em out there. Strange, you know. I never knew of Chelsea havin' folks like that. It's not like we're a big city. I hear there's some young guys, too. Not just middle aged."

George kept his thoughts to himself. He didn't know if Tank considered him – well, both of them – they grew up together – to be "younger" or "middle aged." Where was that cut-off, anyway? The bar was fluid.

On another night, he may have philosophized with Tank. Tonight, though, he let Tank ramble, then be silent, then ramble again. This was the only way George knew to be a friend to his old friend.

Jesus seated Annie's party at the best table in the back dining room. Her party included Chris and Henrie, the two most constant influences in her life, and her parents, her mother, Nancy, and stepfather, Sam.

Recently Nancy and Sam had moved to be closer to her. They now lived in a small house in a neighborhood not far from The Avenue with their large golden long-haired cat, Honey Bear. He was known by Annie's cats as Uncle Honey Bear, or, often, The Dreaded Uncle Honey Bear. Of late, he was either getting better, or they were becoming more used to him. Regardless, they were always happy to see their grammy and grandpoppy, Nancy and Sam.

Nancy was her usual effervescent self. "Jesus, I hear we're going to have Italian tonight. Spaghetti? Lasagna?"

"Sorry, Nancy. We're serving Northern Italian. No pasta tonight."

"Oh hockey feathers. My taste buds were already set."

"I believe you will love what we have. Northern Italy, over the centuries, belonged to one ruling power, then another. What remains is cuisine that is more recognizable as Austrian than Italian."

"You don't say! So, still no pasta?"

"Still no pasta. Gnocchi, risotto and polenta."

Sam said, "I think I know what risotto is. It's a rice dish, right? But what's gnocchi? And polenta?"

"Gnocchi is a potato dumpling, boiled and tossed with whatever you choose. Polenta is made with corn meal. It's used as a side or as a main dish."

Jesus pulled a notebook from his pocket. "I'll start with that one. It's our vegetarian dish tonight. Often, polenta is fried. Our polenta tonight is creamy, made with mixed mushrooms, greens and mascarpone."

Nancy said, "That sounds great. I may have to try that."

"Wait," said Jesus. "Let me tell you about the others. We have beef tenderloin braised with red wine and mushrooms, and we serve it with a simple risotto, made with fresh tomatoes. And…let's see…oh, yes. We have roasted pork tenderloin, also cooked in a red wine sauce, served with gnocchi with lemon and chive pesto."

Nancy said, "I want one of each."

Jesus looked at Nancy with a big smile. A cat-that-ate-the-canary smile. "We thought you might. We'll bring a large plate for each of you that has a little bit of everything."

Sam slapped his thigh. "Just the ticket!"

Nancy asked, "What wine do you suggest?"

"Always, for this group, a dry red, and I would go with a shiraz or a Nebbiolo."

Sam asked, "Nebbi-what-o?"

"Nebbiolo. A great dry red. If you want to try something new, let's go there."

Annie said, "Bring two bottles of that, please. Did Minnie choose cheese from Northern Italy?"

"She did, and that will come out first. We'll serve a plate of four cheeses with a variety of crackers and fresh vegetables. The cheeses are Alpine, native to northern Italy. There is reblochon, beaufort, appenzeller and asiago. We'll put a label on each one, and you can decide which you like the best."

Nancy sat back and looked at Sam. "The best decision we ever made was to move here."

Honey Bear, as usual, was deposited at the Inn while the humans went to dinner. A couple of months previously, Honey Bear had been involved in a detective situation with the neighborhood cats. Annie, Chris and all of her cats were out of town and unavailable.

Honey Bear, a natural leader – at least that's how he would describe himself – took over the group. As he struggled with the issues surrounding the case in front of them and the personalities of the cats of the neighborhood, his appreciation for Tiger Lily grew. He didn't want to let her know this.

He was still, for reasons Tiger Lily was not quite aware, a more reasonable cat. Most of the time.

Tonight, the cats and Sis talked about the situation with the vets, arson and murder.

Sassy Pants said, *"His name was Malcolm, and he was in a boat, an' someone setted fire to da boat."*

"But he was killed first," said Little Socks.

"And there were some young guys that may have filmed it with drones."

"Drones?" asked Honey Bear. *"What are they?"*

Sassy Pants jumped up to answer. *"Dey's like cars and dey take pitchers an' dey fly over tings…"*

Tiger Lily shushed her gently. She never wanted to hurt her feelings. *"Let me tell him, Sassy. They work like toy cars, the kind that you have a remote control for, but instead of driving, they fly. So these guys put cameras on them, and they flew them over the fire."*

Mr. Bean said, *"We have to figure out how to tell Pete. I think we have to send an email."*

"To Pete?" asked Honey Bear. He looked at Tiger Lily. *"Do you know how to spell all of that?"*

"No. That would be a problem. I think we have to find another way."

"Any ideas?"

"Not yet. What do you think?"

Honey Bear stared at her. Tiger Lily had never – or at least rarely – asked his advice. *"Um…I'll think about it."*

Annie groaned. She had too much of a good thing. Now, she relaxed with Chris on the deck of her third floor apartment. Facing the lake, they watched as the sun dipped below the horizon in a splendor of oranges and reds.

The door was open behind them. Now that Sis was a part of the family, they left the doors open most of the time. She had full run of the Inn but couldn't keep up with the cats if they slipped through a cat door.

Annie thought the price of a fly or two was worth it.

"Can you smell the rain coming?"

"I can. Sis noticed it this afternoon. I saw her face the wind to investigate."

"Can she tell you what she's doing? What she knows?"

"Not yet. Actually, I think I'm happy to let her be a dog. Don't think I want to add 'communication with animals' to my resume. Not like you can with your cats, at least."

"She might be disappointed to hear that."

"She'll have to tell the cats, who can figure out how to tell you, then you can tell me, and we'll figure out what to do about it then."

"Fair enough. What do you think about that situation out there at the old marina?"

"You mean the folks that everyone is talking about? I don't know what to think. I suppose Chelsea was overdue for having homeless people that we know about. And it's odd that a group showed up all at once."

"I thought about that myself."

"I suppose there's a route, you know, of people who are homeless but travel, from one place to another during the year, to stay out of bad weather. As far as I know, though, Chelsea has never been on a route like that. I mean, why? I would think they would go to cities, areas urban enough to have opportunities."

"What kind of opportunity?"

"You know. Abandoned buildings, lots of places to pick up day jobs, shelters, food kitchens. That kind of thing."

"We don't have those things because we have never experienced the, for lack of a better word, problem."

"My point exactly. Why did they choose Chelsea? How many guys are out there? Do you know?"

"I don't, but Boone might, and Teresa. Some of us were talking about those small homes. Tiny homes. Tiny houses. I might get it right by the end of the week."

"I hear nouns are the first to go."

"Shut up."

Chris chuckled. Annie was forever reaching for the correct name, the correct word. This was not a new subject. "Tiny houses might be okay." He paused, then added, "This group of vets has an 'off' feel to it."

They lapsed into silence, the touchstone of their relationship. Henrie had once explained it to Nancy and Sam. The two were so in sync they seemed to read one another's minds.

Often, that was the case.

The downside was that, on occasion, their silence led to misunderstandings.

Early in the morning, around two, Annie, Chris and Henrie were awakened again to the sound of alarms and the smell of fire. This time, the fire was closer.

As she looked out the window, Annie could see flames reaching for the sky in the vicinity of the big box store on the access road leading to the highway.

She reached down to pick up Tiger Lily, who paced the window sill. Chris sat in a chair and pulled Sis close. She burrowed her face into his chest as she whined and trembled.

"I don't know if she's afraid of the fire, the smoke or the sirens."

"Maybe all three," said Annie. "Or maybe they know something we don't."

Annie heard a siren come to life on The Avenue. She looked down. Jennifer and Marie had started the ambulance. They peeled out, up The Avenue, around the police department, and straight east toward the fire.

Tiger Lily looked at her siblings. They were all frightened. The dragon fire had consumed – or tried to consume – another human. The smell was not as dreadful as the night before.

5

Tuesday morning dawned bright. The early morning rain had pushed the smell of the fire into a soggy mess. That's how Annie thought of it, as if a smell could be soggy. If it had not been for the fire, the morning would smell fresh-washed. Now…well, now, it didn't.

Henrie served breakfast. It was not "just" raspberry yeast rolls. It was also eggs scrambled with freshly made bacon, spinach and feta cheese, fresh strawberries, steel cut oat groats with dried cranberries and walnuts, and coffee. Excellent coffee.

Chris asked, "What kind of coffee is this, Henrie?"

"Something I picked up at the airport. I have not had the peace of mind to use it until now. It is a Cameroon blend, Arabica."

Henrie's recent trip to his home country of Cameroon had been a disaster. He and his lady friend had been kidnapped. The hope of rescue had grown dim. When it came at last, it came as a surprise.

Henrie's grandmother, thankfully, had not endured any backlash from the rebels who took them. She was safe; she and Henrie had resumed their weekly telephone conversations.

Unfortunately, Henrie and his lady friend had since parted ways.

He rarely spoke of the experience to anyone, with the exception of Annie, Chris and George.

"It has a great flavor. Can we buy it here?"

"I shall look. I would like to have one pleasant memory from my home land."

Annie asked, "Have you heard anything about last night's fire?"

"Nothing. I see the ambulance is back in place. I will find a reason to shop at The Drug Store on my way to Pastor Teresa's this morning."

"Good idea. You always know just what to do."

"Having a finger on the pulse of the community is always helpful," Henrie said with a smile.

"What time is our guest coming?"

"His name is Wyatt, not that you will remember, and I expect him mid-day, perhaps around noon."

"Why is he coming to town, Henrie?" This from Chris, who rose from the table to get ready to leave.

"I do not know. The youngest child of our family would not allow me to speak to him for long."

"Mr. Bean is good about wanting to stay in touch." Chris turned to see Sis, nose poked underneath the cloth covering the detective agency and said, "Come on, Sis. Time to go to work."

Chris was the Officer in Charge of the local Coast Guard Station. He was tall and trim with prematurely white hair. His closely trimmed beard was as white as his hair.

Sis, not trained to water before coming to live with him, had grown accustomed to the Great Lake and to the boats. As Chris would say, like a duck to water.

Annie asked, "Will we see you this evening?"

"Maybe. I promised Pete and Ray we'd get together for poker, but if it's not too late, I'll stop by."

"Ugh, no," said Annie. "You guys reek of cigars after a night of poker. We'll find something else to do."

Chris laughed on his way out the door. Sis looked back at the cats as if to say, *"Poker! This will be fun!"*

Sassy Pants asked, *"Duz we go to da Café today?"*

"No, not today. We might have missed good information by staying in one place yesterday. Let's all go to our own places."

"Dat's a good idea. I hazn't talked to Brown Mousie for a while. He may have heared sumpin'."

"What about me?" asked Sis. *"How can I help?"*

"You just need to keep your eyes and ears open. It's not often that our town crimes dribble into Coast Guard territory, but it's possible."

"I can do that. I'd like to be able to help. Chris said we're playing poker tonight. If I hear anything, I'll tell Jock and Cyril."

"That will work. Was anyone awake when the ambulance came back this morning?"

All she got in answer were shakes of the head. Everyone, after little sleep the night before, must have zoned out after the initial excitement.

"Maybe Jennifer or Marie will come to one of our places today. If so, get close and listen to what they have to say."

6

Annie realized the cats were already gone when the doorbell rang and no paws went pitter patter. Henrie was busy packing a meal for Pastor Teresa, so Annie went to the door.

She opened it to see a tall man in rugged clothes, a little disheveled but clean.

"May I help you?"

"Yes. I have a reservation."

"Oh, yes. Welcome to the KaliKo Inn. I believe your room is ready. I'll get Henrie to check you in." She turned, looking for Kali and Ko, then thought of something else. "Do you have bags?"

"I do. I left them in the car, just in case I was too early."

"We can get them after you check in."

As he walked past, Annie caught a smell. Yuck, she thought. At least Chris smoked decent cigars. Almost on cue, he pulled a cigar from his front pocket.

"Is it okay to smoke in here?"

"No, this is a non-smoking facility. The best you can do is to walk at least twenty feet from your door – you'll have a door that opens to the beach – and smoke out there. Henrie will get an ash tray for you; we don't want butts on the beach."

"Not even on the porch here?"

"Not even the porch. Twenty feet out on the beach, or on the sidewalk, but not if people are walking in."

"Is this posted?"

Annie stopped and turned. The smile remained, but her voice now held an edge. "This is a non-smoking facility. Henrie will be happy to point you in the direction of places that will meet your needs."

Henrie appeared in the dining room door at that moment. His nose took in the issue as his ears took in Annie's firm tone. "Ah, Wyatt. Welcome to the KaliKo Inn. Yes, if you desire a smoking facility, I have a list of hotels and bed and breakfast establishments that will meet your needs. You can, of course, give up your reservation here without charge."

"Oh, that won't be necessary." Wyatt returned the cigar to his pocket. "I'm sorry to have made it an issue. Certainly, I'll be able to follow the rules."

Annie, realizing the Inn would be best served if she left, did just that, leaving Henrie to check Wyatt into his room.

She stopped at each business on her way to the Café, long enough to see that her cats had made it to their appointed places. At Sassy P's Wine & Cheese, she found Sassy Pants in the back dining room, looking intently at a potted plant.

Minnie said, "We still have that mouse. I've never seen it, but I swear, we have a mouse. Either that, or Sassy talks to plants."

"Or maybe a ghost. Have you heard what happened last night?"

"No. I've been here all morning. Jesus is out; he had to go shopping to replace some wines and cheeses, things that couldn't be delivered today. I hope he comes back with news."

At Mr. Bean's Confectionary, Mr. Bean and Tillie vied for her attention. She tried to divide it equally, but erred on the side of a pet or two extra for her boy baby. Isabella was at the counter.

Annie asked, "Any news about the vets?"

"Hank was in to say they aren't at the marina anymore."

"What about that fire last night? Did he know about that?"

"Just that one guy got hurt."

"Who was hurt?"

"Another man, a homeless man, possibly one of the vets from the marina, was inside a vacant garage behind the box store. He must have started a fire that got out of control. He got out of the building, but he was burned pretty badly."

"Were the rest of the vets there?"

"Not that Hank saw, or not that he heard. Or said."

"Was Jerry able to check on Teresa last night?"

"He was, and he met the guy staying there, Gene. He liked Gene, thought he was awfully quiet, but nice."

At Mo's Tap, she unlocked the door to look in. No humans were there, but Mo gave her a lazy gaze from the top of the bar. She noticed his tail draped across the clean glasses. "Keep those glasses clean, Mo. I'll see you later."

Mo yawned and turned back to his nap.

She spent more time at the yoga studio. Diana wasn't teaching a class at the moment, and Little Socks practiced her yoga move in the middle of the floor, sans mat.

Diana said, "What's going on? Two fires in two days? And two men, either dead or injured?"

"What did you hear about the fire last night? I mean, what did you hear about the man?"

"I had breakfast at the tea shop this morning and one of the firemen said it looked like one of those homeless guys. Like this one, or maybe even all of them, moved over to that empty garage."

"Did he see the rest of them?"

"No. Well, he didn't say."

"Did he say how the fire started?"

"He said the injured man wasn't able to talk, and it was hard to tell, until they investigate a little more, if it was an accident or something else."

Annie went on to the Café, bustling with late breakfast customers, here to eat and get the latest. Because information was rolling a little easier today, the servers were able to satisfy, at least with what they knew, which was basically what Annie had heard on her trip up The Avenue.

Annie didn't see Tiger Lily at the hostess stand. A quick glance around the room was all it took. Tiger Lily and fluffy Moriah held court at a table with several of Annie's friends. She walked to the table, pulled over a chair and sat.

She greeted Clara, Moriah's human, and the owner of Bloomin' Crazy across The Avenue; Mem, Diana's mother and the owner of CyberHealth, a tea shop and cyber café; Holly and Jolly, twins, the humans of Simon Finnegan and Oscar McMurphy and owners of DoubleGood; and Laila,

Annie's dearest friend and owner of the grocery store, Babar Foods.

If ever there was a hotspot of good gossip, this was it. This group represented every owner of every business on The Avenue, with the exception of Jennifer and Marie, and Pastor Teresa, if you figured she was a business owner.

"You've all been talking without me. Bring me up to date."

As the women talked, Tiger Lily and Moriah exited to the floor beneath the table.

"You probably know everything your servers know," started Clara. "Fire in that garage behind the box store, homeless guy burned pretty badly, unknown if it was an accident or arson. Right? You're up to date that much?"

"Yep. What else?"

"Well," Clara continued, "Mem couldn't sleep last night," Mem nodded agreement, "and she said she saw that guy staying with Pastor Teresa – you know, that vet, the young one – coming back to the church."

Mem added, "It was before the rain, and just a short while before the fire started. I saw the flame and heard the sirens at about the same time, not too long after I saw him."

"Oh, no! Has anyone checked on Teresa this morning?"

"I did," said Holly. "It's just something I'm going to do for a while. She was fine when I called."

"Mem, did you think to tell Pete?"

"I sent a text just a while ago, after I had a cup of coffee and woke up."

"Have you gotten any word on who the man is?"

Jolly said, "No, but we saw Boone go into the police department, so maybe he's going to know who it is."

"Is he talking? The man, I mean?"

"We haven't heard anything about that."

Clara craned her neck to see something, causing the other women to look in that direction, out the window and toward the police department.

"Who's that man?"

Annie huffed. "That's our new guest."

Tiger Lily jumped to the table to get a look, knocking over a glass of water in the process.

"Big girl! You don't normally do that. What's up?"

Tiger Lily mewed, embarrassed to have caused an accident and angry that she missed seeing the guest, who was already inside the police department.

Clara, wiping water from her dress, said, "Why would he be going there? Who is he?"

"I don't know and I don't know. I know his name is Wyatt, he might be here through Sunday, he smokes dreadful cigars, and he's not very likeable."

Henrie left The Drug Store, filled with information about the night's occurrences and the injured man. He would have a lot to share with Annie.

The two double-bagged grocery sacks had handles, making them easier to carry. He carried ham sandwiches, individual servings of potato salad and cole slaw, bacon, sausage and scrambled eggs, seasoned with only salt and pepper. There were sandwich bags filled with wheat toast, sweet rolls and biscuits. In another container were individual containers of butter and jam.

He had no idea why he had packed the meal this way. Something led him to pack in picnic style instead of the way he would have normally carried a meal to a friend. No matter. It may be easier for Teresa to store this way.

Tiger Lily motioned for Moriah to join her under the table. *"We need to make sure Teresa is okay several times a day. Do you ever go over there?"*

"I do. Almost every day, I go into every place on that side of the street. Should I go now?"

"I don't think so, not right now. It sounds like Holly talked to her not too long ago. But you should go before lunch. Are you afraid?"

Moriah sat tall and glared. Well, for her it was sitting tall. Tiger Lily saw a ball of fluff change into a long-haired rectangle. *"Why should I be afraid? I'm good at this stuff."*

"I was just checking. They told me you were good, but I haven't seen you in action yet."

Two months ago, when Annie, Chris and their combined cats and a dog were out of town, Moriah joined the neighborhood cats in solving a crime. According to everyone involved, Moriah took to the detective business easily. She trained to be a cat burglar – Tiger Lily privately wondered how that rotund body could get around without being seen – and she helped Pete with other clues. The reviews were glowing, but still, Tiger Lily worried about the young cat going off on a dangerous mission on her own.

She heard Mommy say something about a new guest going into the police department. She jumped up to look, which turned out to be a disaster in more than one way.

Pete stood to welcome his visitor. "Hello. You're Wyatt? I'm Pete. How can I help you?"

"I'm from the Veterans' Affairs office. We heard about a group of homeless vets in the area. I thought I'd meet them and see if there is something we can do to help. I figured you would know where they are."

"How did you hear about that?"

"It hit the news yesterday, you know, the guy who died. Hey, mind if I smoke?" Wyatt pulled a cigar from his pocket and waved it in the air.

"Not here, man. Anyway, I wasn't aware the news identified him as one of a group of homeless vets."

Wyatt put the cigar back into his pocket as he said, "I think that came out in various web stories, not in the first report. I don't know how many we're talking about, just that there are more."

"That's true," said Pete, "but I don't know where they are now. I've heard they couldn't be found at the marina, where the first fire was."

"The first fire?"

"The one on the news. You aren't aware there was a second?"

"No. So there was a second fire?"

"Last night."

"Was someone else killed?"

"No, injured. And we don't know if this was arson or an accident."

"Was this injured man one of those homeless vets?"

"He's not able to talk yet, but we don't know him, so it's possible he's one of that group. I just sent a man to the hospital to see if it is."

"So there is someone who knows them?"

"More like someone who met them. One of my officers is with him now. I'll find out soon enough."

"And right now, you can't tell me where to look for the rest of them?"

"Not right now, but if you give me a phone number, I'll call you if I learn anything."

"Great. In the meantime, do you have a problem with my poking around?"

"As long as you don't trespass or break any laws, you can do anything you want."

Moriah trotted back toward the Café on the heels of Teresa. On her mission to make sure she was okay, she found Teresa on her way to lunch.

Much the better. Maybe someone would drop food on the floor.

When they arrived at the Café, Moriah saw several things at once. Jerry waved Teresa to a table in one corner; Tiger Lily sat at a table in another corner with Jennifer, Marie and Annie; and Pete, Boone and Cyril were at a table in the middle of the room.

What to do?

Using her new skills as a detective, she quickly discounted sitting with Jennifer and Marie, no matter how much she wanted to hear their story. A detective was already on the job. She could discount Pete and Boone, too. She really wanted to hear what they had to say, but Cyril was good to share information.

With a feeling of martyrdom, she continued with Teresa, assuming her conversation would be the most boring.

How wrong she was.

Annie seated the sisters and asked, "May I join you?"

"Sure," answered Marie. 'Sit. We'll spill everything."

"Everything we can," said Jennifer.

"We already spilled to Henrie, so we've had practice."

"Great. This is one of the perks of being at the Café every day. What happened?"

Marie and Jennifer dropped into their familiar pattern of speech, one talking on top of the other, finishing one another's sentences. It didn't matter who said what, because you needed both to get the whole story.

"We don't know the name of the guy, which is good, because we can't tell you the name of the guy."

"We can tell you he had second and third degree burns..."

"...on his arms and torso, some on his leg. Hi, Sharon. I'll take the special sandwich, I think that – what is it? Teriyaki chicken? Yeah. I'll take that. It comes in a pita?"

"Yep. It's sliced thin and grilled crispy. It's perfect in a pita."

"Great, and a side of the Asian slaw."

"I'll take the Italian cupboard soup with a couple of slices of garlic bread. Can I get that on thick whole wheat?"

"Sure. To drink?"

"Ask Trudy to send our regulars."

"But tell her I need a double shot of espresso."

"Where were we?"

Annie said, "Second and third degree burns."

"Right. On arms, torso and legs. He was really out of it."

"But if you ask me, I think he was out of it because of that conk on the head."

"Oh, yeah. We had to handle that as well. He was lucky to make it to the hospital."

"The worst burns were on his right arm."

"Too bad, because he didn't have a left one."

"Or a left eye. Looked like he'd been through fire before…"

"…at first we thought his face had been burned, but…"

"…that was an old injury…"

"…he has to be one of those homeless vets…"

"…but we didn't see any of the others…"

"…no, I think I saw one over by the dumpster."

"When?"

"When we first go there. Then he disappeared."

Annie asked, "What did he look like?"

"I don't know. It was dark; he was kind of outlined by the lights from the fire and police vehicles. As soon as I saw him, it's like he registered my eyes and he faded away."

"Age?"

"Can't say. You can't tell with someone who lives on the street. They could be twenty or seventy, but they can have the same look, ya know?"

While coffee was delivered, Annie asked, "Will he be okay?"

Jennifer and Marie looked at one another, then made who-knows faces while wobbling their heads. Jennifer finally said, "He'll recover from the burns if the head injury isn't that severe."

Pete asked, "So you know this one, Boone?"

"Yeah. He's another Gulf War vet. Name is Farrell; I'm not sure if that's with an 'F' or a 'Ph.' Pretty sure he's Army, too. Actually, I think all the Gulf War vets out there are Army."

"Can you tell me anything else? Anything that might help me track him down?"

"He has visible injuries. He lost an arm and an eye, both on the left side, and the left side of his face looks as if it was burned."

"That should help them track him down, even without a last name. Can you tell me anything else?"

"Nope. It was tough to see him at the hospital, Pete. I…for him to live through that and to have this happen. I don't know. I don't know."

"It looks like this was intentional. He had a head injury that can't be explained by the fire."

"Was he out cold?"

"Apparently."

"Then how'd he get out?"

"I don't know. I was hoping you could tell me."

"It wasn't me, if that's what you're thinkin'."

"Not that, Boone. I thought you could tell me which of those guys might, I don't know. Heck. I don't know if someone hit him, started the fire and got remorse, or if someone was watching out for him. I don't know."

"I can't help you there, Pete. I don't have the kind of relationship…heck…they wouldn't tell me stuff like that."

"Would they tell Teresa?"

Boone turned to look at Teresa's table. She had just turned to look back at him.

Jerry stood and held a chair for Teresa. "What's up? You sounded, I don't know, scared?"

"Not scared, but I'm sure glad you could get away for lunch. I'm worried."

"About Gene?"

"Yeah. I think he was out walking around last night, maybe around the time of the fire."

"Do you think he set it?"

"I don't think so. No. I'm sure he didn't. He just isn't that kind of a guy. But he was sure skittish this morning. Henrie brought a lot of food over this morning, Gene didn't eat much, but when I went back to clean up, all of the food was gone."

"All of it? And where was he?"

"He left."

"So he was out walking around, and he took food. This isn't like you, Teresa. You're talking in circles. Here, have some coffee."

Sarah placed Teresa's usual coffee order on the table. "Are you having lunch?"

"Um, yeah," said Teresa. "I'll have the barley minestrone with a basket of bread. Please make sure there's some rye in it. Jerry? This one's on me."

"Thanks. I'll have the same. And some of that bread."

When Sarah was gone, Teresa took a sip and a deep breath. "Okay. Let me get my thoughts in order. Gene left last night. I heard the doors. Then I heard the doors again, I think he came in. Then the rain started, then the sirens, then maybe the door again, or it might have been thunder. Then more sirens. That was the ambulance. By then, I was up and looking out the windows. After the ambulance had been there for several minutes, I saw someone walking toward the church, but I couldn't tell who it was. It could have been Gene, but I wasn't certain he had left."

"Did that someone come into the church?"

"I don't know. He walked past my sight, and I don't know if he walked past or came in."

"Did you check on him?"

"No. That would have been too invasive."

"Too invasive? Teresa, he's living in your home!"

"I know, but, you know, with everybody that I invite, I give an element of trust. You know? I have to trust my gut. Trust I'm doing the right thing for people who need it. Who want it. I'm sure Gene wants it. He wants to be whole again."

"So how can I help?"

"I don't know. I just wanted to tell someone. In case…"

"Teresa, are you frightened for your own safety?"

"No. No, that's not it. I don't know. I want what's best for everyone. I need to talk to Boone. Maybe he can talk to Gene about a job today."

"He's over there."

Teresa turned to look. Boone was looking at her, his expression unreadable.

She turned back to Jerry. "I just had a thought. Maybe he took that food for his friends."

Moriah fairly bristled with excitement. She had real evidence! Her evidence had to be the best!

She trotted to the hostess stand and hopped on top of Cyril. He gave a slight "huff" at her weight.

"You've put on a few pounds," he said.

"I have to keep up my fluffy good looks."

"You're doing a good job of it."

Tiger Lily joined them and asked, *"Who wants to go first?"*

Moriah looked at Cyril. Cyril sat up, dumping Moriah in the process, and began. *"Boone knows this guy, too. His name's Farrell, and he was in the same war as the first guy. He isn't awake yet, and Pete said earlier he might not wake up. It appears someone hit him on the head, then set the fire. But someone pulled him out, either the same guy that hurt him or someone else."*

"That's good information," said Tiger Lily. *"Jennifer saw a guy there. He was by a dumpster, and he kind of faded away, like he didn't want to be seen. He could have been the doer or the saver."*

"Or both," said Cyril.

"Right. Or both. How about you, Moriah. Did you learn anything?"

Moriah fluffed her mane and licked her paw before answering. Tiger Lily's eyes got wide and she looked at Cyril. Cyril rolled his eyes and shook his head, sending her the silent message, *"She did this last time, too."*

Tiger Lily rolled her eyes at Cyril, saying, silently, *"Dear gracious good golly. What. A. Diva."*

Finally, Moriah finished and began her report. *"Teresa said the guy staying with her, Gene, left the church before the fire and came back before the sirens started. But he may have left after that. Or not. She wasn't sure. But she saw someone that could have been him walking away from the fire and toward the church sometime after the ambulance went down there. She couldn't tell, and she couldn't tell if the guy came into the church or walked past."*

As she talked, Cyril and Tiger Lily sat up straighter, eyes got wider, and their mouths dropped open.

Tiger Lily finally got hold of her thoughts. *"We might have a suspect."*

"Or not," said Moriah. *"Remember, she couldn't tell. Humans aren't as perceptive as cats. Or dogs,"* she added. *"If one of us had been there, we would have been able to tell."*

Tiger Lily thought about it and put it into words. *"Gene could have hit him over the head and set the fire, and he could have gone back and saved him. Or he could have hit him over the head, set the fire, and gone back to make sure he was dead. Or he could have been just out walking, and he went out walking again, and he saved him. Or not. Or, um, I lost my place…"*

Moriah stepped in. *"He could have done nothing, and that second guy could have been someone else, or he could have done all of it."*

Tiger Lily looked at her. *"Right. You're good at this."*

"I know."

Cyril rolled his eyes and stood to leave. *"Pete needs me. I'll let you know if I hear anything."*

"Hey, Cyril," started Tiger Lily, *"what about that cat?"*

"Later. I have to go." Cyril walked around the hostess stand to follow Pete out the door.

"Oh! Really, wait! We have to get Pete to talk to some guys who have a drone and took pictures of the first fire, and…"

She and Moriah had followed Pete and Cyril out the door but could do nothing but watch his retreating tail.

She looked at Moriah. *"We'll have to figure out the email."*

The feral cat started as the man leaned into the car. He extended his arm and placed a hub cap on the back seat.

He stood to reach into his pockets. He pulled out a plastic bag with shreds of bacon and sausage mixed with scrambled eggs. He poured half into the hub cap.

"I'm not going to put it all out now. You'd be attacked by rats if you had left overs. I'll be back in a few hours. If this is gone, I'll leave more."

She stared at him as he backed away.

For once, she was glad the tom was away. He'd eat all the food. Now she had a chance to fill her belly. Keep up her milk. The kittens were hungry. So was she.

She wouldn't eat, though, not until this man left. He must have sensed it, because he turned and walked away.

Gene found the others. They had come back to the old marina, because, really, in this town, there was no other place for them to gather and not be noticed.

They sat in a circle, on a pile of tires, dejected.

They brightened as Gene opened his bags and handed out sandwiches, potato salad, cole slaw, bacon, sausage and eggs. Since he had already eaten, he watched as they wolfed down the food, waiting to talk until they had eaten their fill.

Finally, Perry said, "Thanks, man. Where'd you get it?"

"Some black guy brought it to the church this morning. It was like he knew I'd be carrying it here. It was all packed up like this."

Harper looked around as he asked, "Did they follow you?"

"Who?"

Harper shook his head, then said, "Uh, whoever gave ya the food."

"No. No one followed me. Did you expect…"

"Nah. Just, you know, it's been a hard coupla days."

Perry said, "So when are you guys gonna tell me and Gene what's goin' on? What's happening?"

Harper, Ben and Tempo looked at one another, then down at their feet. Ben finally said, "Ain't nothin' happenin'. Bad luck is all."

Gene said, "Bad luck? Bad luck got Mal killed? Bad luck got Farrell nearly killed?"

Tempo, head jerking in rhythm, nearly shouted, "Farrell ain't dead?"

"No, he ain't. He's bad. That pastor lady said he might not make it, but last I heard, he's still alive."

Harper said, "I still cain't figger out how he got outta there."

Gene shuffled his feet. "I pulled 'im out. Couldn't do nothin' else fer 'im, though."

The Gulf War vets traded another set of looks. Ben finally said, "Well, that's good, then. Maybe he'll be okay. He's safe now, at least."

Perry asked, "Safe from what?"

Harper leaned forward. "Safe from the weather, he's got food, he's in a bed. He's safe."

Gene said, "That's not what you meant, man. Safe from what?"

Harper leaned back again, sitting as straight as his back would let him. "You done a good thing, bringin' food here.

I hope you can do it again tomorrow. Feels good, havin' a full belly. But you don't need to be pushin' for stuff that's none-a-yer business. I didn't want you along in the first place. 'Member that?"

"I do. I remember. Mal was my friend. I'd like to know why he died."

"He got caught in a fire, prob'ly set the durn thing hisself. That's all you need to know."

Ben said, "Just a minute now. We might need this young 'un for more than just food. He's got a good head. We might need him to keep an eye out."

"I'll keep an eye out for you, if you tell me what to look for."

Harper stared in the distance. "We all need to get. Go, now!"

Gene watched as his friends scattered in all directions. He finally turned to see a lone figure standing on the dune, staring down. Well, heck. He wasn't afraid of one man, but just this once, maybe he'd better not run into the fight. Slowly, he stuffed trash into the bags, picked them up, and walked back toward town. Every now and then, he turned to stare at the man, who had not moved.

7

Annie's cats gathered under the detective table, joined by Moriah and Tillie. They shared their information but quickly realized Tiger Lily and Moriah had the mother lode.

"So," said Mr. Bean, *"what do we do next?"*

Mo gave a soft trill.

Sassy Pants translated. *"We sends email."*

Tiger Lily shook her head. *"There's too much I don't know how to spell. I don't know how to spell drone, or camera, or computer, or…well…I don't know."*

They were interrupted by the arrival of Simon Finnegan and Oscar McMurphy. They both carried paper in their mouths.

Triumphantly, Simon Finnegan dropped his paper and said, *"We have it!"*

Oscar McMurphy said, *"This is the drone stuff, and pictures of what the drone camera can do."*

"Wow!" "This is great!" "You can figure out how to spell it now!" "Fantastic!"

Tiger Lily thought hard. *"Maybe…"* she said, *"maybe I don't have to send an email. Maybe we can tell Henrie."*

"Tells him what? To sends email?"

"No, tell Henrie to tell Pete what he needs to know."

"How?" asked Kali. *"Will you talk to him?"* asked Ko.

"Kali, Ko, go get him and bring him here."

"How?"

"Just figure it out."

Kali and Ko looked at one another then dragged their big bodies out from under the table. They looked around, wondering where he might be, then heard the back kitchen door. He was coming in.

They dragged themselves into the kitchen and stared up at him, unsure what to do.

Henrie said, "Are you girls hungry?"

Kali and Ko looked at one another and suddenly felt light as feathers. They jumped at Henrie, pawing his legs, mewing what they hoped to be begging sounds. It worked.

"Go into the dining room. I'll be right there with your snack."

They ran back. Tiger Lily had already arranged the papers on the floor. She looked up.

Kali and Ko, at the same time, said, *"He's coming!" "He's bringing snack!"*

"Okay. Everyone in position. Make a part of a circle around me, so he knows this is important."

They did, arranging themselves in a large semi-circle.

When Henrie appeared, little dishes on a tray, he stopped, looked, placed the tray on the dining room table and got on his knees.

"Okay, Tiger Lily. Tell me what you need me to know."

Pete saw Wyatt enter the police department. As he finished his call, he waved him into his office. "Need something?"

"Yeah. I need your help."

"What can I do for you?"

"I found those vets, but they scattered. They aren't going to talk to me, but…well, one of them came back into town. It looked like he had taken food out to them. Maybe, if you know where he is – heck, he might not even be one of them – he might be someone else, you know. Anyway, do you have any ideas?"

Pete picked up the phone and made a call. "Boone, any idea who might have taken food out to the vets?"

"Yeah. Teresa thinks Gene took the stuff that Henrie took to the church."

"That's good. Is he going to work for you?"

"I haven't been able to talk to him yet, but I hope he does."

"Okay. I'll mention it. I'm going to try to find him."

Pete hung up and stood. "Come with me. We might find one of them."

At the church, Pete rang the doorbell to the upstairs apartment. Teresa came on the audio box. "Yeah, Pete, I can see you. Come on in."

Upstairs, Pete said, "This is Wyatt. He's from Veterans' Affairs, and he's hoping to talk to the vets living here."

"Well, maybe he can talk to Gene. I'll see if he's in."

Teresa left the men in the kitchen, pointing to the coffee pot as she left. Pete pulled cups from the cupboard and poured for himself and Wyatt as they waited. "So, what all can you do? I mean, really, can you offer housing?"

"Well, yes. Not here. They would have to come with me, or at least go to one of the towns where housing is available."

"Where is that, exactly?"

"Exactly? You mean what towns?"

"Yes, and what kinds of places? Shelters? Apartments?"

They were interrupted when Teresa came back with Gene. Gene said, "It was you, up on the dune."

"Yeah. I wanted to talk to all of you."

"You didn't come down. You could have come down."

"I'd been looking around town, and, well, when everyone scattered, I didn't want to, you know, give chase."

Gene sat at the table with the men while Teresa hung back. Pete poured coffee for Gene and sat again.

Wyatt faced Gene and began an earnest recital. "I'm from Veterans' Affairs. We've been putting a lot of effort into getting services to veterans in need. Folks like you. We can provide housing, medical services, food, emotional support. We can't do it everywhere, you know, like in small towns like Chelsea, but we can get you to one of the larger towns, one of the cities, and hook you up. Anything you need."

"Anything?"

"Well, within reason, yes. I'd like to offer the services to all of you, but I don't know where to find the other guys."

Pete's phone rang. He pulled it out to silence it but thought better of it. He stood and walked away from the table. "What's up, Henrie?"

8

Gene rose from the table suddenly and left Pastor Teresa's apartment. Wyatt, perplexed, remained at the table, watching him go.

"What did I say?" he asked.

Teresa sat at the table. "It's a combination of what you did and did not say."

"Huh?"

"Gene was interested in the services you had to offer. He tried to ask questions, but you put him off. You were more interested in finding everyone else."

"I have to find all of them in order to take them to. . ."

"Right. You couldn't even tell him where he would be going. He asked that question at least three different times."

"But. . ."

"He asked about shelter, what kind it would be. He asked about jobs. You kept asking where you could find everyone else."

"But doesn't he understand. . ."

"He understands something very well. Someone is trying to kill them, particularly the older guys. You may or may not have their best interests at heart, but you gave him no reason to trust you. I think you should leave now."

Pete found Henrie – and the cats – in the dining room. Henrie held two cat-bitten papers in his hand.

"I believe our friends have discovered a way for you to learn more about the fires."

Pete took the pages, looking at them quickly. He motioned for Tiger Lily to get on the table and faced her.

Cyril watched as she jumped up. *"He's going to ask you to do the yes/no."*

Tiger Lily looked down at him. *"I did it with Henrie, but I don't like to do tricks."*

"Think of it as communicating."

Pete, after reviewing the pages, looked at Tiger Lily. "I hope you'll do the yes/no with me."

Tiger Lily rolled her eyes, then blinked once.

He made fists of his hands and put them on the table in front of her. "Is this important?"

Tiger Lily touched his right hand. Yes.

"Does it have to do with something happening in town now?" Yes.

"Did someone see a fire?" Yes.

"Do you know who owns the drone?"

Tiger Lily looked down at Fat Cat and Scaredy Cat. *"Come up here,"* she said.

Once they were behind her on the table, she touched Pete's right hand. Yes.

Pete directed his gaze to the two big cats. "Did he, or she, buy the drone from DoubleGood?" Yes.

"So, I just need to ask Holly or Jolly about it?" Yes.

"Okay. I'll do that right now. Thanks, Henrie, and thanks. . .all of you. Come on, Cyril."

Pete and Cyril rose to leave, expecting to do police work. They were accompanied by ten cats and a little dog.

Pete shook his head as he walked across The Avenue. To Cyril, he said, "I hope no one is looking."

But everyone was. Heads popped out of doors all over The Avenue to see the spectacle of Pete, like a modern-day pied piper, leading the cats (and dogs) out of town. Or, as it were, to DoubleGood.

Holly and Jolly had opened the door to look and were ready for him. "You're coming here? What's up with that?"

Pete waved the papers in the air as he walked into the door. Holly, from her wheelchair, held the door open until all the furry bodies were inside.

"Drones?" said Jolly. "You want to buy a drone?"

"No, I want to know who buys drones from you."

"A few people."

Pete looked around for Tiger Lily. "Come up here, Tiger Lily."

Tiger Lily sat on the floor and looked up at him.

"Did I forget to say please?"

She blinked once.

"Please."

She jumped to the counter.

"Was it a man?" Yes.

"How many men purchased drones?"

Jolly thought for a minute. "Um. . .three. No. Four. Four men bought three drones. Two singles and a set of brothers."

Turning to Tiger Lily, he asked, "One man or two?"

Tiger Lily stared at him.

"Sorry. One man?" No.

"Two men?" Yes.

To Jolly, "The brothers. Who are they?"

"The Smith boys. They live with their mother and go to the community college. They're geeks, kinda, in a good way. They like their computer toys and cameras."

"So they're set up with cameras? They could have filmed things?"

"Yeah."

"To see in real time or to record?"

"Both, in theory, depending on how they've set it up. With the stuff they've bought here, they could do both."

"Great. Do you have an address?"

"Just a sec." Jolly pulled a laptop out from under the cash register and searched her customer database. "Here."

"Thanks. Come on, Cyril."

They left the store as a parade until Pete stopped and turned around.

"No. No. No. You are not coming with us. I will not have a car filled with cats and. . .a little dog."

Cyril laughed as he trotted after Pete, leaving the little ones in his wake.

The mother cat thought back to better times, easier times. Times when she had a fur-ever family. A nice place to sleep. Food and water every day.

Then the impossible happened. She got lost. She ended up here, in this place with shelter that was passable in good weather, but she nearly died last winter.

The tom found her, kept her alive, then did what most toms did. He went away when she needed him most.

Maybe there was still hope for the babies. If she could keep the babies alive, maybe there would be a chance for them.

Pete knocked on the door of a house on the north side of town. It was a nice neighborhood. The houses were small, older, but well-tended. Here and there were a few that could use paint; some needed weeds pulled. For the most part, they were in good shape.

Finally, the door opened to a middle-aged woman. "Can I help you? Oh, Chief. Is something the matter?"

"No. Callie Smith, right?"

"Yes. Come in, come in."

"Thank you, um. . ."

"Yes, your dog is welcome here."

Pete and Cyril followed Callie into the kitchen. "I just made a pot of coffee. Have a cup?"

"Sure. Don't you work at the hospital?"

"I do. I work strange hours in the ER. Just got home. It sure was awful what happened to that man. Is that why you're here?"

"No." Pete accepted the cup and sat at the table. "Thanks. I think your sons might be able to help me with something."

"My sons? John and Tim? How?"

"I understand they bought a drone from DoubleGood?"

"A drone, cameras, computers, games, cables, you name it. They have to work two part-time jobs each to pay for their toys."

"At least they're working. I hear they're in college, too?"

"Part-time. Everything's part-time. My no-good-for-nothin' husband was no good for them, too. I keep the house up, make car payments, one for me, one for them, and they pay their own way after that. We get by. And they enjoy their toys. Anyway, what do you want to know about the drone?"

"They may have recorded one of those fires."

"Oh, no. Is that a crime?"

"No, no, no. Not a crime. And if they did record it, they may not realize the importance of what they might have seen. I'd just like to talk to them, and if they recorded something, take a look."

"Oh. Okay. Let me call and see where they are. They should be on their way home from class right about now."

She hung up and said, "They're about ten minutes away. Want more coffee?"

"Don't mind if I do. Hey, since I'm here, did you work on that man? The one from the fire?"

"I did."

"Did he ever say anything?"

"He woke up once. He said something that sounded like 'cappin' jenshun.' Said it a couple of times before he went out for good."

"Cappin' jenshun? Huh. Wonder what that means?"

9

Pete lit a cigar, took a deep puff, and smiled. Cigars, beer, pizza, poker, good friends. It didn't get any better than this. A great end to any kind of a day.

Chris brought the carryout pizza into Pete's man cave. Three large, one with every kind of meat the pizza place had, one for vegetarians, or, as Pete liked to say, carnivores that were getting full, and one filled with all matter of great stuff: onions, olives, ham, pineapple, anchovies and Italian sausage. Pete and Ray always let Chris have that one to himself.

"That's okay. Tank will eat it with me."

"Uh, I don't think so," said Tank. This was his first time at the poker game. Pete had insisted.

"This is what you do when life begins to overwhelm you," he had said.

"Broaden your horizons," he had said.

"Bring your money," he had said.

Pete had to do one more thing. He went to the large screen television, turned on the DVR, and set it to play the Westminster Dog Show from February.

"That will keep our friends busy," he said. And it did.

As Ray dealt the first hand, Pete talked about the breakthrough he had this afternoon. He looked at Tank and grew serious. "You're going to hear things here that you won't believe. If you come to this game, you are sworn to secrecy. What you hear in this room stays in this room. Can you live with that?"

"Sure," said Tank. "Are you gonna talk about the case? Because, you know, I'd never say anything."

"Kind of," said Pete. He looked around the table, making eye contact with Ray and Chris. "This isn't really a secret society or anything, but we know things. Things that very few people know. You're going to think we're crazy, but, anyway, what happens at the poker table stays at the poker table. Good enough?"

"Good enough."

"Okay." Pete sat back and started to talk. "Henrie called and I went over to the Inn. What do you think I saw? Those cats, of course. All of 'em from the neighborhood, too. They were sitting around some brochures from DoubleGood. I guess those two from there, they have those strange names, I guess they dragged the brochures over."

Pete took a pull from the bottle and a drag on the cigar.

"Henrie said Tiger Lily pointed to pictures and did the yes/no."

Tank, a confused look on his face, broke in. "I'm going to pretty much listen, but what's the yes/no?"

"Oh, it's a trick. Well, not a trick really. It's how we communicate with our companions. Cyril and I started it, but Tiger Lily and some others have picked it up."

Ray said, "Jock refuses to play. I think he's jealous it didn't come from us."

"Most of the cats don't do it, either. Tiger Lily does it, but she rolls her eyes."

"Cats don't roll their eyes," said Ray.

Chris rolled his. "Tiger Lily does."

"Okay, let me continue. Tank, to play the yes/no, we ask questions that can only be answered with a yes or a no, and the companion in question will touch our right hand or our left hand. Or foot."

"Or foot?"

"Or foot."

A look of confusion remained on Tank's face.

Pete continued. "Henrie was given to assume that she should communicate with me."

Pete took a drink, took a puff, looked at the cards.

"So?" asked Ray.

"Oh, right. We figured out that someone bought a drone and may have filmed one of the fires. I took the brochures over to DoubleGood – followed by all of the cats, I might add – to ask about customers who had drones."

"Holly and Jolly know why you're asking?"

"No, but they're looking at all the cats and the tooth-marked brochures in my hands, and they're piecing it together. A couple of brothers, the Smith boys – you know them – anyway, they like gadgets. Without the cats in tow, I go to see them."

"Were they the right guys?"

"They were. They had footage from the first fire, and they let me make a copy. I have that copy, and I have a little more information than I had before."

"What?"

"First off, I was able to see all the homeless guys. At least I think I saw all of them. They were huddled on that dune. Every now and then, the drone would slip over that far. They all seemed, well, upset. Too upset to have been involved in the fire or anything that might have happened to the dead man. Malcolm. A Gulf War vet."

"Bad deal."

"Lived through that, and now…"

"Right. But the rest of what I saw was really interesting. You'll want to see this, Tank. You know how we figured the fire started at one boat and spread to another, then another, then another?"

"Yeah…"

"The footage shows all of them burning bright at the same time. It didn't show the start, because they didn't send the drones until they heard sirens. They were there soon enough, though, to capture one very large fire. Everything burning at the same rate. I'll bet the investigators find accelerant in all of the boats."

"Anything else, Pete? Other people?"

"Not that I could tell, but by the time the drone was there, there were firemen and police all over the place. The biggest takeaway was the fire itself. I made a copy for the arson investigator."

Tank finished one beer and started another. "One thing, Pete."

"Yeah?"

"Tell me about those cats."

During the commercials, Cyril told Sis and Jock everything he knew about the investigation to date. When he finished telling them about the conversation between the cats and Henrie, Sis said, *"That's impressive. How did Henrie know to listen to them?"*

Jock answered. *"He's had a lot of experience with the cats. He and Annie have a special relationship with them. For the most part, they're happy to treat them like cats, you know, like royalty, who get to sleep in, eat whenever they want, stuff like that. But on occasion, they do something un-cat-like, and they know to pay attention."*

"Is that how you talk to Pete, Cyril?"

"Kind of, but we've had a one-on-one working relationship for a lot longer. He knows how to rely on my instincts."

"Same with me and Ray," said Jock. *"Ray talks to me all the time, and when I answer, he understands. Sometimes, like when there's danger, we take turns saving one another."*

"You've had to do that?"

Jock nodded soberly. *"We've had some close calls."*

"I hope that doesn't happen to me and Chris," said Sis. She recognized her grammatical error, but she wanted to fit in. She had mirrored Jock's error with her own. She was grateful to get a genuine smile from the big black dog.

The block party committee rarely met anymore. Things came together without much thought. Still, the group felt a need to gather at least once, not to plan, but to visit.

Tonight, they met at Mo's Tap. Candice took their table so she could participate on occasion. Tonight, she served family-style platters of cheeseburger sliders, sweet potato fries and deep fried dill pickle spears. "Nothing but carbs and fat," she said. "Enjoy."

Several tables had been pulled together in a haphazard fashion to accommodate the group. It included Annie, the kind-of-sort-of chair, or coordinator, or caller-of-meetings, most of her friends from across the Avenue and several of her staff, at least those who were not working. Others from the community joined them, like Nancy, Janet, Pete's wife, and, for the first time, Annie's former nemesis, Geraldine.

Geraldine was tall, compared to Annie's medium height. Geraldine was svelte. Annie was not. Geraldine's hair was always "just so." Annie's straight hair fell to her shoulders in a kind-of-a-style. Geraldine was always dressed to the nines. Annie didn't go there. Geraldine wore stilettos. Annie kept her feet close to the ground.

Geraldine used to have something stuck in her nether regions. Now, she shared a desire to make her community a better place to live.

She also – for the first time in her life – found a need to work. Her work, consulting for a high-end fashion company, afforded her the opportunity to travel and to continue to dress in style.

Nancy made a point of sitting next to Geraldine. Unlike Annie, she still didn't trust her. She wanted to be close, just in case Geraldine decided to bring out those verbal switchblades to throw in Annie's direction.

Geraldine helped herself to a sweet potato fry and asked, "What does anyone know about the homeless people in town? How long has that been a problem?"

Those questions got the "meeting" started.

Like any "meeting" among several women, several conversations ensued at once. The end result – after a few rounds of pomegranate martinis – was to assign a task to none other than Geraldine. The task was to find a charity that served veterans that was more about service and less about hype.

"Well, okay. I can do this. Does anyone have a suggestion?"

Trudie answered, "Go online to Charity Navigator. I think it's a dot org. Then search for veterans groups. They rank charities based on the percentage of dollars that go to services, transparency, quality of leadership and fundraising, stuff like that."

Nancy said, "There are lots of organizations that say they help vets, but they don't. They line their own pockets."

Geraldine said, "So I have to really do my homework. Okay. I'll do it before the next meeting."

Janet looked at her watch. "I think they're finished with the poker game by now, but I doubt the smoke has been cleared."

Cheryl, Ray's wife and the owner of the well-kept marina, shook her head. "I don't know how you can handle going back into your house after one of those games. Remember the days we used to do our own thing in the kitchen?"

"That was before the cigars came out," said Annie. "Speaking of cigars, we have a smoker at the Inn. He's a piece of work. Wanted to light up inside or on the porch."

"Is it that guy over there?" asked Laila. She pointed to a man at the bar, talking to George and waving an unlit cigar in his hand.

"That's him. Has he tried to light it?"

"No, but I think he asked George about it. I think he argued, too. That must have been what was going on, when George pointed to you."

"When was that?"

"Oh, maybe a half hour ago. He turned to look, must have recognized you from behind. Anyway, he stopped pressing the point."

Annie shook her head. "What a piece of work."

Annie turned to Geraldine. "Hey, do you ever talk to Hank?"

Geraldine made a face. "That creep? No. Why do you ask?"

Annie's mind went to all of the times Hank had been cruel, had put her businesses at risk, had put her friends and family at risk, had tried to hurt her mentally and emotionally. He had never come out on top. Over the years, Hank had to pay some civil, although never criminal, penalties. Annie never knew the source of his hatred for her.

She came back to the present. "It just seems like every time I turn around, people are saying 'Hank said this,' 'Hank saw that. . .'"

"In relation to what?"

"The fires. The vets. You know."

"Well, he does get around. When I did, um, know him well, he spent part of each day walking in one part of town or another. He went everywhere. High places, low places. He wanted to know everything."

"Well, he must be doing the same thing, even though he's not on the Town Council."

"I imagine he plans to run again. He would want to continue to meet the voters."

Nancy dropped her precious Honey Bear at the Inn before going to Mo's Tap. He had barely gotten to the third floor apartment – he was still in the kitchen – before Mo approached him and began to trill.

Over and over again, he trilled, stopped, trilled again, looked around for his interpreters, and, seeing none, continued to trill.

Finally, Honey Bear yelled, *"Will someone please tell me what he's talking about?"*

Sassy Pants finally came to the kitchen. She didn't need to hear Mo again. She was able to read his mind.

"He wanted to tell you we founded a way to tell Pete about da drones, an' we wented with Pete to Holly an' Jolly's store, an' den Pete wented to talk to da guys."

"How'd you do that?"

"Simon Finnegan an' Oscar McMurphy founded a way. Dey gotted papers dat showed da drones and we showed Pete."

"Good job! Do you know what the guys said?"

"No. We hasn't hearded yet. You wants to come to da dining room? We'ze sittin' on da window sill watchin' peoples."

"Sure. Thanks."

Honey Bear was feeling more and more at home at the Inn. This was a good thing.

10

Annie made a point of being in the kitchen early. She wanted to see this man – this smoker – to see if he would press his luck again.

He didn't.

He didn't smell like cigars, either. His clothes today looked and smelled fresh. As Henrie poured coffee, Annie asked if she could join him for breakfast.

"Sure. I'd love the company. You might be able to help me."

"How so?" Annie helped herself to hazelnut French toast, poured syrup and added a few slices of bacon.

"I've been working with the Sheriff…"

"You mean Pete? He's the Chief of Police."

"Oh, yeah. Him. Anyway, I'm trying to track down that group of vets that's been here. You know, they've had a couple of issues. One death, another injured…"

Henrie interrupted. "I am sorry to inform you the second gentleman passed away during the night. I heard the report on the morning news."

"Who was he?"

Henrie's eyebrows raised just a touch. "I do not believe the name has been released, pending either identification or notification of next of kin. They did say, however, that he was an Army veteran of the Gulf War, Desert Storm."

"That's too bad," said Annie. "I understand that this may also have been an arson, not an accident."

"You don't say," said Wyatt, turning to Annie. "They were both arson?"

"I believe so. Henrie, what have you heard about the first death?"

"Only that the gentleman was not living at the time the fire was set."

"Well, then it was a murder-arson," said Wyatt. "What about the second one?"

Annie answered, "It appeared he may have been assaulted before the fire, but he was able to rouse himself, or someone pulled him out. He was burned, but the burns probably didn't kill him."

"Well, this makes my mission ever more important. I must find them. I've been to the old marina, the site of the first fire. I saw them, but they scattered. If they know someone is looking for them, well, perhaps they will have found another place to stay."

"What do you mean, if they know someone is looking for them?"

"Well, you know, I was looking for them, but they saw me, and they split."

"So you need someone to find them and maybe let them know you want to see them?"

"Let them know the services we can offer. Housing, medical care, you know."

Henrie asked, "Do you provide job placement services?"

"We do, yes."

"What jobs are available?"

A blank look came over Wyatt's face. "Um, you know, I don't know the answer to that. Someone else handles jobs."

Annie looked at Henrie, then at Wyatt. "I'll keep my eyes and ears open."

Kali and Ko gave low growls when Wyatt came into the dining room.

"What's up with that?" asked Little Socks.

The big girls answered at the same time. *"He stinks." "I don't like him."*

Mr. Bean stuck his head out from under the cloth to look at the guest and take a sniff. *"I don't smell anything."*

Kali joined him and took a sniff. *"You're right. He has clean clothes on today. Yesterday he smelled like a rotten cigar."*

"Dat's why mommy duzn't want Chris to come over after poker. Rotten cigars."

Mo trilled. Kali interpreted. *"Chris doesn't smell that bad. His cigars are better."*

Tiger Lily looked at Kali and Ko. *"You're going to be busy the next few days. Every room will be full. The carriage house, too."*

Kali and Ko gave solemn nods. Together, they said, *"We're ready."*

"Okay," said Tiger Lily. *"Come on, guys. It's time for us to go to work."*

"We duzn't waits for Mommy?"

"No. She's going to the museum today. It's her turn to volunteer."

Annie stopped in the kitchen before leaving. "Whatcha doin', Henrie?"

Henrie turned from his task.

"Oh, I thought you had gone. I am packing lunch for Gene."

"He eats that much?"

Henrie laughed. "No, but Teresa believes he took yesterday's meal to his friends. I am making it easy for him to do so."

"Do you know where his friends are?"

"No, but I believe he either knows or has the ability to find them. I need to get this to him before he leaves for the day."

"Before you go, what do you think of Wyatt?"

"I do not trust him."

"Me neither. Hey, more guests will arrive today, right?"

"Yes. If my count is not off, we can expect to welcome fifteen today alone. We will have to use the detective table for breakfast for the next several days."

From the Inn to the Historic Lighthouse Museum was a walk of about a mile, if one walked up the beach. Annie took advantage of the soft June day to do just that. She opened the museum with her own key. Owned by the local historical society, the museum kept the beginnings of Chelsea and the region alive. Exhibits spotlighted the shipping and logging industries from which the town began.

As she unlocked the door, she noticed cigarette butts and beer cans around the entryway and the side of the building. Well, she would come out with a bag and a rake as soon as she opened up.

Nancy drove up. "Hey! I thought I'd help today. Put me to work."

"Great. I need to check things inside, then we'll clean up outside, okay?"

"Sure. Hey, what's with the butts and cans? I thought you didn't allow smoking or drinking."

"We don't. Someone must have hung out last night. I have rakes and those long-handled dust pans. It will go fast."

Annie checked the notes left by the closing volunteer the day before. Nothing of note. Nothing about butts or beer. No mail, no bills. Apparently, the museum had hosted twenty five visitors the day before, students from the local fourth grade class.

She walked through the museum, checking the exhibits from memory, moving a piece here and a piece there. This museum was an experiential one. That meant that most of the exhibits could be picked up, held, examined. One of the duties of the volunteers was to know the exhibits so well, they could tell if a piece had been returned to an incorrect location, or if it had not been returned at all.

For the most part, they did not have a problem with theft. They never – yes, she could use the word 'never' – had an issue with the classes. They came often, and they came with supervision, both teachers and parents.

On rare occasions, a tourist would take a liking to a small piece: an oil lamp, a bottle made of colored glass, or a captain's coffee mug. Each piece was a loss, but that was the price they paid for allowing guests to touch, to experience.

She noticed nothing out of place, nothing missing. Satisfied, she opened the cleaning closet and got two rakes, two dust pans and a trash bag.

Outside, raking the butts with Nancy, she heard movement in the grassy dune nearby. She looked up and saw several men.

Nancy noticed her gaze and turned to stare. She smiled and waved, a pure Nancy move. Who else would wave to several men, none of whom were familiar, and all of whom looked as if they lived on the street?

Nancy called, "Hello, there! It's a beautiful morning, isn't it?"

The men eased back into the grass and disappeared. One, Annie thought he looked younger than the rest, waved a hand before disappearing.

"They seem nice," said Nancy. She went back to work. Annie could only stare at her.

"Mom, I am continually in awe of you."

"That's nice, dear."

Inside the museum, Annie called Henrie. "Hey, they're here by the museum. Have you delivered lunch to Gene already?"

"I have, but I am still on The Avenue; he has not yet left Soul's Harbor."

"Think you can let him know without, you know, spooking him, that we've got eyes out?"

"I will do my best."

"Are you going to tell Wyatt?"

"I will not. I will, however, relay the information to Boone."

11

Pete and Tank spent the morning with the county coroner and the state arson investigator. The coroner had earlier confirmed the cause of death of Malcolm: blunt force trauma to the head. She suspected the same for the second victim, now confirmed as Boone's acquaintance, Farrell.

What was not yet confirmed, but highly suspected, was the presence of a savior on the night of the second fire. The coroner insisted Farrell would not have been able to walk away on his own. The blow, while not immediately fatal, was too damaging to allow him to navigate, especially while injured further by burns.

The arson investigator confirmed what they suspected. An accelerant had been used on all of the boats that were destroyed by fire, and also on the interior of the garage. What allowed the second victim to live – beyond the appearance of a savior – was the absence of accelerant on his clothing.

Because the Café was still busy with locals seeking gossip, Pete and Tank met Boone for lunch in the back dining room of Sassy P's.

Boone led with interesting information. "They've been spotted. Annie saw them over by the Lighthouse Museum. There's a few places out there for them to sleep under shelter, well, a little shelter. A bus stop and a carport by the accessible parking."

"Does anyone else know?"

"Henrie. He's been sending food, sorta, through that young one, Gene."

"How's he doing that?" asked Pete.

"He took lunch to the church yesterday, and Gene, when Teresa wasn't lookin', took it. They both thought it went to the others. Henrie packed more up today, and kind of let it be known they'd been seen at the museum."

"We have to keep their location to ourselves as much as possible. I don't know why, but it seems our vets may be targeted by someone."

"Why?" asked Tank. "They just got to town, as far as we know. They haven't had time to make anyone mad or ruin a Sunday picnic."

Boone said, "Maybe…I hate to think it…maybe one of 'em is doin' it to the others."

Pete countered, "Then who pulled Farrell out? I would think it would have been one of them."

"Maybe one's a bad 'un and one's a good 'un."

Tank said, "Or maybe it's someone else. Someone else that followed them here. What do we know? When did they get here?"

Tank and Pete looked at Boone. "I saw 'em first a week ago, around there."

"Were they at the Marina when you saw them first?"

"Yep. I was out there with my boys, pickin' up parts. They was just sittin' around that bunch of boats. They musta took me for a vet, 'cause they didn't run. Anyway, I went out there a few times before that fire. They didn't seem 'off' or anything. Nothin' to say they was afraid of anythin' or runnin'."

"Did you ask why Chelsea?"

"I thought it, but I didn't ask. That might be something to ask that young fella."

"I will. I wanted to yesterday, but someone else was there, and then I got called away." A movement caught Pete's eyes and he looked up. Wyatt approached from the tasting room.

"Hey, Pete. Good to see you."

"Wyatt. This is Boone, and this young fella is Tank."

"Howdoyado? Hey, I was wondering if you had anything to tell me? Have you found the vets?"

Boone and Tank watched Pete closely as he answered.

"Pull up a chair Wyatt. Join us for coffee."

"Don't mind if I do."

Wyatt pulled a chair to the table as Pete said, "Wyatt, here, is staying at the Inn. He works for – what is it? Veterans' Affairs? – and he wants to offer services to the vets. Housing, medical, that kind of stuff." He turned back to Wyatt. "We haven't heard from them. Nothing."

"Well, that's too bad. Do you have ideas where I might look?"

Boone and Tank exchanged glances. Boone said, "You could try the state park's campground. They have some cabins out there. They're usually rented, this time of year, though."

Tank added, "Or you could walk through the state park. They might be out there somewhere."

Pete thought Wyatt hid a quick look of anger. What was that about? No matter. Boone and Tank were on his side here. They would keep quiet. For now.

Pete wondered, but he didn't ask, why Wyatt didn't just ask Gene. They had met, after all.

Sassy Pants sat in the pot of the flowering bush near Pete's table. She listened carefully. It was important, of course, for her to get it all right. She leaned her head around the bush's trunk to look at Brown Mousie.

"You seeze doze guys? You needs to watch all dem, whenever dey come in. Listen good. Specially dat one we duzn't know, dat guy named Wyatt."

Brown Mousie nodded quickly. He was a capable spy.

Gene looked in all directions before coming from behind the rotted boat. He trotted to the old Edsel and crouched down to look inside. The cat was still there, and the food he had left the day before was gone.

He reached in to get the hub cap and set it on his knees. From his pocket he brought a mashed napkin filled with leftovers. He placed a healthy amount into the hubcap and returned it to the car seat. He also poured water from a bottle into a Styrofoam bowl, placing that next to the hub cap.

He knew the cat wouldn't eat while he was there, so he moved back to the rotted boat, again looking in all directions, and sat inside the splintered hull. He would wait for an hour or so and take more food after that.

He pulled his knees to his chest when he heard the car. Doors slammed. The voices of at least two men. A big white dog covered with brown speckles came up to the rotted hull and pushed its face into the opening. It was the dog that belonged to the Chief of Police. The dog sniffed, seemed to nod his head in approval, and slipped away.

Gene moved to the other side of the hull as quietly as he could, where he could peer out in the other direction. He saw the police car, the Chief, and a man that could have been from the fire department. He wasn't in uniform, but Gene had seen him before. The dog went to the Edsel and poked its face into the car.

Gene watched the dog. It appeared to talk to the cat. Was that possible? Maybe it was just trying to decide if the cat or her kittens would be a good snack. No. . .the dog didn't offer a menacing presence. Not to him, and not to the cat.

The dog walked to the other side of the car and poked its face through that window, appearing to sniff the kittens. Gene didn't hear anything from the cat, but he probably wasn't close enough to hear a hiss. Still, the dog didn't appear to be a danger.

Gene turned to look at the men. They were using their feet to move bits of charred wood around, staring at the ground and every now and then pointing to something interesting. Certainly there was nothing else to be found. The fire investigators had been here and gone. And this was the first fire. Certainly no evidence remained.

For a minute, Gene considered going out to talk to them. Maybe he should tell them what he knew. Or rather, what he didn't know but was beginning to suspect.

Maybe he should tell them his concerns about Wyatt.

No. Not yet.

He heard the police chief call, "Cyril, come!" He had to call a second time, and a third. When the dog finally left the Edsel, they all got into the cruiser, and once again, Gene was alone. He hoped.

He had stayed long enough. He trotted to the car, reached in and emptied the napkin of leftovers into the hubcap. "I'll be back tomorrow," he said.

The cat stayed on her haunches, leery, still, and watched as he walked away.

Cyril was glad to go back to the old, ratty marina. He wanted to check in with the cat. As he got out of the car, however, he followed his nose to the broken down hull of a boat that was off to the side, out of the way of the original fire.

He looked inside. Gene was there, and he smelled of food, like he had something in his pockets. That was good, because he probably didn't have food very often.

Satisfied, he trotted to the Edsel and looked in. He smelled the same food inside the car. Looking at the crumbs in the hubcap and the leery cat, he said, *"Did that man feed you? His name is Gene. He's staying in town now."*

The cat said nothing.

"Did I tell you my name is Cyril? I don't remember if I introduced myself last time. Do you have a name? Sometimes, dogs and cats who don't have humans don't have names."

The cat said nothing.

Cyril moved to the other side of the car and looked intently at the kittens, lying in a pile on the floor in front of the passenger seat. They were dirty, and two of them looked sick.

Cyril kept his eyes on the kittens but said, *"If you let me tell my human about you, he'll get you and your babies some help."* He turned his head to look at the cat.

She said nothing but glared back.

"You don't have to. I'm just saying, is all. I'd like to help you. I can tell that man is bringing food to you, but that's not enough. Your babies need help."

She said nothing.

"Did you see the fire the other night? Do you know what happened? If you know, I can find a way to let my human know, and he'll take care of the person who did it."

She said nothing. Pete called him to come.

Cyril lingered. *"I'll be back. Let me know if you want me to get help for you. I can do it really easy, but I won't if you don't want it. You can trust me."*

As Cyril left, the cat wondered if she should speak up next time. Her babies might not make it if she didn't have some help soon. Maybe the dog was right.

12

Henrie was in his element. He was at his best when overwhelmed. Today, and for the rest of the week, he would be overwhelmed with guests.

Shortly after lunch he helped the airport's minibus driver unload luggage. He rolled the luggage cart from the parking lot to the carriage house three times, installing five couples. Ko rode the luggage cart each time, climbing over luggage to get a good sniff of each. Many a crime had been solved by her good sniffer.

Kali deposited love hairs on the legs of all the men. One man wore long pants. It was easy to get him. The others had shorts and sandals, but she managed.

Kali was notorious for ignoring the female guests.

Finally, the last trip completed, Henrie stood in front of the group.

"As you can see, there are several beds between the two floors. Between the two, you will find three full bathrooms, two kitchenettes, one hot tub, albeit small, one pool table and two entertainment areas. I leave it to you to decide sleeping arrangements."

One of the men said, "Thanks. And breakfast is at the main house?"

"Yes. Your group requested breakfast at eight o'clock, with one allergy to peanuts. For the rest of the week, not a single peanut will be in evidence. No peanut oil, no peanut butter." Henrie turned to the woman he recognized as the one with the allergy. "Do you carry an epi pen at all times?"

"I do, thanks for asking."

Another woman spoke, "What about me? I'm vegetarian."

"Several dishes will be prepared for you. In every dish that does not contain meat or poultry, only vegetable broth will be used."

Another man said, "I'm vegan. And I'm lactose and gluten intolerant. I can't handle salt, pepper or most spices and I can't eat fried foods."

Henrie turned to look at him. "I apologize. I was not aware such a diet was required. I will review the menu and assure something will be available to you."

"Hey, I'm sorry, man. I thought Bonita woulda said something."

Ever the diplomat, Henrie said, "My notes must have been incomplete." He broadened his gaze to include the group. "I expect the remainder of your group to arrive shortly. Please feel free to tour the main house at your convenience."

Henrie turned to go, then turned back. Looking directly at Tim, he said, "Rest assured, just as the peanut allergy has been relayed to everyone on The Avenue, I will be certain to relay your food issues."

Henrie returned to the main house and sat at his computer in the kitchen. He pulled up the reservations again. For this large group, he had requested photographs, particularly with someone evidencing a peanut allergy. He also had contact information for medical emergencies.

The guests were from several states. They vacationed together two times a year and referred to themselves as

Ultimate Scavenger Hunters. One of the organizers, Bonita, had explained the concept.

"We go to towns that none of our guests have visited, and we have a different hunt every day. We'll arrive Wednesday to get the lay of the town and hunt Thursday, Friday and Saturday. Saturday night we'll have dinner together, name the winner, and we'll be out of your hair on Sunday morning."

Henrie had asked, "What do you hunt?"

"Oh, innocuous things. For example, we'll have a list of businesses in town and they'll have to take photos of certain ones. Or we'll identify prominent landmarks or recreational areas. We might have them find the most expensive thing to buy for a man or a woman, or the most unique thing people can do for fun. Then on Saturday, everyone will decide who won each day. The couple with the most points wins the trip."

As they talked, Henrie had difficulty with the term "ultimate," but he did not ask further. Today, he wondered about it again, but he turned to his task. He studied the photographs and made notes.

Bill and Kristen were from the Midwest. They were professionals, both attorneys. Kristen had an allergy to peanuts. Henrie knew how deadly an anaphylactic shock could be. He had already put Jennifer and Marie on alert as well as Annie's other business managers.

Chet and Justine were from the Southwest. They were professionals as well. Well, Henrie thought, to vacation somewhere with a group of friends twice a year, one had to have a decent income.

Damien and Tasha were from New Orleans. Their photographs – and their presence – alluded to a Cajun background. Tasha was the vegetarian.

Thad and Treena were from the Northeast, about as far up and east as one could go without entering Canada or the Atlantic Ocean.

The last couple, Tim and Barbara, were from northern California. Tim was the man who claimed to be a gluten-lactose-salt-pepper-spice-and-fried-foods intolerant vegan. Henrie's first thought was why someone professing to be vegan would be concerned with lactose.

The dietary requirements could be accommodated, but he wondered if the man had tried to throw him – what did the Americans call it – a curve ball – just to create trouble. Perhaps that was part of the hunt. Well, two could play at that game.

To be safe, he sent a blast text to everyone on The Avenue. It was possible the Ultimate Scavenger Hunt guests would try their patience in more ways than one.

He searched his menus for recipes that would work and realized he had groceries on hand for Thursday, Friday and Saturday morning. By Sunday, the hunt would be over, and both he and Tim could give up the façade.

He turned as he heard the front door open. Kali and Ko had returned from the carriage house to greet the next set of guests. Bonita and Rich, not a couple, but the two moderators of the scavenger hunt, arrived together.

Kali deposited love hairs on Rich while Ko sniffed their luggage. She found nothing interesting. This was going to be a boring group, after all.

Henrie gave the full tour, showing each to their rooms in the process. Rich had the room Henrie liked the most, the one facing The Avenue. Bonita faced the lake, an outstanding view that also overlooked the Inn's private beach.

Before leaving them, he turned to Bonita. "I apologize for missing Tim's dietary requirements."

"What…"

"No matter. I have reviewed menus and the larder. I can prepare a separate breakfast for him every morning. For the afternoon repast, in lieu of the planned dishes, I will prepare fresh fruits and vegetables for everyone."

A smile seemed to play on Rich's lips. Bonita nodded and said, "Thank you."

Henrie returned to the kitchen with a song in his heart. He had been correct. A curve ball. He would make Tim suffer.

Rich knocked on Bonita's door. He called out, "I have red! A fine regional varietal. . ."

Bonita opened the door. "Come in. Did you get glasses?"

Rich held up two stemmed glasses. "Of course."

Bonita took the bottle and poured a healthy glass of wine for herself. "This guy may be smarter than the innkeepers we're used to having. Do you think we need to change our plans?"

"No. He won't figure it out. He's on top of the menu, but that's his job."

"Still, I wonder if this was a good idea."

"This? Chelsea? It was your idea, after all."

"I keep hearing good things about it. I wanted to see for myself."

"It's a smaller town than we're used to. Harder to hide. Everyone knows everyone else. This could lead to trouble."

"Not for us. For the players, yes, but not us. We just get another great vacation on their dollar."

"Are you getting tired of this?"

"No, not yet. We get two great vacations every year. We eat at the nicest places in town. We can do whatever we want during the day while they play. And. . ."

". . .they pay for everything."

"They pay for everything. But our profit margin is slipping. I think we'll have to raise the price to play. Or lower the value of the winning package."

"A chance of a free trip for the winning couple is probably the only reason they pay what they do."

"But it's starting to fray a little at the edges. They are getting pretty competitive."

"Better for us. Speaking of that, what's our big score this time?"

Bonita flashed a wicked smile. "I found a place on the internet called Gema's Creations. The woman makes her own jewelry with precious and semi-precious stones, and she uses silver, gold and platinum."

"Perfect. We can case it tomorrow. What does your little heart desire?"

"Emeralds. Or rubies. I'm tired of diamonds."

Ten people gathered in the downstairs apartment of the carriage house. Chet handed beers around to everyone. "From Mo's Tap. They have a great selection."

"So why'd you get just one kind?" This was from Tim, who continued, "Hey, what do you think that guy meant, he'd tell everybody on The Avenue about my food stuff?"

Treena said, "You're going to suffer this week. That's what it means."

"We can eat other places."

Tasha said, "You didn't check the websites. There isn't much of anything else here in town. Some fast food places, a restaurant or two around town, but really, everything for us to eat or drink is right here. On this street."

"You've got to be kidding me!"

"Nope. You're going to enjoy the week. Not."

Damien said, "On to a different subject, but not so very different, what are we doing in this small town?"

"I dunno," said Barbara. "Bonita wanted to come here for some reason."

Bill said, "Kristen and I have talked about it. This will probably be our last time. It's getting too dicey, and, well, we almost backed out this time."

"We're about through, too," said Tasha.

"Do you think a town this size has a jewelry store big enough for us?"

"We wouldn't be here if Bonita hadn't checked it out already."

Tim asked, "Does everyone have their curve ball? And Kristen, yours is really getting lame."

"We don't need the points on a curve ball. We get top points on everything else. We just put that out there to get on the board."

Justine added, "And let's face it. You don't get the points unless you follow it through all week. Usually, that's only at the B&B, but in this town, it will be all over. You won't get a single point if you don't follow through, Tim."

"I'll try not to eat in front of you, honey," said Barbara. She didn't say it like she meant it.

"It can't be that hard. I'll just eat what Tasha eats."

"No you won't. I'm vegetarian, not vegan. I eat eggs and dairy. I repeat. You're vegan. A vegan who's somehow lactose intolerant. How does that work again?"

"I have trouble with milk."

"Vegans don't eat dairy products."

"Oh, come on. Vegans can't have milk?"

"Or cheese, cottage cheese, sour cream, cream cheese, Jell-O, anything that has anything that comes from an animal."

"No Jell-O?"

"Horses hooves, idiot."

"Oh. Well, what can I eat?"

"Let's see," said Tasha. "Because of your improbable list, which includes salt and pepper, you won't be able to eat most prepared foods. Add gluten intolerance, you can only have gluten-free breads or crackers, which will probably be hard to find in a town like this. You won't be able to spice up your foods to make up for the lack of salt and pepper, so everything you eat will be bland. If anything is made with milk, it will have to be soy or almond, coconut, some animal-free variety. And eggs will be only imitation, so probably no baked goods, even if they are gluten-free."

Chet said, "It's good we're a forgiving group, otherwise, you couldn't even drink beer with us in private."

"What?"

"Beer," said Chet, "has gluten. Are you feeling the pain yet?"

"Clearly, I didn't think this through."

After eating the wonderful snack prepared by Henrie – fresh bacon with cream cheese on the side – Tiger Lily watched as Henrie placed carrots, celery and sliced pineapple on a tray. She followed as he put the tray in the refrigerator in the Keurig corner, the place where guests picked up their afternoon snack.

Why, she wondered, was Henrie putting such a poor snack out?

She wondered even more, when ten adults burst into the foyer. Several made comments. "Smell the bacon! I wonder what it is." "I smell bacon!" "It smells wonderful!"

From underneath the love seat in the foyer, she watched as another woman, one who came from upstairs, reached into the refrigerator to pull out a tray.

Eventually, everyone grew silent. Finally, a woman said, "What gives?"

The woman who had come from upstairs said, "Tim, did you tell Henrie you had dietary restrictions?"

"Well, yeah. That's our curve ball."

"I'm sure everyone will take the points into account when they realize we will all suffer. Get used to it. No matter what we saw on the website, we're having fruits and vegetables for our afternoon treat. And from the looks of it, he didn't have a lot to choose from today. Maybe it will be better tomorrow."

The group grumbled a bit, but everyone took several pieces from the plate. One man finally said, "We were going to eat at that winery. Let's go now. We can start with appetizers."

Mr. Bean had crept under the love seat beside Tiger Lily. *"So Henrie did that on purpose?"*

"I think so. And I think he put the bacon smell in the house for spite."

"What's spite?"

"Um…to make a point. To tease them, kind of."

"Okay. That makes sense. Doesn't seem like Henrie, though."

"I imagine he has his reasons. Let's get the report from Kali and Ko."

After the humans had moved out of the Inn, they came out from under their hiding place and walked to the dining room.

Tiger Lily said, *"Tell us about these people."*

Kali and Ko said at the same time, *"They're okay." "They're kind of nice." "Nothing interesting in the luggage." "But there's something funny going on."*

"Why do you say that," asked Tiger Lily, focusing on the last thing she heard.

Kali said, *"Henrie asks everyone if they have trouble eating anything, and two of these people said so before getting here."*

Ko added, *"But one guy gave him a whole list of problems after they got here. I don't remember all the words."*

Kali said, *"I think he can't eat meat. Or milk."*

"Oh, yeah," said Ko. *"He can't have salt or spices either. And something else."*

"But he didn't say before he came? He's going to make Henrie change his entire menu."

"No," said Kali. *"I think Henrie's going to make this one guy a special dish every day."*

"Interesting. We'll have to keep an eye on them. What about the other guests?"

Kali said, *"Everyone that's here is from that one group, the couples in the carriage house and the man and woman. They're in The Avenue room and the lake room."*

"That's all? I thought all the rooms were supposed to be full."

"They are," said Ko. *"There's a wedding couple coming – they couldn't stay in the honeymoon suite because of these other guys – and a friend of Candice is coming."*

"Yeah," said Kali. *"A friend of Candice. Henrie doesn't expect any of them until this evening."*

"Okay. A full house. What can you tell us about the guy in the back room? The stinky cigar guy?"

Kali and Ko looked at one another. Ko spoke. *"The only clothes that smell like cigar are the ones he wore that first day,*

and I don't think they smell like cigar. I think they smell like
smoke, like that fire."

Kali said, *"He hasn't smoked that cigar once. Not once. He
carries it with him all the time, but I think it's one of those cheap
ones you can get at the box store."*

Sassy Pants said, *"Pete duzn't trust him."*

Heads snapped around and a chorus ensued. *"What?"*
"How do you know?" "What did you hear?" "Trill!"

Sassy looked at Tiger Lily, who nodded for her to
continue. *"Pete and Tank and Boone were at my place. Dey
talkted about da fires, and dey say someone saveded da second
guy. He died."* Sassy Pants looked at the floor for a second,
allowing for a moment of silence.

She looked up again. *"An dey wuz gettin' ready to talk
some more, but dat Wyatt guy comed in, and dey started lyin' to
him."*

Little Socks said, *"Pete lied? What about?"*

*"He tolded da guy he didn't knows where da vet guys were,
but he did. Mommy founded dem at da museum."*

Mr. Bean couldn't contain himself. He jumped from one
foot to the other and finally asked, *"Did you hear anything
else?"*

"Um...let me tink..."

Little Socks stomped her front feet, but Tiger Lily was
ready. She moved close to Little Socks and sat on her tail.

Mo said, *"Trill."*

*"Oh, yeah. Tanks, Mo. I talkted to Brown Mousie. He'ze
gonna keep a eye on dem, specially dat Wyatt guy. Oh, an'*

Henrie takes food to da guy dat stays wit Teresa and he takes it to da udders."

Tiger Lily tried to digest all of this and put it in a coherent format. She said, *"So Wyatt may be a bad guy."*

Moriah said, *"Or not."*

They all jumped. Moriah had come in without making a sound. Maybe she would make a great cat burglar after all.

"Why not?" asked Mr. Bean.

"Well, Sassy Pants said that someone saved the guy that eventually died. This Wyatt guy could have started the fire, or he could have pulled him out of the fire."

"You're right," said Tiger Lily. *"The same could be true of Gene. He could have started the fire; he could have pulled the guy out; or maybe he wasn't involved at all."*

Little Socks said, *"It seems to me we're missing the broader picture."*

Cat heads swiveled in her direction.

"No matter who is killing these guys, Wyatt or Gene or someone else, the big question is why."

13

Minnie seated a large group in the back room. Because they took the largest table, they were in the far corner, out of hearing of most diners on a Wednesday evening.

As she handed out the day's menu, she asked, "Are you the scavenger group from the Inn?"

"We are. We'll be around through the weekend."

"That's great. We're ready for you, almost. Because our menu isn't set, we can alter it for special groups. This week we've made certain to stay away from peanuts and anything made with peanut products. We always have vegetarian options, and it just so happens that we have one vegan item on the menu this week. Unfortunately, it's already put together. It has gluten, salt, pepper and spices, and the side dish is deep-fried. Let's see. . .it's Tim, right, that has those intolerances?"

The group turned to Tim, smiles playing on their faces.

Minnie turned as well and looked at the man, who seemed confused.

"We work together, Tim, to make sure our guests have the best possible experience. When Henrie let me know about your food issues, I ran to the grocery store to get a selection of fruits and vegetables. I picked up some hummus as well. I can offer red beet or avocado. Which would you prefer?"

"Um. . .do you have anything else?"

"Not on the menu tonight that meets vegan, glucose-free, and neither fried nor spicy guidelines. We had about an hour's notice. I can look for other things tomorrow."

"Well, I'll take the first one, whatever that was, and crackers."

Minnie hid her smile as she made notes on an order sheet. When it was under control, she looked up to say, "I don't think we have salt and gluten-free crackers on hand. I'll look for some tomorrow. But I'm sure you're used to dipping fresh veggies."

"Right. Well, um, yeah. I can do that."

"I'm very sorry for the lack of selection. We're kind of a small town, and it's hard to prepare for everything. But like I said. . ."

"Yeah. Tomorrow."

Minnie took orders for wine flights and left the table with a light step. This was just the beginning. She was certain one or more of them would have "difficulty" with everything. No problem. She was ready, and she intended to have fun.

Perry found a half-full bottle of Old Granddad by a large rock on the beach. Some kid hid it before getting caught, or it got left after a party. It didn't matter.

If a bottle of anything was hanging around anywhere, Perry seemed to run across it. He thought of it as his mutant power.

He and Ben were on their own for the afternoon. They would meet their friends at the lighthouse museum in the evening. They had decided that one more night should be safe. The women saw them, and Gene had learned where they were. He brought food. Today, all of the people who found them were good people. Today. They hoped it would extend to a safe night.

Ben was a good guy to stick with. He seemed to have ears like a hawk. Did a hawk have ears? No matter. Ben's good ears had saved them from many a scare. It wasn't so good for Ben, because every sound scared him. But when he started of fright, Perry and the others usually got warning of bad people or bad things.

That hadn't happened for Malcolm. Malcolm had been sleeping alone in one boat when the man came. The others, sleeping in two other boats, were able to get away because Ben woke up screaming. Malcolm had either been too far away to hear or he was high. Malcolm's mutant skill had been finding drugs.

Either way, it didn't help.

And Farrell, he was just unlucky. He was tired from lack of sleep, and his scar tissue wore him down, as did having only one eye and one arm. He had gone to sleep in that old garage while the rest of them scavenged for food. And the man had come again.

They settled in a clump of weeds near the base of a rock cliff and Perry offered Ben a swig. "You can tell me now, can't you? Why we here? Why ain't we in a bigger place? And why this man comin' for us?"

"It got nothin' to do with you, boy."

"It do, too. Me and Gene, we from a differ'nt war an all, but we's in it witcha. We gonna be jus' as dead."

Ben looked at the ground between his legs and shook his head. "It's a bad thing. It's jus' a bad thing."

"It got to do with the Gulf?"

Ben didn't answer right away. Finally, he said, "Sorta."

"Sorta, how?"

"It got to do with what happened after the Gulf. When we shipped out."

"I'm listenin'."

Ben sighed. "We was all in the same company, an' we went out one night to a bar after we got home, 'bout a week before we shipped out. We was at the Anniston Army Depot in Alabama. Some reporter or other was at the bar, lookin' for a story. He'd got wind that them Patriot missiles wasn't all they's cracked up to be."

"Patriots? They were first used there, in the Gulf, right?"

"Right. The dang military was sayin' they was miracles. Killed ever-body they aimed at, real effective, you know. But we was on the receivin' end of some of them missiles. The dang software was scrappy. They hit stuff we didn't aim at, an' if they was shootin' at a Scud, lotsa times they'd miss. Scud would come right down on us."

Ben stopped talking. Perry prompted him. "So twenty-five or thirty years ago, you guys talked to a reporter in a bar. Told him that stuff. What's that got to do with today?"

"That reporter, he took lotsa notes, an' he dug around a few days. We seen him at the base a couple days later. An' then Malcolm seen him again, outside the base, but he weren't gonna tell no stories about missiles to nobody no more. Nope. He weren't."

"Why not?"

"He was deader'n a rat that et poison."

140

Perry sat back and took a deep drink, draining the bottle. "What the heck? Who done it?"

"Malcolm figured it out. He was sent out to get some stuff fer the cook, he had access to a truck an' all, an' he see'd that reporter in a alley behind the grocery. He see'd a officer walkin' away, a Captain, an' that Captain turned aroun'. Malcolm got down deep in that truck, an' the Captain went on. But he musta found out who was drivin' it. He mighta come lookin' for 'im real soon, but Malcolm went right back to the barracks where we was."

Ben picked at some weeds before he started again. "We shipped out the next mornin', and they rotated us out of service real quick from Fort Dix. Malcolm decided to lay low, an' we went with 'im. Well, all of us but Harper. He tried to make it at home first. Didn't take 'im long to join us on the streets. Mostly that New York area. It's easy to hide there."

"But what's that got to do with where we are now?"

"That Captain, he was some kinda big fish. It took him some time, but he tracked Malcolm down. Remember that drug bust a few months ago?"

"Yeah. He got caught with some coke."

"Yep. Musta tracked him from that. Anyway, he sent a guy after Malcolm, an' the guy found us on the street. Said he had some sweet cash for us, but we hadda get here to Chelsea."

"Why'd you guys trust him? Go with him?"

"Malcolm got soft in the head. He was sure we'd get paid, and then we'd be on easy street fer the rest of our lives. We come along because we's used to stickin' together now."

"Why Chelsea?"

"That guy – that officer – he lives here. His toady tole us to get here an' he'd find us, take care of us."

"What's his name?"

Ben didn't answer. His eyes got wide, and he dropped face first into the weeds. Perry barely registered the bullet hole in his friend's head before he scrambled behind the rocks of the cliff and ran for his life. For once, Ben's ears had failed him.

Kali and Ko rushed to the foyer. Two guests had arrived, and Henrie was in the process of greeting them. Ko jumped to the top of the largest piece of luggage. Kali curled around the ankles of the gentleman. She purred, because he was such a handsome man.

At least he was handsome to Kali.

Ko moved to another piece of luggage. Kali left extra-special love hairs on the man's pants legs. Henrie got to the part about it's-unusual-for-guests-to-arrive-in-the-evening-so-excuse-me-if-I-forget-anything.

Ko became bored with the luggage and jumped to one of the love seats to listen to Henrie. He was just getting to the part about what-time-would-you-prefer-breakfast and have-you-made-contact-with-The-Escape when Tiger Lily slipped in beside her.

"Have you checked out the luggage?"

"Yeah. It's pretty boring. Lady stuff, smelly lotions and things."

"Are these the wedding folks?"

"I think so. Henrie asked about The Escape. I think they'll be getting married in the middle of the lake."

"They probably won't take up any of our time, but just in case, we should keep an eye on them. Why don't you listen at their door tonight and see what they're doing tomorrow."

"Okay. Kali will want to flirt with the man anyway."

Tiger Lily nodded and turned to go upstairs. She stopped when she heard Candice at the front door. Jeepers! Another guest! She had forgotten all about the friend that was to stay over the weekend.

She sat again and listened to Henrie's spiel. "Welcome to the KaliKo Inn. I am Henrie. You must be Kara."

Candice said, "Kara's my best friend from college, I was hoping you could get her settled, and she'll come back to the bar to hang out."

"Certainly. We will tend to the paperwork tomorrow. Come with me as I show these guests – please meet Don and Suellen – to the second floor. Your rooms are quite close."

Tiger Lily turned back to Ko. *"Listen to her, too,"* and then she trotted upstairs.

Ko mumbled under her breath. Was she expected to take care of everything?

Tempo thought he was in the clear. He saw the man shoot Ben. He thought it was Ben. He thought he saw Perry run away.

Tempo had run, too, in the opposite direction. He headed up the shore, past the cliff and to the lagoon that cut into the rocks.

When he got to the lagoon, he turned to make sure he was clear.

That's when the bullet hit.

Minnie brought wine flights to each of the couples and mini flights to the two singles. Some were sweet, some dry, and some mixed. She explained the offerings and watched, picking the problem couple immediately.

They were unable to play the part correctly, looking at one another as they nodded. The couple – throughout the evening, Minnie learned their names were Damien and Tasha – took quick sips of the first glass of a sweet white wine.

Tasha puckered her lips and screwed up her face. "Eew! Too sweet! We asked for dry!"

Bill stuck his tongue out as he agreed. "Take this back. We wanted reds. Dry reds."

"I apologize," said Minnie. "I'm sure it was my mistake, and it's probably too dark in here for you to see the glasses are holding white. Dry reds, you say?"

"Yes," said Tasha, reaching for the next glass.

Minnie beat her to it, deftly slipping the rack with the wine flight off the table and onto her tray. "I'll be back as soon as I can. We got busy in the front room."

Minnie waited until their food orders were ready to take another flight of wine to Damien and Tasha. Without missing a beat, she picked up the empty flight racks from the other couples and took orders for individual glasses of wine.

Damien took a taste of the first glass of red and with his best game face said, "Yuck. This is awful!" He passed the glass to Tasha, who followed suit.

Minnie gave a sad smile and said, "Would you prefer to order glasses from the menu?"

"Not if this is the kind of stuff you serve."

"I hate to say it is."

"Well, we'll just have to drink it for free."

"I'm sorry, I can't bear to see you drink something you don't like. I'll bring water." Once again, she took the rack, placed it on her tray and left.

"Wait a minute," said Damien, voice raised. "What…."

But Minnie was gone. She heard the rest of the group break into laughter while one of the women said, "You've been snookered. You'd better stick to water."

Kara sat at the bar, talking with George when he was available, and Candice when she was. Just as she finished a burger with sweet potato fries, a man walked in, sat at the only free stool – the one next to her – and said hello to George.

"Tank, it's good to see you. You're sittin' next to a friend of mine, Kara. Kara, this handsome guy is the chief of our fire department. We call him Tank."

As George moved up and down the bar, serving guests, and as Candice got busier on the floor, Kara and Tank drew deeper into conversation.

George took a look from time to time and did what he thought best. He approached them only when one or the other seemed to need a drink. He thought, "This couldn't have gone better if I planned it."

Henrie made a pass through the hallways. He thought Wyatt had come back for the evening, but he could not be sure. As much as he loved to know what went on at the Inn, Henrie did not micro-manage his guests. That is what he told himself.

No, it was only the necessity of clipping flowers on the far side of the Inn that caused him to walk around the back. And because the flowers were underneath the guest room window, he was forced to look in. Briefly. Enough to see that Wyatt was not visible.

That did not mean Wyatt was out. He could have gone to a common area after Henrie left the kitchen.

Henrie thought he could use the skills of the detective cats, but he wasn't sure how to send them on a mission of this type. To be honest, he knew how to send them, but he did not know how to receive an accurate report.

The cats were nowhere to be found, at any rate. They must be in the apartment, tired from detecting all day.

He sighed and got back to work. With the Inn as full as it could possibly be, he needed an early start on tomorrow morning's breakfast.

He pre-cooked four pounds of bacon, four dozen sausage links, and six dozen sausage patties, prepared the ingredients for large vegetarian egg casseroles, and got the ingredients ready for two large pans of baked cinnamon French toast. He could have made oat groats with cranberries and walnuts, but he didn't want to offer his problem eater another option.

He stood to listen when people came into the Inn. It turned out to be the moderators of the scavenger group, Rich and Bonita.

Bonita, in a loud voice, probably a little tipsy, said, "I think Tim and Barbara have won the curve ball so far, don't you? Damien and Tasha are in second place, and Bill and Kristen are bringing up the rear, as usual. That peanut allergy is gettin' old."

Rich shushed her and they went upstairs. Henrie heard one set of shoes go up the stairs with certainty. The other was a little less sure. Eventually, he heard, "I DID shut up! Stop it!"

One guest door opened and slammed shut.

Henrie smiled to himself. He would continue to serve Tim his ridiculous meals, and while he was relieved Kristen was not allergic to peanuts, he would not change his menus. He wondered what Damien and Tasha had done to merit points in the game. He looked at his cellphone. Minnie had just texted him the "what." He shared it with everyone else.

When activity from the bar started to wind down, Kara suggested she and Tank move to one of the areas with overstuffed chairs. "Candice cleaned there. If we hang on to our glasses, she won't need to clean it again."

"Good idea. I can't stay much longer, though. I have to get to the station early tomorrow."

"So how does that work? Do you work eight to five? Twelve on? Twenty-four on?"

"The guys have a twenty-four forty-eight schedule. I need to be available for other things, so I work a kinda sorta eight to five. I'll come out nights and weekends for emergencies, and sometimes I take a shift or two."

"Were you at the fire Candice told me about? The one with the boats?"

Kara thought she saw Tank flinch a bit before he nodded.

"You don't have to tell me. I shouldn't have asked."

"No, it's okay. It's just pretty fresh, is all."

"Well, let's change the subject. Are you free on Saturday?"

"Saturday? Yeah, I think I am."

"Great! Candice and George kinda promised me a trip out on the lake with this friend of theirs, Ray? Know him?"

"Sure do. Played poker with him last night. But I thought he said. . ."

"Yeah. He has a wedding on the boat."

"Yacht. He likes to call it a yacht."

"That. Anyway, we haven't decided what to do, but they've taken the whole day and evening off from the Tap, and we're going to do something."

"Are you sure it's okay for me to join you?"

"Sure! I can tell you have the official okeedokee from George, just from the way the two of you talk."

"We've been friends for a long time."

"Then great! We can all plan the day together!"

"I'd like to spend more than just Saturday with you. Maybe we can get together tomorrow?"

Before the night was over, another fire broke out, this one in a shed behind the condominium development. Chris and Sis were there before the Police and Fire Departments. Chris pulled the body of one of the younger vets from the burning structure. He would later learn the name was Perry.

14

Henrie placed dishes of freshly-heated bacon bits on the floor of the kitchen. The detectives were without their table this morning. Henrie had to put it into use because of the number of guests.

Seven cats prowled the kitchen floor, usually, but not always, staying out of the way of his feet.

Henrie had finished plating the hot and cold foods on the buffet tables when the guests arrived. All of them. At once. This was not typical, but it happened. Hot on the heels of the guests was Annie. She introduced herself as she rolled through the dining room to the kitchen.

"Tell me what to do, Henrie. I'm all yours this morning."

Henrie's eyes rolled to the back of his head – thankfully out of Annie's view – and he answered, "Everything is in order."

"Oh, Henrie, I'm not going to try to cook, but I can take what you've made to the tables as soon as you tell me."

"For now, let us wait until the first rush is through."

Henrie opened the refrigerator and took out a plated bowl, uncovered it and added three bright red raspberries.

"What's that?"

"Breakfast for our vegan, gluten-salt-pepper-spice-and-fried-food intolerant guest."

"We have one of those?"

"No. We have a guest masquerading as 'one of those,' and I am accommodating."

"What is it?"

"A very tasty bowl with almond butter surrounded by chopped granny smith apples and topped with coconut and pecans."

"Tasty, indeed. This is supposed to be a problem for him?"

"My guess is that he would prefer bacon – lots of it – with eggs, French toast and pancakes."

"Oh. Poor guy. He probably has the same problem all over town."

"Yes. Our staff is fastidious about providing only the best and most healthy options for our guests, no matter the diet restrictions."

Henrie left the kitchen with the bowl and set it at Tim's place, just as he had picked up a plate at the buffet.

"I do not know what you will find to suit your diet this morning, Tim, but I prepared this especially for you. Your protein needs are being met with almond butter, in keeping, of course, with our peanut-free menu for the week."

Tim said, "Thanks, Henrie." It was not said with meaning.

Kara was the last guest to arrive. As she came into the dining room, Henrie turned to her with a smile. "I trust you enjoyed your evening?"

"I did, thanks. I really liked Mo's Tap. Nice atmosphere."

"And the clientele is second to none, I understand."

"I'm sure you understand just about everything, Henrie. Candice told me all about you."

"I see. Then you will be certain to let me know if you need anything to make your stay more pleasant."

Henrie returned to the kitchen. "Have you spoken with Chris this morning?"

"I have. He didn't know the name of the man yet, but Pete told him it was one of the younger guys."

"This is a terrible situation. Terrible."

"It is. Are you taking lunch to Gene today?"

"I am. Teresa has not yet seen him today, but she is certain he will be back in time to take the meal to his friends."

"I wish there was something I could do."

Kara put her purse at the table for four at the end of the room. She smiled and nodded at the other guests as she helped herself to breakfast.

She counted twelve – six couples, or at least six men and six women – at the large table and the side table. They seemed to know one another, as the conversation was animated and crossed between tables.

As she made her way back to her small group, she sat and introduced herself to the man she had not yet met. "I'm Kara, and you are?"

"I'm, uh, Wyatt."

Kara waited. He said nothing else. She turned to the wedding couple. "So, I have to ask. Are friends and family joining you for the wedding?"

"Friends will join us tomorrow," said Suellen. "They'll be with us for our bachelor dinner, and they'll come back Saturday for the wedding."

"They aren't staying here?"

"Good for us, they live close. They couldn't afford to stay, and we couldn't afford to pay for a room for them, so. . .anyway, Marsh Haven is close. They're happy to just get out on the lake for the wedding."

"I've heard about this boat called The Escape."

"Yacht," said Don. "He prefers to call it a yacht."

"Yeah, that. I'm visiting friends here, and he's a friend of theirs. Actually, you're the reason I'm not getting a free trip!"

"Really?"

"Yeah. My friends asked if I could go out, and he said he has a wedding. That's you. Bummer."

Suellen and Don looked at one another, then back at Kara.

Suellen said, "You know, we were just talking about this. That's a big boat, and there will only be four of us. We like our friends – I mean, they're standing up for us – but we'd all like to have more on board. You know, make it more of a party."

"Yeah," said Don. "Who are your friends? You say they know Ray? The captain?"

"Yeah. George is the manager of Mo's Tap, and Candice is the floor manager."

"We saw them last night!" said Suellen. "They look like fun people, and they're friends of Ray?"

"Yeah. You can check with him, if you want, and if he says they're okay to bring along, I'll talk to them. They're both taking Saturday off so we can do something. We didn't make any plans yet."

"So, that would be three more people?"

Kara smiled. "I met one of George's friends yesterday. You can ask Ray about him, too, probably. His name is Tank."

Don said, "We're supposed to meet Ray at the Café this afternoon, you know, to talk about food. We'll ask him."

Suellen added, "If it looks like it will work, we'll get enough for eight total."

Kara nodded quickly. "We'll help you pay for it. I mean, we would have paid to go out somewhere, and you shouldn't have to pay for us, too. We can work it out."

Suellen reached into her purse to pull out her cellphone. "Give me your number. We won't order anything until we decide together on a budget."

"Good deal! What a great place this is! Who would have figured?" She turned to Wyatt. "And why are you here? Business or personal reasons?"

"I'm here on the job, really. I work for Veterans' Affairs. I'm trying to locate vets here in town to offer our services."

Don shook his head. "I didn't realize organizations like yours went out looking for clients. I thought they came to you."

"Generally, they do, but this is a small town. We don't have a local facility here."

"So you pay for people – like you – to stay in B&Bs and look for them? How do you do that? Do you set up a temporary office?"

"No. . ."

Kara thought Wyatt appeared nervous now. His face was flushed, a bit of sweat appeared on his brow. She wondered if he was naturally shy.

Wyatt finally said, "We. . .um. . .I go out and look. We mostly look for homeless folks."

Suellen leaned back in her chair. "In Chelsea?"

"Yeah. There are homeless vets everywhere. This is where I am this week. Next week I'll go somewhere else."

"Really?" This from Suellen again.

Kara stepped in to help Wyatt. "Tank, the guy I met? Well, he told me about these fires in town, and homeless vets are dying."

Don and Suellen leaned in. "You're looking for them?" asked Don.

Wyatt took a deep breath. "Yeah, well. . .yeah."

"How are you doing that?"

"I'm walking around; I talk to people; I talk to the Chief of Police, and other folks who seem to know what's going on."

Kara took a breath. She realized she had not been breathing. Probably because Wyatt wasn't breathing. She touched his shoulder and lowered her voice. "It must be hard, knowing this is going on, and trying to find them. You probably worry it will happen to the rest of them."

Wyatt jumped back in his chair. "Why do you say that?"

"Well, I mean, you know, you're here looking for vets and vets are dying. You know. You probably worry."

"Well, yes. I do. Um. . .I have to go. Nice to meet all of you."

Kara looked at Don and Suellen as Wyatt hurried away. "What's up with him?"

"Don't know," said Suellen. "Weird guy. I hope he finds somewhere else to sit tomorrow."

Henrie kept an ear tuned to the tables of twelve as he and Annie kept the buffet filled. Once, Annie brought an additional bowl to Tim, who barely nodded as she set it down.

In the kitchen, stepping over Kali and Ko, Annie said, "How long can we keep this up?"

Henrie dodged Mr. Bean's front feet. "As long as he does. I have a feeling part of the point system depends on their ability to maintain the lies they tell."

"The prize must be worthwhile." Annie eased around Tiger Lily, who, for some reason, had decided to sleep in front of the refrigerator. "I would hate to take a vacation and not be able to enjoy the food."

Henrie used the toe of his shoe to move Sassy Pants from one side of the counter to the other. "I have a feeling this group will be more trouble than they are worth, in the end."

Little Socks jumped to Annie's shoulder and wrapped her tail around Annie's neck. "Just what we need this week." She took hold of the tail so Little Socks wouldn't fall as she reached for a cup of coffee.

"Indeed." Henrie nearly stepped on Mo's tail.

To Henrie, Annie said, "Have you picked up their chatter?" To the kids in general, voice raised, she said, "Really? You can't find a windowsill or someplace else to sit?"

Henrie stood up straight to allow several cats to scurry from the kitchen floor through the door to the dining room. "They have discussed the day's activities and have decided, with the weather's cooperation, to spend the day at the beach."

"Giving up the hunt for the day?"

"That was not my impression."

"Huh?"

Henrie lifted a finger to silence Annie and returned to the dining room, a plate of bacon in hand. He walked closer than necessary to Tim, allowing the small to waft in his direction.

He moved the bacon from the plate to the warming bin and returned to the kitchen. He looked at Annie and said, "The coordinators have given sheets of paper to each couple with what appears to be a list of items. I would be willing to bet many beach-goers will be missing a few of those same items before the day is over."

"You don't think they'll just take photos?"

"I do not. She told me that is what they do, but something tells me she was not being honest."

Annie laughed. "It's probably harmless, you know, like 'find a yellow towel,' or 'green sand pail.' And really, it has to be photos. Why would they go on vacation to steal things like that? Just in case, I'll text Pete and ask him to check in with one of us sometime today."

"Excellent idea. What are your plans for the day?"

"I'll go to the Café and see what trouble I can get into." She stopped to look around. "Where did the cats go? Oh, well. What about the other guests? Anything new?"

"I heard the wedding guests say they could not afford to keep their friends overnight for the wedding. It is a shame we do not have a room for them."

"It is. We could at least give them a discount if we did. How about Wyatt? Anything new?"

"Pete called this morning and asked what time Wyatt got in last night."

"Did you know?"

"I did not, but when he narrowed the time frame, I could tell him that I thought he was out."

"How did you know?"

"Do you know the flowers underneath his window? They needed tending."

"Henrie!"

Tiger Lily caught the tone in her mother's voice. It was a whip-stitch from over-the-edge. She called to her siblings and they all hit the door, running through the dining room and into the foyer.

Tiger Lily stopped them before they left the house. *"Did you hear Mommy and Henrie? These game people may start stealing stuff."*

"Just pails and towels and things," said Little Socks. *"Nothing to worry about."*

"We don't know that. We don't know what's on the list."

"We needs to get da list an' you can reads it."

Tiger Lily stared at Sassy Pants. *"Why didn't I think of that?"*

"You can't think of everything," said Mr. Bean. *"You have lots of stuff to manage in your head today."*

"Speaking of that," added Little Socks, *"we need to talk to Sis today, to find out about last night's fire."*

Mo gave a sad, *"Trill."*

Kali and Ko translated at the same time. *"He's sorry the guy died." "He's sad Sis had to find a body."*

Tiger Lily nodded. *"Let's stay sharp today."*

As she said that, they all had to step out of the way, under pieces of furniture or against the wall. Twelve humans left the dining room at the same time, two going upstairs and the others out the door, presumably to the carriage house. They could be heard to say, "Beach at 10:00!" "I can't wait to wear my new suit!" "Did you pack our beach blanket?" "I want to walk to the lighthouse." "Are we packing picnic lunches?" "I heard all of these places here will sell picnic basket lunches." "Let's get food first." "Beach at 11:00!" "Who's getting the beer?"

When the group was gone, Tiger Lily emerged from under the love seat and trotted into the dining room. Three guests were still at the small table. Wyatt was gone.

She jumped to the main dining table and walked carefully around the dirty dishes, looking intently for a list. Seeing nothing, she jumped down, then to the top of what was supposed to be her detective office. Giving a derisive sniff, she continued to look.

Finally, she found one. It was underneath a dirty plate, with used silverware carelessly tossed, causing butter and jelly to land on the page. She took the corner of the paper in her mouth and pulled. The corner tore.

Carefully, she moved the plate a few inches to the side. She wasn't as careful as she thought, and the plate fell to the seat of the chair. *"Bummer,"* she thought.

As Annie rushed in to see what had caused the clatter, she grabbed the sheet of paper, jumped to the floor and ran from the room.

Underneath the love seat, she started to read aloud. Mr. Bean, Little Socks, Sassy Pants and Mo surrounded her, ever helpful, as she tried to figure out the typed list.

"Towel...pink or...purple...there's a number here. I'm not good with numbers. Then, um, blue or green, with another number, then ssstttrrripes. Stripes, with another number. Then it says no ponts...no pints...no po-i-nts...no points! No points for pat...turns....pat...turns...."

Little Socks said, *"Patterns?"*

"Right!"

Mo gave an excited, *"Trill!"*

Sassy Pants translated. *"He knows da numbers. He helps George wit invitations."*

"Inventory," said Little Socks.

"You reads his mind, too?"

160

Little Socks pushed her forehead into the floor. *"No, you idiot. I speak English."*

Tiger Lily bopped Little Socks on the nose. *"Stop that!"*

"Stop speaking English?"

"Stop being mean."

"I'm not mean. She's an idiot!"

Tiger Lily bopped her on the nose again, then looked at Sassy Pants. *"You're not one of those. Tell me what Mo says about the numbers."*

Mo trilled. Sassy Pants sat back and looked at him. He trilled again. She shook her head, perplexed. *"Trill, trill."*

Sassy Pants finally shook her head and said, *"I sees pitchers in his head. I duzn't know wot he means."*

Tiger Lily had long gotten over the picture in her mind of pitchers of water pouring into Sassy's brain. She knew the little girl mispronounced the word 'pictures.' She shook her head, turned and called to Kali and Ko, underneath the love seat across the way. *"You have to come over here and translate."*

Kali and Ko crept from under the seat, looking both ways to make sure they couldn't be seen. Tiger Lily closed her eyes and counted. Little Socks pounded her head into the floor a few more times. Mr. Bean and Mo cleaned their hind quarters.

Finally, the two big girls squeezed in beside their siblings. Together, they said, *"What?"*

Mo trilled. Kali said, *"He said the first number is ten, the second one is five and the last is one."*

Tiger Lily looked at the list again. *"So...the biggest number is with pink or purple, and the numbers get smaller each time, until you get to this that says 'no points.'"*

Mr. Bean said, *"So they have towel colors, numbers, points, and....what does that mean?"*

Sassy Pants said, *"Dat's easy. Dey gets points for da towels dey takes, and numbers, dey means how many points."*

Kali and Ko said, at the same time, *"So they want to find the towels with the most points." "They want the pink or purple towels to get the most points."*

Tiger Lily nodded to herself. *"That makes sense. They're doing this whole thing on points, and there will be a winner at the end of the week. So they're making it hard. Everybody knows beach towels are really pretty, mostly."*

"Yeah," said Sassy Pants. *"Dey gots seashells and star fishes and stripes and circles and lots of colors."*

Little Socks said, *"The people that don't have the pretty towels are the ones that can't afford to buy them. They bring their towels from the bathroom."*

Mr. Bean cried, *"So they're going to steal towels from poor people?"*

"Maybe," said Tiger Lily. *"Now that we think we understand it, let's look at the rest of the list."*

She didn't get the opportunity.

Annie was on her hands and knees, peering under the love seat. She came eye to eye with seven cats, squeezed together in the false hope that they were invisible to the rest of the world. Tiger Lily's right paw was on a piece of paper. She looked at Annie with an expression of pure innocence.

Annie reached in. "Let me see that, darlin'."

She pulled the sheet of paper out, sat on the floor and was joined by Henrie. Well, he didn't really sit on the floor. He sat on the love seat but stood quickly as three guests appeared at the dining room door.

To their quizzical looks, he responded, "We are discussing – with the cats, you see – their abysmal behavior. They know better than to get on top of the tables."

From the floor, Annie said, "Especially when there are plates and things…"

Kara laughed. She turned to the wedding couple. "I've heard stories about these cats. We'll just leave them to it, okay? I'll talk to you this afternoon."

As the three went their separate ways, Henrie closed his eyes and shook his head. He sank again to the love seat. "Let us see what the children have found."

Annie looked at the paper again. "Did you figure this out, kids? It looks like the scavenger hunters are to find the things on this list, and they get the most points for certain items."

She read from the list. "Towels, higher points for certain single colored ones, pink, purple, blue, or green, and you get one point for stripes and no points for patterns."

Henrie said, "Most beach towels are brightly colored."

"So they aren't making it easy. And just as an aside, all of our beach towels are purple. They could just take ours from the closet and get their points."

Henrie said, "They would not dare!"

"They might. Let's move on. Beach blankets, again, different points for various colors, highest points for the most unique; sand shovels of various colors. Umbrellas of various colors. Sandals or flip flops, higher points for adult male or female. Coolers. They're going to take coolers. You get the most points for coolers with certain items."

"What items?" asked Henrie.

"Most points for alcohol, beer, wine or mixed drinks; medium points for fried chicken and, specifically, seafood salad; fewer points for sandwiches; no points for potato salad. And there are bonus points."

"Dear me. What, pray tell, constitutes a bonus?"

"Cell phones, cameras, iPods, earbuds or headphones."

"So…assuming the moderators do not participate, five couples will be on the prowl. It is possible that at least five of each of these items will be stolen from the beach today."

"Yep. I'm thinkin' I should call Pete now."

"That is an excellent idea."

Annie looked at Tiger Lily. "Sorry, darlin'. Did I rain on your parade?"

Pastor Teresa and Boone stood leaning against the side of Pete's police cruiser while keeping their eyes on Gene. Gene stood several yards away, being interviewed by Pete and the State Police.

Tank and his crew were gone, the remains of the small structure fire left for clean-up later, when the State Police and fire inspectors were gone.

Boone noticed Wyatt leaning against a tree, watching the inspectors and gawkers with a haggard face. To Teresa, he said, "I should go over there and talk to him."

"Huh? Who?"

Boone pointed. "Him. He's the Veterans guy."

"Oh, yeah. Him. Why do you think he's hanging around?"

"Probably to talk to Gene. I don't know what this guy's deal is, but somebody has to be setting these fires. Right now, the only suspects left are the three living vets and this guy Wyatt."

"In my mind," said Teresa, "the only suspect left is Wyatt."

"Mine, too, but Pete has to keep an open mind."

"So if you talk to him, what are you going to say?"

"Don't know. Want to join me? Or wait here?"

"I'll go with you."

They walked over slowly, giving Wyatt a chance to register they were headed in that direction. When they reached him, Wyatt kept his face down. Boone said, "So we lost another one. Have you found the other guys?"

"No," said Wyatt. "I was hoping you, well, Pete, or you, could tell me, but, man, this is just too much."

Boone took a close look. It appeared Wyatt had been crying.

"I'm sorry, Wyatt. Real sorry. I didn't realize how important this was…"

"Oh, it's nothing. I just get…real emotional. I was hoping to talk to the younger fella, Gene, to see if he's willing to tell me where the other guys are." Wyatt peered closely into Boone's face. "And you don't know?"

"Nope," lied Boone.

Teresa said, "Wyatt, I'm just a simple little old pastor at a simple church in a resort town. I don't know much about anything, but I've sure learned a lot about people. You need to stop this story about being with a veterans' service organization. Tell us why you're here, and maybe we'll be able to help you."

As she spoke, Boone's head jerked in her direction. He marveled at the straight shooting but was unsure if the tactic was the right one.

Wyatt's head jerked, too. Apparently, he wasn't sure about the tactic, either. After several seconds of silence, he finally nodded his head several times, looked straight at Teresa and said, "Okay. Okay." He looked at the ground and said one last time, "Okay."

Looking back at Teresa, he said, "I think my dad's here, and I think he's in trouble. Real trouble."

Boone looked at him closely. "What kind of trouble, Wyatt, and why didn't you…"

Teresa put a hand on Boone's arm and said, "Tell us about your dad, Wyatt."

Wyatt leaned against the tree and said, "He was…he is…well, he was a great dad. Took care of Mom and me, proud to be in the Army. Then he got sent over there, and he came back, and he was different. Something happened."

He remained silent for a while, then began again. "We don't think it had anything to do with the war, you know, the fightin' and stuff. We thought it was something else. And then, when my Mom passed, I was cleaning up her stuff, and I found...I found this."

Wyatt reached into his pocket and brought out a well-worn piece of paper, folded over and over again. He handed the paper to Teresa, who took her time reading it. Boone read it over her shoulder.

Bonita and Rich went to Antiques On Main. The store was empty except for a woman behind the jewelry counter and a man and woman walking among the antiques.

The woman behind the counter said, "Welcome. May I help you?"

Bonita stopped at the counter; Rich went to the locked case at the back of the antique store. Bonita said, "Yes. I have an interesting proposition for Gena's Creations. Are you the manager?"

"Yes. I'm Gema, and I'm all ears."

"Great. My friend and I are moderators of a scavenger hunt. A group of ten – five couples – are part of the hunt. We're all staying at the KaliKo Inn, and we'll do several hunts during our stay."

"A scavenger hunt? Intriguing. How can I help?"

"We put together a list for each day, and tomorrow, we want them to find expensive gifts for men and women. The trick is for them to find the most expensive gifts.

They'll take photos of the gifts they choose, and then we'll match the prices, add them up, and the couple with the highest priced gifts – only two – wins the points for the day."

"That won't be hard. The prices are there for all to see."

"I know. That's what I want to ask about. For tomorrow, could you hide the prices somehow, so they can't see them?"

Gema thought about it for a minute. "I'm willing to work with you, but I have to say that I'm in business to make money. I would hope to make a sale, and to do that, people have to see the real prices. And I don't know that Frank will be able to hide all of his prices."

"We've done this before, and I have a solution to offer."

"Again, I'm all ears. Maybe I should get Frank over here." Gema waved the man over.

When Frank arrived, Gema continued. "Hi. I was telling Gema about our scavenger hunt. It's something we do on vacation a few times a year. We picked Chelsea for this one. Anyway, just to bring you up-to-date, Frank, I've asked Gema to hide her prices, so couples can pick out what they believe to be the most expensive gifts. Once they've chosen, they take a photograph, and then they shop."

Rich came to the counter as well. "Trust me. Our folks love to shop. They're professionals; they have money; they like to spend it."

Gema said, "That sounds interesting. It would mean a little work for me, but nothing I can't handle. I imagine it would be harder for you, Frank."

"I have too many pieces to hide all the prices, but how about this. I can offer my locked case, the case with smaller expensive items, including heirloom gems. It wouldn't be difficult to hide the prices in there."

Rich said, "We can arrange that. We'll give them the parameters of the hunt. Only locked cases, either jewelry or antiques."

Bonita beamed. "Well, then, I think we have a hunt! But for now, let me look at that ruby ring, and that emerald over there. I'm going to do some shopping of my own."

As Bonita tried on the rings, Rich took photos. "We'll make a decision tonight and get one of these tomorrow."

Bonita glanced at the woman who waited for Frank on the antique floor. She was older, fit, and wore a bemused smile. She sat on an antique settee beside a large golden long-haired cat. The cat divided his attention between the lovely Himalayan cat whose tail entwined with his, the woman, and, apparently, the goings-on at the jewelry counter.

Suellen grabbed the beach bag and cooler and followed Don out the door. "Where to?"

"How about one of those lunches from Mr. Bean's?"

"Good idea. They have a couple of sandwiches that looked really great, and I saw a special on cold fried chicken."

"Their bottled soda looked good, too. It's that kind from Mexico, with pure cane sugar. Better than what we can usually find."

Lunch in their cooler, they walked to the town park entrance to the beach. Suellen said, "We could have gone to the Inn's private beach."

"But I want to walk to those cliffs."

"Good idea. We can set up a spot, take a walk to the cliffs, then come back for lunch."

They paid a small entrance fee and rented an umbrella for the day, one with a purple and pink tie-dye pattern.

"Do you want to swim first?"

"No, let's leave our stuff and we can walk up the beach."

"Do you really think it's safe to leave our stuff?"

"Look around. Lots of people are here, and several have left their stuff. If they think it's safe, then it has to be."

Don spread the multi-colored quilt he had used for years as a beach blanket – it had been made by his maiden aunties and given to him as a child – planted the umbrella in the sand, dropped the cooler, their sandals and their KaliKo Inn purple beach towels beside it.

"I don't care how safe you think it is, my billfold is coming with us. Your wallet, too. Give it to me. I'll put it in my fanny pack."

"Are we taking the cellphones?"

"Sure. We might get some great pics!"

Gene knocked on the kitchen door to the Inn and entered when Henrie opened it.

"Come in, Gene. I am very happy to see you. I am sorry you lost another friend."

"Thanks, Henrie. I sure don't know what's happening, and I'm certain Perry didn't know, either. It's a sad thing, alright."

Gene sat at the kitchen table as Henrie poured a cup of coffee. "Do you know anything more, Gene?"

"No. Just that they pulled his body out of another fire. I don't know who's killing us or why. I saw that guy, Wyatt, leave with the police. Do you think he's involved?"

"I have no idea. Do you know anything about him?"

"No. Nothing."

"I know very little as well. Are you certain you should be walking around by yourself?"

"I have things to do, Henrie."

"I know. You want to assure your friends have food."

"Not just my friends. There's a cat – a mother cat and her kittens – feral. My friend Mal made sure she got food every day, and now so do I."

"A cat, you say?"

As Henrie spoke, Kali and Ko wandered into the kitchen. They sniffed the ankles of the new man carefully. Kali deposited a few love hairs on his cuff.

Gene smiled and looked back up at Henrie. "They're beautiful! Do they live here?"

"They do. They and five others. We are, in effect, a cat house."

"Wow. I'll bet that cat would love living in a place like this."

"Not necessarily. A feral cat does not take easily to comfort. However, if you are aware of a cat with kittens, I am bound to see if I can assist. Where does she stay?"

"In an old Edsel at that marina, not far from where the first fire was."

"Indeed. Well. Let me retrieve some supplies, and you can show me."

Pete appeared at the kitchen door. "Hey, Henrie. Oh, good. Gene, you're the guy I was looking for. I need you to come with me to the station. Someone I need you to talk to."

Chet and Justine stood at the back of the town park, surveying the swimmers and sun bathers. Justine said, "There. Right there at the back edge. See that purple and pink umbrella? No one's there. We might get it all."

"We might, but I saw the people before they walked away. They're staying at the KaliKo Inn. That couple that's getting married."

"Good catch." She looked around again. "Oh, hey! See that umbrella in the middle? Red, pink and green? Looks like the folks are getting ready to go in for a swim."

"Okay. That's good for me. Look. Damien and Tasha are going for the purple and pink."

Justine looked up at Chet. "Think we should stop them?"

Chet laughed. "Nah. Let's stay quiet for now. I hope they get caught. And I have to say, their curve ball was pretty lame."

"You're right about that. And they have to keep it up. At every restaurant, they'll have to send their food or drink back."

"These people are too smart for that. They all talk to one another. They'll start charging them for the stuff they won't eat or drink."

"We shouldn't come to such a small town after this. Stick with the cities."

"I thought it was a risk, but Bonita insisted. For some reason, she had to try this town."

"Why?"

"She said it gets rave reviews. She was probably checking it out for a personal vacation."

"She'll never be able to come back here. Everyone will remember her."

Chet nodded, then he changed the subject. "We have to get a curve ball."

"We're late to the game. We'll have to do something spectacular that we only have to do once."

"What do you think Thad and Treena will do? They haven't come forward yet."

"I heard Thad tell Treena he'll 'choke' on something tonight at supper."

"Lame. He's done that before."

"I know. What about theft? We could hide your purse and say it was stolen."

"I don't want to be without my stuff."

"You don't have to. We'll stash your cards, driver license, cash, everything that you can't replace; you keep your phone in a pocket. Do you have one of those expensive purses with you?"

"I do. A Gucci."

"Let's go shopping, pick up a new one, a cheapie, make sure everyone sees it."

"Okay. That can work. Hey, look. Our marks just left. Let's head that way."

They nodded at Damien and Tasha as they left the park, a purple and pink umbrella and cooler in Damien's hands, and a brightly colored quilt wrapped in purple towels in Tasha's.

After they passed, Justine said, "Do you think they even noticed all the beach towels at the Inn are purple?"

"Dim. They're dim. They might get extra points if they're able to talk their way out of it, though."

Rich and Bonita settled into Bonita's room, a jewelry case with maker's tools handy.

"Here," said Rich. I think this set and this fake emerald will match this one."

"Good. And I have a set for the fake ruby."

"It might be hard, having the creator in the mix. She might recognize the thefts before anyone else we've cased."

"She'll be fine. I've got lots of counterfeit money to pass around. She'll think she's made thousands of dollars in sales, and she won't be looking for these two rings."

While Nancy picked up lunch to go at the Café, Honey Bear hopped to the hostess stand. Tiger Lily hissed. She was a bit proprietary of her stand.

"Don't hiss at me. I'm here with news."

"What?"

"We were at the antique store, and that big group of people staying at the Inn are up to no good."

"How can you tell?"

"I think they're going to set up Gema and Frank, maybe steal some jewelry or other small things. Expensive things."

"What makes you think that?"

"Two of them were in there, said that tomorrow, everyone will go in there, and they'll have to do silly stuff, guess at prices, get things out of the counter, take pictures. It just sounds fishy."

"What did Claire think about it?"

Claire was the lovely Himalayan. She rarely left the antique shop, but she was Honey Bear's honey. They found time to make it work.

Of course, they were both "its," but love is love.

"She thought the same thing. She doesn't think Frank and Gema saw through the act."

"We'll have to search the rooms tomorrow night. See if we can find stuff that was stolen."

"Good idea."

"Thanks, Honey Bear. Really. Thanks."

Hank settled at a table in the back room of the winery. He waited for his partner. Well, a man who sat at a desk in

Hank's building every day, drinking and stealing a paycheck every week. He probably shouldn't be meeting him in a place that served drinks, but drinks would probably keep him loose and off-kilter.

The man had been good for a few things lately, but now Hank was going to have to turn him lose.

Permanently.

A man sat at the table. "Are you buying, Hank?"

"Sure, Ed. Lunch is on me. Order a glass of wine if you want."

"Don't mind if I do."

Ed looked around, noticing they were in a private corner. "So, what's up? Got something for me to do?"

"Yeah. I think I got a line on the last Gulf War vet. Are you gonna be available tonight?"

"Sure, but I tell ya, it's gonna cost more this time."

"How much?"

"For starters. . .oh, hey, Minnie. Give me your best lunch, and a glass of something white and sweet."

"Okay, Ed. How does a muffaletta sound? It's Italian, made with salami and provolone, and it's served with olive dressing."

"Sounds good."

"How about you, Hank?"

"Get me the same, and some chianti."

"Change my white wine to that."

"Sure thing, guys. I'll be right back."

Hank noticed that Minnie wiped her nose as she walked away. He couldn't blame her. Ed needed a bath.

Ed turned back to Hank. "For starters, I want a raise. A substantial raise. You leave me in charge of everything, you're never around, I have to take care of all your crap."

"Okay, okay. What, five thousand?"

"A year? Heck, no. I want at least twenty a year more."

"I'm gonna have to think about that."

"Well, think away, and then get back to me about this evening."

Hank drummed his fingers on the table. "Okay. Twenty a year. Do the paperwork. I'll sign it."

Eddie pulled an envelope from his pocket. "It just so happens. . ."

Hank grabbed the envelope, opened it, read the document and scribbled his name on the bottom. "You said that was for starters."

"Ten thousand for each of the guys I did or helped you do."

"That's fifty thousand! Sixty after tonight!"

"Right."

Minnie returned with two glasses of chianti. "Sandwiches will be right up."

When she left, Hank said, "He found a vacant house at the end of Washington Street. He probably doesn't go out of it at night, afraid of what might happen. Hey, that glass went down pretty quick. I'll order another for ya."

Hank smiled to himself. The idiot didn't even think to ask how Hank came by this information.

Brown Mousie scurried out of the planter in search of Sassy Pants.

15

Kali and Ko sat in the foyer. *"We should go to the Café."*

"No."

"It will be a couple of hours before she gets home."

"No."

"We can do it. I know we can."

"No."

The argument turned to hisses, then swipes with front paws, until a full body roll-around fight ensued.

This is how Clara and Moriah found them. Clara had her wagon with fresh flowers. She put her hands on her hips, looked down at the cats, now quiet but still entwined, and said, "Girls! Your mother would not be happy to see you fight."

Kali and Ko looked at one another, and said, at the same time, *"Let's tell Moriah!"* *"Moriah will do it!"*

They quickly told Moriah all she needed to know, and she took off.

As Clara worked with the fresh flowers, taking down the old and putting the new in the vases, she chatted. She was used to talking to the big girls. They watched every Thursday afternoon and enjoyed samples on which to chew.

Today, they chewed red, yellow, pink and white snapdragons while Clara chatted away.

"For some reason I decided on dragon flowers for each of your mother's places. Geranium dragon hearts, snapdragons, dragon's breath celosia. Throw in a couple of purple lotus and fire red flowers of very kind. . .. Anyway,

I had a need for dragons. Do you suppose someone's trying to send me a message?"

Moriah trotted into the Café and jumped to the hostess stand. Tiger Lily hissed. What was up with all the cats jumping to her hostess stand today?

She asked Moriah, *"What are you doing?"*

"Delivering a message."

Moriah fluffed her mane, licked a paw and said a gracious *"hello"* to the next guests who came in. They heard, "Mew, purr, mew."

It didn't help that the guests reached over to pet Moriah and tell her what a beautiful girl she was.

Tiger Lily jumped down and trotted behind the coffee bar. She sat there in a huff until Moriah joined her.

"I said I have a message."

"Then give it, and go home."

"If that's the way you're gonna be. . ."

Tiger Lily rolled her eyes and shook her head. *"I'm sorry. What is it?"*

Moriah fluffed her mane again, but sensing she was on thin ice, she put off cleaning her paw. *"Kali and Ko said Henrie heard about that cat, the one Cyril saw. She's – they didn't know the word, exactly but said it meant 'not tame' – and she has babies. And she needs food. And she lives in someplace called an Eddie."*

"Eddie?"

"That's what they said. 'Eddie at the marina.'"

Tiger Lily thought about it. Cyril had seen the cat at the old marina, after the first fire. She didn't know what an 'Eddie' was or where it would be in the marina.

"How did they hear about the cat?"

"They said – have you ever tried to listen to them talk? I mean, you have to almost close your ears to everything and back up and. . ."

"Yeah, yeah, yeah. I know all about that. How did they hear about it?"

"Oh. Right. They said a man, one of the vets, was at the Inn this morning and told Henrie about it. They said Henrie was going to see if he could find it and help, but Pete came to the door and wanted to talk to the vet. Gene. They said Gene."

Tiger Lily thought about it. *"We have to make sure Henrie goes out there. There are babies involved."*

"Well, that's my message. Oh, here's my mommy. She's got the flowers."

Moriah jumped to the hostess stand to help Clara change the fresh flowers. She had purple, lavender and pink snapdragons.

As Moriah left to help Clara, Sassy Pants ran around the corner of the stand. Tiger Lily jumped. *"What are you doing here?"*

"I has news! Brown Mousie sez dat awful guy, Hank, he killin' da vets!"

Gene left the police department with Wyatt and Boone, still feeling a little dizzy. Now it was clear. The reason they had come to Chelsea. The reason the older vets didn't want to talk to him or Perry. And even though Perry wasn't a part of it, he was dead, too.

Now Pete and his force were looking for three: Ben, Tempo and Harper. A search of the marina, buildings around the box store and museum grounds had gained them nothing. Pete wanted to know what Gene knew, first, where they might be, and second, did he know their reason for coming to Chelsea.

Now, he knew, and now, he wanted to spend some time with Wyatt. And hunt for Harper. Lost in thought, he nearly tripped over two cats.

Tiger Lily and Sassy Pants ran through the cat door at the police department and kept running until they found Cyril.

Cyril seemed to be in conference with Pete, but a closer look told them Pete only pretended to talk to Cyril as he spoke into the telephone.

Sassy Pants jumped in front of Cyril to get his attention. *"Cyril! We knows who kills dem!"*

Cyril yawned and shuffled his big body to the floor. *"I know. It was Hank. And maybe someone else is helping him."*

Tiger Lily and Sassy Pants sat up straight and looked at one another. They turned to Cyril and said, at the same time, *"What?"* *"How?"*

Cyril yawned again, enjoying the one-ups-manship. Generally, the cats told him "who done it." Today, it was the other way around.

"We found a guy, a guy who had a story to tell."

"What guy?"

"Some guy named Wyatt."

"Wyatt? He's staying at the Inn!"

"Then you've really been sleeping on the job."

"We thought Wyatt might be doing it."

Cyril laughed so hard he started to sneeze. When he got himself under control, he said, "I'm sorry. I'm just teasing. This guy Wyatt, well, Pete thought he might be doing it, too. But turns out, he's here looking for his dad. He had a story, written and left by his father. He came here looking for Hank, because he had Hank's name and the name of the town where he lived."

"Chelsea."

"Yeah, Chelsea. Anyway, he saw a news story about the fire, the first one, and the side story about a group of vets, so. . ."

"He decided to come check it out."

"Right."

Sassy Pants looked at the floor for a few seconds, then made one of the leaps of thought that she was known for. First, you think she's an idiot, then you wonder how she knows what she does. "He wuzn't smokin' dat nasty cigar. He wuz pretendin' to smokes it so we wouldn't smell da smoke from da fires. He was pokin' 'round for evidence."

"You're right. Why didn't you read his mind?"

"I duzn't do dat on command. It ain't polite."

"Don't say that."

"Dat I duzn't do dat on command?"

"Ain't. Don't say ain't."

"Why not?"

Tiger Lily shook her head. *"Let's move on. Cyril, who's Pete talking to?"*

"He's calling in the big guns."

Sassy Pants jumped up and down. *"Dey talks on da phone? Big guns?"*

Cyril hid his head in his paws. Tiger Lily bopped Sassy Pants on her nose. *"Let's go home. We have to save the cat and her kittens."*

Suellen jumped down the last couple of feet. "That was so great!"

They had climbed to the top of the rock cliff, which afforded a dazzling view of the lake and several upscale homes and condominiums. Behind them had been a wooded area marked as state park area.

"Now I'm ready for lunch. Let's head back for the blanket."

Don said, "The climb took a little longer than we thought. We're going to be late to meet Ray."

"We'll have time for a piece of fried chicken. Hey, look. What is that?"

Don looked in the direction her finger was pointing. "I don't know, let me. . .AHHHHHH!"

Suellen got closer to see what he had seen and screamed along with him.

Pete stopped at the Inn on his way to the beach cliff. "What did you need to see me about, Henrie?"

"Annie and I believe our large group of guests will be up to no good."

Cyril nuzzled Henrie's leg until Henrie reached into a cupboard for a treat.

"Dangerous?"

"No. They are probably harmless. We suspect they will commit several petty thefts at the beach today."

"Just where I'm headed, but for something else. A couple of your guests found a body."

"No! Which guests, and whose body?"

"That wedding party, and they found another veteran."

"Dear me."

"I'll check with you later about your concerns. In the meantime, if you see Gene, send him my way."

"I will, Pete."

Pete and Cyril left, driving the cruiser as far as the town park entrance. From there, Pete climbed onto an ATV handed over by a lifeguard. Cyril was happy to run along.

Cyril reached the base of the cliff first. Like a good boy, he stopped short of the body, turned, and guarded until Pete arrived. There weren't many people to guard it from. Just a man and a woman.

The perplexed couple looked from Cyril to Pete. He climbed off and said, "I'm Pete, the Chief of Police. Some crime scene folks are coming in from the State Police, but I'll take your statement."

The man pointed to Cyril. "Is he yours?"

"Yep. He won't bite, not if you're the good guys."

"We are. Hey, everywhere we go in this town, people have cats and dogs that work with them. What's up with that?"

"We're just enlightened, that's all. You're, um, Don Straight and Suellen Young?"

Don answered. "Yes. We're staying at the KaliKo Inn up the way. Getting married this weekend."

"I hear. On The Escape. You'll meet my dog's best friend."

"We already have, I think," said Suellen. "Jock."

Cyril gave a happy yip.

Pete moved over to the body. "Did you touch him?"

"No. I could tell he was dead. We didn't get any closer than right about where the dog is."

"Cyril."

"The dead guy is Cyril?"

"No, the dog."

Pete gave a hand signal and Cyril moved away. While he checked vitals and looked around the scene, Cyril did what he always did. He guarded. When Don turned to walk away, Cyril growled. Don turned, and Cyril put a happy smile on his face. Don stayed.

Two officers arrived, ready to help process the scene. Pete said, "We still have a few vets missing. Take a walk as far as the lagoon, and it wouldn't hurt if one of you climbed this cliff."

They left, and Pete snapped a photo of the dead vet's face. He sent it to Boone and followed that with a call.

When Boone answered, Pete said four words. "Which one is it?"

"That's Ben. That leaves Gene and two Gulf vets, Tempo and Harper."

Pete disconnected the call and picked up another. It was Henrie.

"I think I know where Gene may be."

"Yeah? Where?"

"Before you arrived this morning, he told me of a stray cat that he has been feeding. At the old marina, in an Edsel."

"Well, isn't that something. Cyril took an interest in that old car. I'll call Marco and have him check."

"Please call animal control as well. I understand there are kittens."

Pete disconnected, looked at the ground and shook his head. Henrie. His priorities were all about the cats.

He made the call. Cyril gave a happy yip.

Pete finally turned when he heard, "Hey, Chief? Mr. Officer?"

"Yeah?"

"Do you need us?"

"I need to get a statement."

"It's just that we're supposed to meet the guy with the boat. Ray."

"Oh. Right. I can get your statements later. You'll be around for a couple of days. Thanks for calling it in, and for staying this long." Pete turned back to the body.

Don continued. "No problem. Just one thing?"

Pete turned back to them.

"Will you tell your dog it's okay?"

"Oh, sure. Cyril, let them go."

Cyril, who had not changed from his happy smile face, stood to shake his tail, indicating it was perfectly fine for the two to go.

Pete soon heard one of his officers calling from the area of the lagoon. "Pete! We have another body!"

Wyatt treated. They stopped at Mr. Bean's to pick up a picnic lunch of cold fried chicken, cole slaw, chips and Mexican soda. Wyatt purchased enough for several adults.

"I wish I knew where they were," said Gene. "They're probably mighty hungry about now."

"We have enough for them, if we find them. Let's walk and talk while we eat."

"Okay. Let's go to that old marina first. They might be there, but I have to feed a cat, too."

"A cat?"

"Yeah. Malcolm, the first one to get it, you know, in that fire at the marina, he started feeding this darned mother cat, and, well. . ."

"You feel beholden to keep it up."

"Yeah. I told Henrie about them. I hope he can arrange to pick them up, or have someone else do it."

"He'll probably do that, but it's a good idea, anyway, to start at the Marina. They don't know me, but they know you. I've probably been in their vicinity dozens of times, but they always run."

"They don't know if you're working with that guy or not."

"Hank."

"Yeah. Tell me again what you know."

"I only know what I read, what Dad wrote down. There was a murder near an Army base, and your friend Malcolm, he saw the guy that did it. It was an officer. Dad only remembered him as Captain Jenson. They shipped out real quick, it was just the timing of it all, and that guy Jenson didn't get to do anything about it. I guess you know more than me, now."

"Not really. I can tell you that a couple months ago, after Mal was arrested – he had a nose for drugs – anyway, after he got out, he said we needed to get here, to Chelsea. I didn't know why, and most of the guys didn't want me to come along. Or Perry. We was from a different war an' all. We was younger. Your dad, Harper, he really didn't want us to come along."

"Maybe he didn't see any reason to get you wrapped up in this."

"Maybe. Well, for whatever reason, here I am. And now, well, seems the police know this Captain Jenson."

"They at least have a good idea. We aren't supposed to talk about it where anyone can hear us. He used to be a big deal here in town."

They walked on in silence for a while. Wyatt finally said, "Tell me about my dad."

Gene was silent as they walked on for several yards. Finally, he said, "He's a good man. He always took care of the other guys, and him with a bum leg and back. He has a good heart." He paused, then said, "He didn't want me to come here, but besides that, he was always a friend. Malcolm was the first. My first friend on the street. Harper, though, if Malcom weren't around, he'd take care of me."

"Did he ever talk about me? About his family?"

"No." After a while, he added, "Well, that ain't true. One time we got to talkin' about our lives before. Before the street, you know. I remember Harper sayin' he had a boy, a real good boy, would take good care of his momma."

Wyatt, softly, asked, "Did he say anything more about momma?"

"No, Wyatt. He didn't. You gotta understand. On the street, we didn't talk about the good things. The good times. We can't go back there, no way no how. We might be able to get ourselves off the street, but there ain't no way we can go back to somethin' that ain't, not no more."

16

Henrie answered the Inn's main telephone line. He was surprised to hear the voice on the other end. "Gracious! It is good to hear from you. Are you coming to Chelsea?"

"I am," said the voice. Do you have a room?"

"I am so sorry to say we do not, but we will find a place for you. I will turn the back porch into a room if need be."

"That won't be. . ."

"Nonsense. Are you in town now?"

"No. Just headed out. It will be this evening at the earliest."

"Make the Inn your first stop. If we cannot find a place for you here, you still have friends. I am certain we can find a guest room."

Don and Suellen reached the place they were certain they had left their blanket and umbrella. They stood and looked all around.

"I thought you said it would be safe?"

"I thought it would be. I'm glad the aunties are dead. They'd be really mad I lost their quilt."

"Maybe we'd better go back and tell that police officer."

"I think a dead body trumps our missing beach stuff. We're going to have great stories to tell our kids."

"That's the truth," said Suellen. "Come on. I'm hungry. We can grab lunch at the Café when we meet with Ray."

Marco drove into the old marina at the same time as animal control. Sure enough, Gene was at the Edsel, reaching into the back window with what he assumed to be food. That other fellow, Wyatt, was with him.

Stopping his vehicle well back, he called over.

"Gene, I have some bad news for you. And I brought someone with me to help with your cat."

Gene looked past Marco at animal control. A young woman emerged from the driver's seat.

Gene nodded at Marco, turned and spoke to the cat. "I don't know if you can understand, but these folks are from the government, and they're here to help. Really. I won't always be here to feed you, but they'll make sure you and your babies are safe.

Wyatt had already joined Marco at the car. Gene backed away and watched as the team gathered the mother and her babies with surprisingly little effort.

As animal control pulled away, Gene turned to Marco. "Bad news? What?"

"It appears two of your friends were killed, probably last night, possibly around the time your friend Perry was killed."

Wyatt tensed. "Was one of them my dad?"

"I don't know." Marco pulled up the photos on his phone and held the phone out to both of them. "Know them?"

"Yeah," said Gene. "That's Ben. That one there is Tempo. Harper is the only one left, and we haven't been able to find him." He put his hand on Wyatt's shoulder. "It's not your dad. He's still out there somewhere."

Wyatt asked, "Is it that guy we talked about this morning? Did he do it?"

"We don't know, but Pete made a call. We're calling in a friend, someone who can investigate in ways we can't. Thing is, we need to find Harper. Gene, we need to get you someplace safer than the church."

"But I don't know anything."

"He doesn't know that. You've been lucky, staying on The Avenue, walking all over town by yourself. You've been darned lucky. Pete told me to arrest you if necessary, but to get you someplace safe."

"Where would that be?"

"We don't know yet, but for now, come with me to the station."

"When's that guy coming? The investigator?"

"He should be here by this evening. In the meantime, let's talk about where your friend Harper might be."

Maggie knelt beside the Edsel. She and her volunteers had two cat carriers, nets, animal control poles, protective clothing and headgear. She also had a variety of foods. Not cat food. This cat wouldn't respond to cat food. She had pieces of burgers, bacon and ham.

For now, the cat stared up at her from the floor in front of the passenger seat. She protected her babies. Some of the babies appeared healthy. The mother had gotten enough food to keep her milk going, at least.

The mother would probably never be adopted, but there was hope for the kittens. Perhaps the mother, once the babies were weaned, could be taken by a farm family, someone in need of a mouser, and someone who had outdoor buildings in which the cat could find shelter.

Softly, she spoke to the team and outlined her plan for capture, and blissfully, Plan A worked. Momma went into one carrier and the babies – five of them – went into the other.

As they walked back to the vehicle, she spoke to Gene. "Did you tell her we were here to help? She was almost docile. Almost."

Maggie stopped long enough for Gene to look in and say good-bye to the cat.

Tiger Lily and Sassy Pants ran home, picking up siblings along the way. Not because they stopped and asked them to come, but because they saw the girls through the windows. Everyone but Mo. Mo was always in some dark, quiet place in the bar, flirting with some woman or another.

By the time they reached the foyer of the Inn, the rest were hot on their tails. Bringing up the rear were their friends from DoubleGood, Simon Finnegan and Oscar McMurphy.

Henrie hurried in, having heard the snips and snarls of cats running into one another and taking umbrage.

Tiger Lily looked up at Henrie, earnest and hopeful. She turned to her siblings and friends. *"I need to ask him if he can save the cat."*

A chorus ensued. *"What cat?" "Who?"*

Thankfully, Kali and Ko came to the rescue. At the same time, they said, *"The cat Cyril found." "The cat in the Eddie."*

"What?" "Huh?" "What's a Eddie?"

Henrie, thankfully, stood by, aware a momentous conversation was near at hand.

Tiger Lily turned back to him. Desperate, she turned to the cats. *"Do as I say, now!"*

The cats, surprised, backed away from her.

Tiger Lily looked at Kali. *"Lie down, now!"*

"What?"

"Lie down. Now!"

Kali dropped to the floor.

"No, belly up, like you have kittens!"

"What?"

"Now!"

"Okay, okay!"

"Now you guys." She pushed Little Socks, Mr. Bean and Sassy Pants toward Kali. *"Pretend she's your mom!"*

"WHAT?" *"NO!"* *"You wants me to WHAT?"*

Quickly bopping noses, she pushed them into place. First, Mr. Bean. She pushed his head into Kali's stomach, and he took a bite. Kali screamed.

Sassy Pants was next. *"Okay! Okay! I bites her!"*

She did, and Kali screamed again.

Before Little Socks was pushed into Kali, Henrie stopped her. "Tiger Lily, you do not need to do this. I understand. Marco is on his way to take care of momma and her babies. They will soon be at the rescue facility."

Tiger Lily dropped to the floor, mentally and physically exhausted. Her siblings flounced away, angry at having been used. Their friends (and Ko) were unable to do anything; they were laughing too hard.

Don and Suellen arrived at Tiger Lily's Café, breathless, and quickly spotted Ray at a table. As they sat, Don said, "I'm really sorry. We went to the beach and. . ."

"Found a dead body," finished Suellen. "We had to call the police."

"And then our stuff was stolen. . ."

"And we're starving. They got our lunch! Mind if we order?"

By this time, Ray had leaned back in his chair, head thrown back, with his characteristic loud laugh.

Jock jumped from behind the hostess stand, dropping a treat in the process. When he saw all was fine, he returned to the dish Trudie had left.

Ray finally stopped laughing. "I can tell this won't be just another boring wedding."

"Oh, it won't," said Suellen. "It will be fun! We met the nicest person at the Inn today. Kara. She's a friend of those people from Mo's Tap? George and Candice? And she met this guy named. . .what was his name, honey?"

Sarah arrived and asked if she could take their orders. Don asked, "Are you eating, Ray?"

"No. I'm sticking with coffee."

"Okay. We're starved. What can you do fast?"

"Our sandwich and salad special is fast. Curried chicken salad with mandarin oranges, grapes and pecans on a croissant; mixed greens salad with dried cranberries and pineapple, topped with Asian vinaigrette dressing."

"Sounds great. Two of those, and did I see a coffee special?"

"Bees Knees."

"What?"

"Espresso, honey, milk, lavender, rosemary, simple syrup and a touch a pepper. On ice."

Don and Suellen looked at one another.

Together, they said, "Two, please."

As Sarah left, Suellen looked at Don. "That name, Don?"

"It was strange. . .um. . .Truck. . .Trunk. . . ."

Hopefully, Ray said, "Tank?"

"Yeah. Know him? Them?"

"I know everyone but Kara."

"Are they good folks?"

"Sure. They're friends."

Don said, "Great. We invited them to come along. We thought a party of four just wouldn't cut it."

Suellen added, "So we need to order food and drinks for eight. Fun food and fun drinks."

Don added, "But they said they would help pay, so we want to keep our expenses down."

Ray laughed again, motioned Felicity over, and they got down to business.

As they finished, Ray said, "We should probably call the police department and let them know about your stuff being stolen."

"We already talked to them about a dead body. You think we should tell them about something so mundane?"

"Well, at least consider it."

17

Annie and Henrie finished getting supper together. It was easy. Bacon burgers on brioche buns warmed in the oven alongside zucchini fries, both from Mo's Tap; bottles of a dark regional beer sat proudly in ice; wheat crackers and a variety of cheeses were ready to serve; and a dark red wine was open to breathe on the dining room table, which was set with the most colorful dishes Annie could find.

Henrie slapped Annie's hand when it reached for the box of Italian white truffles.

"I'll behave," she said. "Chris should be here any minute. . ."

And he was. Annie had left her apartment door open. Chris and Sis walked right in. Sis nodded a polite hello to the humans and went in search of her feline friends.

Chris said, "Guest room is set. It will be good to have company for a few days. Any idea why he's here?"

Henrie said, "I believe it has something to do with the veteran issue. Pete and Janet will join us this evening. I imagine we will have a front row seat to their plans."

Pete, Janet and Cyril arrived next, walking in just as Chris had. Cyril, ever as polite as Sis, nodded hello to the humans and went in search of his feline friends. And Sis. Pete asked, "Is he here yet?"

"Not yet, Pete. He should be here soon."

Pete looked at Chris. "He's going to stay with you?"

"There's no room at the Inn. . ."

Henrie, in a very un-Henrie-like move, threw a wheat cracker at Chris's head.

Chris caught it, walked to the table for a piece of brie, and ate it. "And you, Henrie, you're the wicked inn-keeper. You sent poor Jeff Bennett off to the manger."

Jeff Bennett walked into the room and said, "But what a manger! High priced condo on the edge of the lake. And a garage for my donkey."

Henrie poured wine, served beers and moved people to the table. While he participated in the conversations, mostly he was Henrie. He heard everything.

Pete and Jeff: "The thing is, we now have a suspect, but what I couldn't tell you on the phone is that he's a former Town Council member." "You couldn't tell me on the phone?" "Walls have ears." "So this Gene, can he tell me the backstory?" "I don't think he knows anything. I made a copy of the document Wyatt found, that his father left at their house, but I think the only witness – or the only person that can tell us about the original crime – is his father. Harper. He's still missing." "So, you want me to look for Harper?" "No. I want you to see if you can make a case with Hank. I'll look for Harper."

Annie and Janet: "Don't you think it's funny Hank still knows everything about what's going on in town?" "He always had a way of finding out all the secrets." "And he always had secrets of his own." "Did you hear the guys talking? Are they talking about Hank?" "I thought I heard his name." "What did they say?" "Didn't catch it."

Pete and Annie: "Your wedding guests said all of their things were stolen from the beach today." "You don't say. Well, you're going to have to have that conversation with Henrie and I that you've been too busy to have all day."

"You think they were stolen by your other guests." "We could have fun with this."

Henrie spoke up at this. "I have a plan. Pete, come to breakfast tomorrow around eight thirty. Bring a warrant."

Annie and Chris: "Were you talking about Hank?" "No." "No? Janet and I heard you." "We were. . .you must have heard us talking about Frank." "Frank? What about Frank?" "I don't remember. We were just talking." "Chris!"

Henrie looked over in time to see Chris's famous what-who-me face.

Jeff and Chris: "Thanks for giving me a place to stay." "No problem. Hint: if you don't want a dog in your bed, shut the door."

Pete, Jeff and Annie: "We need to keep Gene safe, and we need to find Harper." "Where is Gene now?" "Marco took him out to Boone and Hilly's house. He'll stay there, work with Boone during the day." "What about Wyatt? What's up with him?" "He'll stay in town to look for his father, Harper. He's still out there." "Any idea where to look for him?" "He's got to have found another abandoned building somewhere." "Maybe he left town." "How?" "He could have gone to the highway to hitch a ride." "Or maybe he stole a care." "Maybe he got on a boat."

Cyril and Sis were over it. It took at least half an hour for the cats to tell them what Tiger Lily made them do. Over and over and over.

"She made me lie down like a momma kitty! And she made them bite me!"

"She pushed me!"

"She maded me bites Kali!"

"I wasn't going to bite Kali, but she tried to make me do it!"

Ko and Mo rolled on the floor in laughter as the story was told. Over and over and over.

Now, Tiger Lily was ostracized. She cuddled into Cyril's warm rear haunch, alternating between sad and mad. At the moment, she was mad. Then she remembered.

"Sis, I'm real sorry you had to find a body."

Sis nodded. *"It was pretty awful. Chris made me go far away so I wouldn't be scared. I still was."*

Sis leaned in to lick Tiger Lily's head. *"How long will those cats be mad at you?"*

Tiger Lily said, *"Probably forever. I don't know what the big deal is. It got results."*

Cyril said, *"Don't let it bother you. Your intentions were good. You wanted Henrie to save that cat."*

"And her kittens."

"And her kittens. Are you sure they were saved?"

"I'm sure Henrie sent someone to do it. They would have told him if they couldn't."

"So we don't have to worry about them anymore. That's great. She wasn't in a place I could get to every day, and I never go around with extra food."

"Did you ever learn her name?"

"No. I don't know that wild cats have names."

"Kind of like Fat Cat and Scaredy Cat."

"Right. They didn't even have those names until you met them. You gave them the names."

"That was back in the day that those silly cats trusted me."

"They still trust you. They're just jealous. You had a plan, and you didn't have time to get their opinions."

"Maybe next time I'll let them come up with the plan. So the 'big guns' is Jeff Bennett? He's going to help?"

"Yes. He can look into Hank's activities better than Pete. He can be sneakier."

"And he's nice."

Sis said, "I hope so. He'll be staying with us. Who is he?"

Cyril answered. "He works for the FBI. He comes to town when bad stuff is happening that is more than Pete can handle. He's a good friend."

Tiger Lily changed the subject. "Do you think we can go where the cat is? Now that she's saved? And talk to her?"

Cyril answered, "I don't know how to get you there."

Tiger Lily sighed, then skipped to another subject. "I think the big group that is here might steal jewelry from Gema tomorrow. Maybe stuff from Frank, too."

"Why do you think that?"

"Honey Bear saw them, and he thought they were up to no good."

"He's probably right. I think they stole a lot of stuff from the beach today."

"Can we tell Pete about the jewelry?"

"Let's wait and see what happens. Maybe he'll nip it in the bud."

"What?"

"Nip. . .he'll stop them before they get started. Maybe."

Kara and Tank sat at the far side of the bar, in a place to be able to talk to George when he had a minute and at the best people-watching place in the Tap.

Kara said, "There, see that big table in the middle?"

"Yeah. Those are the ones from the Inn. I've heard about them."

"There's something strange about them. Several of them have food allergies or preferences, and they are doing this scavenger hunt."

"George said something about locking all the peanuts and peanut butter up for the week. Is that for them?"

"Yep, and there's one guy that can't eat hardly anything, but he doesn't act too happy when he's accommodated."

"I heard about him. George and Candice have one thing that meets his conditions: a flavorless soy burger, grilled without oil and served like a steak. For a side, since nothing can be fried, they gave him black beans, cooked without spices. Oh, and he can't have beer."

"That must be why he's unhappy. Have you seen that couple at the end of the table? Facing us?"

"The ones that keep sending food back?"

"Yeah. When you went to the loo, George and Candice huddled down here to discuss it. They're going to charge them full price for everything they send back."

"How can they do that?"

"Candice took that table, probably expecting trouble. She was very specific about everything with this couple, how do you want it to be cooked, what do you want with it, what kind of bread, that kind of thing."

"But what happened to 'the customer is always right'?"

"A little thing called a pocket tape recorder. If they question the charges, she'll threaten to play it to the cops."

"Good for her. But why?"

"I asked. Apparently, they pulled the same stunt at the winery last night. Several tastes went without being paid."

"Oh no! Look!"

The dining room jumped to life as one of the men at the table appeared to choke on something. Kara heard people yell, "Help!" "Someone help!" "He's choking!" "Save him!"

Candice and every other server in the room rushed to the table. Candice pulled the guest from the chair, but by the time he was standing, George was there. Taller and stronger, he performed the Heimlich maneuver.

Tank said, "Huh."

"Huh?"

"He came out of it pretty quickly. And I didn't see anything come from his mouth. Did you?"

"I wasn't looking. I was scared. . ."

"He was playing."

"Do you think George knew that?"

"George couldn't afford to know that. He had to act, just like Candice and everyone else."

"Huh."

"You probably didn't see the other thing."

"What other thing?"

"I knew he was acting. You can tell if you've seen it before, or, like me, if you've been through the training. I watched the other folks at the table. One of the other men grabbed his wife's purse and ran to the restrooms."

"No!"

"Yep. Came right back out, without the purse."

"Shut. Up."

"I think this group has some 'splainin' to do, and I think they're going to have to 'splain it to Pete."

"Who's Pete?"

"Oh, the Chief of Police. I assume you'll be meeting him as soon as they report that purse stolen."

"What?"

"Want another beer? This is gonna be fun."

18

Hank ordered breakfast to go from the Café, retrieving his order and cup of coffee from Trudie.

"Hey, Trudie, my scumbucket of a business manager walked out on me. If you hear of anyone lookin' for work, shoot 'em in my direction, okay?"

"Sure, Hank. I'll do that."

Trudie rolled her eyes as Hank left. As if anyone would want to manage a business for that piece of work.

Oh, well. Someone out there might need a job.

She sent a mass text to the people she told everything worth telling.

Chris tried to drink a cup of coffee but couldn't stop laughing. Sis stayed as far from the man as she could. Last night he was pleasant enough. She even joined him in bed for an hour or so. Now, he had a hairy face, wore silly glasses and a hat, and his clothes were all wrong.

Chris said, "That explains the expensive car you drove in with, and why you parked in the city lot."

"Yeah, this is my version of undercover. How else will I be able to figure this out?"

"You do what we do. Talk to the cats."

Sis nodded. The man – she thought he must still be Jeff – didn't seem to notice.

"Right. Those magical cats. Tell me, did they let you know who the murderer was?"

"Um. . .no. They were a little slow on the uptick there."

Sis jumped up and down in protest. They knew who it was before this man got to town. They just hadn't had the opportunity to. . .

The men continued their conversation. "What's the plan?"

"I'm going to drive away from here and come back from another direction, head into the Café and do some digging. I remember Hank from the other times I was around, but I don't think he'll recognize me."

"Do you need any more information? More than you got last night?"

"No, I think I'm good."

"Oh, hey, wait." Chris re-read the text he just received. "Good luck just smiled on you."

Henrie had breakfast under control, so Annie visited in the dining room. She sat with Wyatt. "I understand why you're in town now. Please let me know if there is anything I can do."

"Thanks. It's good to know there are people I can trust."

"You have friends here. I'm sorry I didn't trust you. I could have told you, a couple of days ago, where he was."

"I heard. That's okay. I didn't give you any reason. . ."

Kara came in and Annie rose. "Here, Kara. I'm sure Wyatt is ready for a friend, if you have time."

Kara looked at Wyatt, and Annie saw her facial expression change. "Sure. I'm happy to sit with you. And hey, if you don't have anything to do tomorrow, you can come with us! There's going to be a wedding on the lake!"

Annie left the table and went into the kitchen.

"Is everything ready, Henrie?"

"Yes. I had a chat with the wedding guests last night. Our morning should be entertaining."

"Great. Oh, here come the scavenger hunters. What do you have for our problem eater?"

"Quinoa made with coconut milk, bananas and pecans."

"The smell of bacon is very heavy this morning."

"I put plates all around the dining room."

"You're evil."

"Thank you."

Annie listened to the conversation, as much as she could, at least. For the second morning in a row, she and Henrie had to navigate around cats. Except for Tiger Lily. She was in the dining room, underneath the buffet, concentrating on the guests.

Annie finally stopped trying to walk around the cats. She poured a cup of coffee, made a plate from the items still in the kitchen, and moved her chair as close to the dining room door as possible.

Bonita and Rich were outlining the day in store for their crew. Annie had to smile to herself. They were so screwed, and they didn't know it.

Bonita spoke in an elevated voice so everyone could hear her. "Today is the expensive gift day. To get the most points, you have to find the most expensive item you can purchase for a man and for a woman. Rich and I visited the best shop yesterday."

Rich took up the lecture. "You'll go into The Antique Shop. Go up to the corner, turn left, and it's the first place past the church. There are wonderful antiques as well as hand-crafted jewelry. Precious and semi-precious stones in silver, gold and platinum. We asked the proprietors to hide the price tags, only the ones in the locked cases, so you'll have to guess at the prices."

Bonita said, "As usual, the couple that has the top price for the two items together will get the top points."

Annie walked with Henrie to the far side of the kitchen and whispered, "Gema and Frank are going to owe us for this. They won't lose several thousand dollars today."

"And here is Pete."

From under the buffet, Tiger Lily watched Pete and Cyril walk into the dining room. There was no room for them to sit.

She watched as the other cats huddled in the doorway between the dining room and the kitchen. They hissed and spat for the best seat.

They could have joined her under the buffet, but they were still not speaking to her. No bother. She had the best seat.

Henrie pointed to the cats. "We will be unable to enter the dining room. I shall retrieve a chair and join you here."

As if on cue, Don and Suellen arrived in the dining room. They said good morning to everyone, helped themselves to breakfast, coffee and juice, and sat at the small table.

They made a special point of speaking to Pete. "You're here to talk to us? We can make room here at our table. Do you want breakfast?"

"Don't mind if I do." Pete helped himself to a little of everything and a lot of bacon.

Henrie lifted a chair over the cats. Don retrieved it and made room for Pete at the small table.

Pete said, "I need to talk to you about those items stolen from you at the beach yesterday, and I need to talk to. . .is it Chet and Justine? Had a purse stolen last night?"

Chet raised his hand. "Yes. Us."

"My officers talked to you last night. I'll just get some additional information. After I talk to Don and Suellen. Oh. I should say how sorry I am that so many of you have met with petty thieves here in Chelsea. It's very unusual."

Annie, watching the faces of the scavenger hunters, enjoyed the looks of concern.

Pete took a drink of coffee, then turned to Don and Suellen. "I have the report you made yesterday. Let's see. . ." He pulled his cellphone from his pocket. "An umbrella, pink and purple, owned by the town. Two beach towels, purple, owned by. . .let's see. . .the KaliKo Inn. Well that's convenient. If we find the towels, Henrie or Annie will be able to identify them."

Pete turned to the kitchen doorway. "That right, Henrie?"

"Yes. We will be able to identify them from the color, the style and pattern, and the stitching in the hem that identifies them as KaliKo Inn property."

Annie continued to watch faces. Two flinched.

Pete turned back to his cellphone. "Okay. A cooler, owned by you, with cold fried chicken, potato salad, chips and sodas from Mr. Bean's Confectionary. Right?"

"Right," said Don.

"A beach bag containing minor items. . .you had your cards, cash and important items with you?"

"That's right," said Suellen. "And our phones. We had our phones."

"And the item that concerned you the most, a quilt that was put together by your great aunties. Irreplaceable, you said."

"That's right," said Don. "There is no way that can be replaced. I can turn in an insurance claim, but the quilt meant everything to me."

"And I happen to know where you were when the items were stolen. Have you recovered from finding the dead body?"

"Pretty much," said Don. "That bullet hole gave me a nightmare last night, though."

"You might be interested to know that we've identified the man. We're taking every possible step to identify the shooter. Well, that narrows the time frame for me, at any rate. You discovered the loss after leaving the crime scene yesterday?"

"Yes. We went straight back, saw everything was gone, then went on to our meeting with the boat guy."

"I see. And I have lists of stolen items from several families that went to the beach yesterday. The lists were similar to yours, and specific. Anyway, I know what we're looking for. I just need one more thing."

Marco came through the front door. "Here, boss. I have what you need."

"Great. Have a seat. Get a cup of coffee first. Or some breakfast. As usual, Henrie made enough for an army. Let me see." Pete checked his cellphone again. "It looks like I need to talk to Chet and Justine."

Pete didn't move from his table, but he turned to the couple. Then he turned back to Tim. "What's that you're having for breakfast?"

"It's great," said Tim, clearly not feeling the greatness. "I'm vegan, and, um. . .I have. . .other food issues."

"Looks good. Quinoa?"

"I don't have a clue."

"Henrie, could I get a little of that? Let's see. . .Chet and Justine. You were at Mo's Tap last night, and sometime after. . .um. . .Thad, is it? Thad had a choking incident, you discovered Justine's purse had been stolen. Correct?"

"Yes," said Chet.

"And the items missing? What was in the purse?"

Henrie appeared – as if by magic – and handed a bowl of breakfast quinoa over the cats to Don. He put the bowl at Pete's place.

"Oh," started Justine, "just the usual. A wallet with my driver license, credit cards, cash, family photos. Makeup. A cell phone charger and accessories. My phone was in my pocket. Um. . .I'd have to think about it. You know. The stuff that's in a purse."

"And you're sure you were at Mo's when it was taken?"

"Oh, sure," said Justine. "I had it over my shoulder when we went in, and I showed it to everyone. I just bought it yesterday afternoon at that cute flower shop. It was fun. Colorful, and fun. Anyway, I know I had it when we got there."

"This quinoa is great, Henrie. You ought to serve it more often." Pete conferred with his phone one last time.

"Okay. I think I have enough information. I'm going to have to ask everyone to stay where you are, right here. Help yourself to more breakfast, coffee. Get comfortable. I'll wait in the dining room with you while they administer the search warrant." Several uniformed bodies appeared behind Marco on the foyer side of the dining room.

Cries erupted from the scavenger group. "What?" "What do you mean?" "You can't search our rooms!" "What's this about?"

Pete stood and reached for the piece of paper in Marco's hand. "Here's the warrant. Gives me permission to search every room, all pieces of luggage, personal property, you name it. While we're doing this, would you all please place whatever is in your pockets – and your purses, fanny packs, whatever you have with you – on the tables?"

Chet stood and exclaimed, "For what reason?"

Pete turned and looked at him. "For the reason that I think you've all come to town to steal stuff and I'm going to nip it in the bud. And I think I'll be able to determine that purse wasn't stolen after all."

Pete turned back toward the foyer. "Marco, you look through these personal items. You four, take the carriage house. You four, second floor. Rooms and common areas.

And because I'm going to be fair, you two take the back room and all of the common areas on this level."

Three of the scavenger hunters tried to leave, but they encountered Cyril at the door. He stood and smiled, but it was not a friendly smile.

They sat back down.

Pete refilled his coffee. He turned to the people at his table – Kara, Wyatt, Don and Suellen – and said, "So, how's your trip to Chelsea been so far?"

Tiger Lily was flummoxed. She had done nothing to help with the vets. She had done nothing to stop the scavenger hunters.

Maybe she should retire as a detective.

Or maybe, she could do something to help them find that last veteran, Harper.

She couldn't work with her siblings. They were still not speaking to her. Fat Cat and Scaredy Cat? No. They had laughed at her.

Moriah. She could ask Moriah to help. She was a little diva, but she was smart. She might have ideas. When this mess was over with, she'd go find Moriah.

Ray carried equipment to The Escape. He had a cooler for beer and wine, a wine safe for room temperature reds, and a duffel specially made to carry crystal and china.

Eight people onboard for a wedding was a perfect number. He had food for twelve, always planning for big eaters. Also, he hoped, as he always did, that someone would say, "Me! Take me! I want to help on your cruise!"

That rarely happened.

Of course, he had Jock, who trotted happily beside him, but Jock couldn't pour wine for crap.

Jock could, however, warn him of danger, and that's what he did right now.

He barked; he danced; he stood in front of Ray and wouldn't let him get onto The Escape.

Ray stood on the dock. "Hey! Somebody in there? HEY!"

A hand raised up from below decks, then another.

"Anyone in there with you?"

"No, sir," came a quavering voice.

"Okay. We're coming up. Stay where you are, hands where I can see them." As if I have a weapon, thought Ray. Well, I do have Jock. That's something.

Ray climbed up, dropped his baggage on deck and walked to the doorway. He looked down and saw an older man, possibly appearing older than his years, in filthy clothes. He needed a shave. He needed a bath. He needed a laundromat.

He relaxed. "Hey. I'm Ray. This is Jock. You're that vet they're looking for, Harper?"

The man nodded. "I got a reason for not wantin' to be found. I'm sorry to be on your boat. I'll find somethin' else. Someplace else. Appreciate it if you don't tell no one."

"I might get in trouble with a pal of mine, but hey, don't worry about it. We vets have to stick together. You were Army, right?"

Harper nodded.

"I was Navy. Hey, you hungry?"

Harper nodded again.

"Well, get out of the way, let me come down there and we'll see what I can find."

As Harper moved, Ray noticed what appeared to be a painful limp and possibly a back injury. "You okay, man?"

"War injuries. I've learned to live with them."

Ray moved into the galley kitchen and used his keys to unlock two refrigerators and a freezer. "Do you care what I fix?"

"No, sir, I surely don't. I'm mighty grateful."

"Don't worry about it. Say, while I'm cookin', why don't you tell me what your plan is. I don't need to know why you're hiding. Several dead folks in town give me a clue about that."

Harper nodded. He took a bottle of water from Ray, drank most of it, and sat at the counter.

"Well, if you're interested, I was hopin' to stow away and get somewhere other than Chelsea. Anywhere. I picked the biggest boat here, because I thought it would go the furthest, maybe to another state."

"So, you hoped I wouldn't find you. . .and you would slip off when we made port somewhere. . . ."

"I admit, I wasn't thinkin' that clear."

Ray used a spatula to scramble eggs with a packet of chopped frozen vegetables, a bit of shredded cheese and spices. He tossed a couple slices of bread into a toaster.

"Coffee?"

"Please."

After fixing the pot to deliver a strong brew, Ray reached into the refrigerator for butter and jam.

"Well, I might just be able to help you. It might mean you help me a little, too."

"Name it, sailor. I'm all ears."

Ray slipped the eggs and toast onto a plate and set it in front of the vet. "I have a wedding this weekend."

"You're gettin' hitched?"

"No, not me. A couple is getting married out in the middle of the lake. There will be about eight folks, and I can always use help, you know, getting beers, pouring wine, keeping food out."

Harper looked down at himself. "How is it you think I would be good at that? Are ye blind?"

"No problem. I'll get a couple sets of clean clothes that will fit; you can stay here in my stateroom, clean up, shave. You'll look great."

"An' then what? I help with the weddin' an' then?"

"I can drop you at a port along the way. We're going to the middle of the lake, and we don't have a time limit. I can come back going north or south, drop you, then come home following the shore."

"You'd do that for someone you ain't ever met?"

"I know enough. You served our country. You're one of the good guys."

"Well, hey, that sounds like a good deal for me. You say I can take a shower?"

"You can take several. You probably should, as a matter of fact. And start on that face this morning, so it doesn't look so raw tomorrow. I'll let you into my quarters as soon as you finish breakfast."

Marco met with each of the officers in the library as they finished their work. Eventually, he came into the dining room.

"Boss, I think we found everything on the list of items stolen from the beach yesterday, including the towels that belong to the Inn. We found five sets of – let's just say 'booty' – on the first and second floor of the carriage house."

Marco gave his cellphone to Don. "Is this the quilt made by your aunties?"

"That looks like it, yes. Can I take it with me?"

"Sorry, sir, we're going to need it for evidence, but we'll return it to you as soon as we can."

Marco turned back to Pete. "We also found, in Chet and Justine's luggage, her driver license, credit cards, insurance cards. . .the kind of things women keep in their purses."

"Do tell," said Pete. "The things that were supposedly stolen. Where were they?"

"They were inside a lady's purse, a Gucci, inside a large piece of luggage."

"Well, well, well. And Mo's almost had to shut down so we could interview folks. Caused them a bit of trouble. Cost them some money, I'm sure."

"Hey, we didn't mean to. . ."

"Oh, yes, you did. Everything you folks have done this week has cost people money. Sending wine back, sending food back. . ."

Damien cut in. "They charged us for all that food. Said they had a recording."

"And the special food? You can't tell me, Tim – it is Tim, right? – that you can't eat all those things. Everyone who watched you anywhere in the last couple of days knows how unhappy you are that we're keeping you healthy."

Tim pushed the bowl of quinoa away as he stood. "If everyone knows, I'm gettin' a real breakfast right now. Henrie won't have to worry about it tomorrow."

Henrie appeared again in the doorway. "You are correct about that, Tim. You will be leaving today."

"What?"

"We will not have thieves, petty or otherwise, at the Inn. We are given to understand your next target would have been larger: jewelry and possibly antiques. We will not be lackeys to your plans."

"Fine," said Bonita. "Get me a revised bill."

"That will not be necessary," said Henrie. "Your credit cards were already charged for the full reservation. We turned potential guests away. Oh, and I added a few wine tastings at Sassy P's to the final bill as well."

"You can't. . ."

"Please refer to your reservation contracts."

Rich said, "No problem. We'll leave town right now."

Pete held up a hand. "Not so fast. You have to leave the Inn. You can't leave town until we book everyone that needs to be booked and whoever can bond out does so. I'd suggest you go to your rooms to pack. These officers will accompany you."

Marco said, "Before they do that, boss, you might want to take a look at this."

Marco reached to the hall table next to the dining room door and brought a small case into the room. Pete rifled through the contents. It was a jeweler's case, complete with settings, stones, tools, and two rings, one emerald, one ruby, probably fake. Henrie lifted the handle inside the case to expose a hidden section filled with money. He picked up a bill and held it to the light.

"My, my, my. What have we here? You may want to change into comfortable clothes. I doubt anyone will be bonding out today. And just so you know, I'll trace your credit cards and contact the towns your little hunt has visited in the last few years."

Tiger Lily had heard enough. She knew Pete had everything under control. And Henrie. She stopped by Cyril on her way out the door.

"I'm going to get Moriah to help me find Harper."

"How are you going to do that?"

"I don't know. We'll figure it out."

She left the Inn, trotting up and across The Avenue to Clara's flower shop.

Inside, she heard a blood-curdling scream. She broke into a run. Moriah was in trouble!

She screeched to a halt in the back room.

Moriah screamed for her life, but there wasn't a bad guy in sight.

Clara held onto her with one hand, an arm and her body while she used her other hand to administer a grooming brush.

Piles of curly light-colored hair were on the floor, on the table, flying through the air. The fluffy girl was still fluffy, but her body looked a bit neater. Or what she could see of it did.

Clara looked up. "Oh, good morning, Tiger Lily. Did you come to see my baby? She hates this, but I make her sit still for it three or four times a week. Sounds like I'm killin' her doesn't it?"

Clara took Moriah's hefty little body in two hands and put her on the floor. Moriah would have run, but she had disgraced herself in front of Tiger Lily enough. She sat, fluffed out her mane, licked a paw, and, finally, said, *"You want something?"*

"Yes, I do. Do you want to help me with an investigation?"

"Sure. What are we investigating?"

"It seems Pete and Cyril have taken care of figuring out who was killing the vets, and they called in a friend from the FBI to help arrest him. And a couple other crimes were cleaned up this morning. But no one knows how to find the last vet. His name's Harper."

"So we're going to look for him?"

"I thought so, yeah."

"How are we going to do that? We aren't supposed to leave The Avenue. Surely he isn't anywhere here."

"You're right. I thought we could talk about it and see what we could come up with."

"Okay. Can we do that at the Café? I'll bet people will drop food for us."

"Sure. Let's go."

Trudie served coffee to the man at the window table. He looked familiar, but she was sure she didn't know him. "Here's your coffee. Double shot hazelnut cinnamon latte. Don't get many calls for that."

"I don't get to a place to order coffee like this often. What's for breakfast?"

"Well, you have the menu, but we have some specials: granola with almond butter and honey, or pancakes made with carrots and zucchini, served with honey butter."

"I'll have the pancakes. With a side of fresh fruit, if you have it."

"Sure. Are you in town for work or play?"

"Work, actually. Well, I'm looking for work. Got downsized a few weeks ago, so I'm using some savings to go check out jobs in towns I might like. Know of any positions for accountants? Or other business types?"

"Actually, I might. I know someone who's looking for, well, I can't say a partner, but someone to manage his businesses."

"Really? Who?"

"His name's Hank. I. . .well, I shouldn't say this, but I wouldn't trust him as far as I could throw him, which isn't far, but if you really need work. . . ."

"I understand. Really. Would you be able to give me his number? Or tell me where to go?"

"Let me get that for you. I'll turn in your order first."

Trudie returned to the coffee bar, found Hank's information in her cellphone, and went directly to the kitchen. "Here's an order for table seven. Do you have a minute, Felicity?"

"Sure. What's up?"

"Take a look at the guy at table seven. Do you recognize him?"

Felicity looked through the window. "He looks familiar, but no, I don't know him. He could just have a familiar face."

"He says he's looking for work. I told him about Hank needing someone, told him I'd give him contact info."

"Did you tell him Hank's a son-of-a-witch-with-a-b?"

"Kind of. What do you think?"

"He looks nice. And smart. It won't hurt, and maybe he'll be a good influence on Hank."

"Oh, here come Sam and Nancy. I'll bet Honey Bear could use a treat."

Before Trudie could move, they watched as Nancy and Sam sat at the table with the man they didn't know. Nancy chatted with him as if she'd known him all her life.

"I wonder if Nancy's lost it again. We should tell Annie her meds need to be checked."

19

Pete wanted to be out looking for Harper, but instead, his office was filled with people coming in and out, claiming the items stolen at the beach. He wasn't able to release anything yet, but he tagged and boxed everything that belonged to each family.

In the back, Marco served sandwiches, chips and water from the Café to their twelve temporary tenants. Twelve unhappy temporary tenants.

Pete could hear a voice he now recognized as Bonita's. "I didn't do a darn thing! Let me out of here!"

Rich added, "These other yahoos are the thieves. They stole stuff everywhere we went!"

"At your direction!" "You did, too!" "Gettin' tired of those diamonds, Bonita?" "Don't think we're going down for this without you!"

Pete sighed. The Sheriff's Department transport vehicle couldn't get here soon enough. The case had mushroomed from a Chelsea petty incident to multi-state misdemeanor and felony thefts. Hopefully he could turn them over, wrap up the Chelsea incidents and move on to the murders.

Cyril walked back and forth, watching Pete with the Chelsea residents for a while, then checking in with the prisoners. He learned nothing of interest and finally pestered people until an officer let him out, supposedly to pee. To humor the officer, Cyril peed, then sat under the tulip tree to watch traffic and people.

He saw Tiger Lily and Moriah on the street. They walked into and out of all the businesses on The Avenue. Some, they left right away. Others, they stayed in for a while. He had no idea what they were doing but decided not to bother them. He would probably see them for lunch.

He saw someone else.

Cyril had been a police dog for a long time. He was used to seeing people work undercover. He was even used to seeing Jeff Bennett work under cover. He wasn't used to seeing him look like this, though.

Cyril jumped up as Pete walked out. "Come on, Cyril. We have another body."

Kara waved to Don and Suellen from the window at Mo's Tap. Mo was in her lap, tail curled around her arm and body in a full-chest hug. Kara's right hand stroked his head. The hand was lost in bliss.

When the couple joined her, she merely turned her head, keeping hold of the large, long-haired and luscious cat.

"Have you met Mo yet?"

"I've seen him," said Suellen, "but I haven't met him. Can I hold him?"

"Um. . .no. Not right now. He's comfy."

Don laughed. "Yeah, I can tell that."

Kara leaned in, still holding onto Mo. "So, what do you think about inviting Wyatt to your wedding. I know I'm being forward. . . ."

"No!" said Suellen. "That's a great idea! He was such a different guy this morning, like, less intense, less nervous. And he really had fun with that arrest."

"So did we," said Don. "We loved playing the part. Knowing who did it but acting stupid until the warrant was served."

Suellen leaned in to whisper. "Not only was it fun, but Henrie heard us tell you our friends couldn't afford to stay, so he offered a room for them for the weekend! Free!"

"Really?"

"Yes! Of course, we said yes! And they said yes!"

Suellen and Kara enjoyed a "girl squeal," but not such a big one that Kara let go of Mo. Kara threw her head back in joy to say, "This is such a fun town!"

Don said, "We're going to come back, maybe for our anniversary."

"I'm coming back, too. Candice always wanted me to visit, but I couldn't find the time. And the stories she told? I didn't believe her. I thought she had become, you know, weird. But she isn't! The stories are true! Even the ones about these cats!"

"The cats?"

"Yeah. Annie's cats. You know they 'manage' these businesses, at least, according to them. You've noticed the names, right?"

"Yeah. And we were on the websites. The KaliKo Inn – those big girls hate me, but they love Don."

Mo trilled.

"He's telling us something, but I don't know what."

"Yeah, right."

"Well, back to my question, you think it's okay?"

"What? Do I think what's okay?"

"That I invited Wyatt."

"Oh! I got lost for a minute. Sure," said Don. "I'll call Ray right now and tell him we'll have one more."

Don moved away to make the call and Suellen moved closer to Kara. "At least I'm gonna pet him. He's so pretty."

"And he knows it. Oh, look. Here's Tank. I asked him to stop in and say hello."

Tank came to the table. "Hi, I'm Tank. You must be Suellen. I can't stay, just wanted to say hello, and thanks for letting us join your party!"

"We're looking forward to it. Have you met that guy that's staying at the Inn? Wyatt? We hope he'll come along, too."

"Yeah. I met him. At the time, I didn't know what to think about him, but now I know he's just been looking for his dad. Tough break, all the stuff that's going on."

"Exactly," said Suellen. "So Kara thought, and we agree, that he needed a break from all of that. He didn't say no, did he, Kara?"

"No. He didn't say no. He hasn't said yes yet, but I'll talk to him again."

Don returned to the table. "Ray said it was great. He thinks he ordered enough food to cover an extra guest, and if he wants to bring a friend, that should be okay."

Kara turned to Tank. "Maybe he'll want to invite that younger vet, Gene. I'll say something to him. And what about you, big guy? Will I see you tonight?"

Moriah and Tiger Lily returned to the Café. Trudie was someone worth keeping around. She had treats!

They sat behind the hostess stand and ate. Moriah didn't stop until her bowl was empty. She then pushed Tiger Lily out of the way to get the last of hers.

Tiger Lily sat back, rolling her eyes. A diva. A selfish diva. Oh, well. She needed someone's help, and Moriah was the only one around.

Moriah finally finished, fluffed her mane and licked both paws. *"So what did we learn this morning? We went everywhere."*

"We learned a lot, but not much we can use. We know Jeff Bennett is looking for work. And we heard that Hank's business manager quit."

"What does that tell us?"

"Not much if that's all we know, but it's possible it's connected."

"I see," said Moriah. *"The business manager could have been helping Hank. Or maybe he found out what Hank was doing."*

"I thought about both of those things, but I don't know how to check it out. Especially since no one else is speaking to me. None of the cats, anyway."

"They just don't know how hard you were working to tell Henrie about those kittens."

Tiger Lily dropped her head to her chest. She was tired. Really, really tired.

"It doesn't get us any closer to finding Harper."

"No, it doesn't. We need a little good, old fashioned luck."

Just then, Ray and Jock walked in. Jock, as usual, came around the hostess stand to see if anyone left a treat for him.

"Hi, guys. What's for lunch?"

"We've already eaten," said Moriah, *"but here comes Trudie with something for you."*

Jock nodded a polite thank you to Trudie as she left a small dish on the floor. *"What have the two of you been doing this morning?"*

"We've been detecting," said Moriah, putting a proud puff on her chest.

"What are you looking for?"

"We want to find out where that vet is, Harper."

"I know where he is."

Two cats jerked their heads toward him.

"He's on The Escape."

"What?" "How?"

"He's hiding out from whoever is killing the vets."

"That's Hank," said Tiger Lily.

"Really? Does Pete know?"

"He does now. He called Jeff Bennett in to help."

"I thought that was Jeff. He put something on to mask his scent. Probably so the town dogs wouldn't give him away."

"And he's wearing a beard and a hat," said Tiger Lily.

Moriah added, *"And he's pretending to look for work."*

Jock said, *"He's meeting Hank at Mr. Bean's right now."*

"I'll bet he's going to take that job!" said Moriah.

"What job is that?" asked Jock.

"*Hank's business manager quit.*"

"*Or got killed,*" said Moriah.

"*What?*"

Tiger Lily said, "*It's a working theory, that he may have known something and Hank got rid of him. But enough about that. Why's Harper on The Escape?*"

"*He was hiding out there, but we found him. He wants to get away, and he's a nice enough kind of guy. Ray is going to clean him up and give him a job this weekend, and then help him get away.*"

Tiger Lily asked, "*Do you think you can tell Ray that Hank is the guy?*"

Moriah added, "*Do you think you can tell Ray Harper's son is in town?*"

"*What? Get out! Who's his son?*"

"*He's staying at the Inn. His name is Wyatt. We thought he might be killing the vets, but turns out he's just been looking for his dad.*"

"*Wait a minute!*" said Tiger Lily. "*This morning, I heard Kara ask Wyatt if he would go with them on the boat tomorrow. They might end up at the same place!*"

"*That could be a good thing,*" said Jock. "*As long as Harper wants to see his son.*"

"*Yeah. So. . .the good news is that Harper is safe. Hank would never go onto The Escape.*"

"*You're right about that,*" said Jock. "*And he never comes to The Marina either. Ray won't let him.*"

"*So we're finished here?*" asked Moriah.

Tiger Lily said, *"We can rest. But we never finish. Detectives are never done."*

Thoughts of quitting the game were now far from her mind.

Jeff called Pete to touch base. "I got lucky."

"Yeah? How so?"

"Seems our friend Hank has a position open. His manager walked out, left a job opening. It's mine, now."

"That's great, Jeff. Really, really, really great."

"But?"

"But you need to watch your hind end. I'm at a murder scene right now. Seems the reason you have a job is because your predecessor now has an extra hole in his head."

"Oh. Okay, then. I'll watch my back."

"When do you start?"

"Monday. He's giving me the weekend to move my stuff to Chelsea. Says he has an apartment I can move into, where his former guy used to live."

"Where's that?"

"Second floor over the office. I took a look. I'm going to bring roach repellent, rat traps and air freshener. A very strong air freshener."

"Are you sure you want to live there?"

"It's the job, Pete."

"Okay. So what's next for us? How do we communicate?"

"I'm gonna live a double life. This afternoon, I'm moving over to the Inn as Jeff Bennett, friend of the family. Seems they now have some vacancies, thanks to you."

"Yeah, well, I knew you needed a room. What else?"

"I'll stay there until Sunday afternoon, take off the disguise, enjoy the weekend, and move into the dump Sunday evening as Wally Krause."

"Wally?"

"Wally. Don't use it until you meet me. If you do, you know, around town."

"Got it. So I think we're making plans to meet at Sassy P's this evening. See you there?"

"Sure thing."

20

Hilly was in the room facing The Avenue when Henrie appeared in the doorway. "Perfect," he said.

"Well, I do a good job, if I do say so myself."

"You misunderstand my intent. It is perfect that you have finished this room. A guest is arriving this afternoon. This is his favorite room."

"A regular?"

"Yes. Our friend, Jeff Bennett."

"Something in the wind must have told me to do this one before the other. I finished the carriage house. It was a mess."

"I believe it. I wanted to ask after your house guest."

"Gene. He's a pleasant young man. He's confused, of course, but now that he knows who may be committing the murders. . .I know we can't talk about it. . .he has relaxed a bit. We thought we'd bring him to town tonight for dinner."

"You should consider joining us at Sassy P's. I imagine a large group will gather."

"Good idea. Do you think Wyatt might come?"

"I do not know. For the most part, I do not involve myself in the private life of our guests."

"Well, I have no qualms about doing so. I'll say something to him, if I see him, I mean."

"I have a cellphone number for him. Oh, Kali and Ko are here to inspect your work."

"Hey, girls. I understand a friend of yours will be staying here, so do a good job."

Kali and Ko looked up at Henrie.

"Yes, girls. Jeff Bennett will be here for the weekend. This is his favorite room, and you are his favorite hostesses."

Kali said, *"I love Jeff Bennett. He's my favorite."*

Ko said, *"I just do my job."*

Henrie and Hilly heard "Mew, purr, mew." And "Mew, grr, purr."

"Alright, girls. That's enough. Let's let Hilly finish her work."

Kali and Ko waited in the dining room for the cats to get home. They wanted to point out the detective table was back in place, against the wall and covered with the cloth, all cushions "just so" underneath.

As if it were their doing.

The cats came home, one by one, confused.

Sassy Pants said, *"Where wuz Tiger Lily? She duzn't pick me up today."*

Little Socks, the next to arrive, asked, *"Did everyone come home? Did you forget me?"*

Mo trilled when he trotted in. Sassy Pants said, *"It okay, Mo. Tiger Lily duzn't get any of us today."*

Mr. Bean was the last to arrive. *"Did you guys forget me? I waited and waited!"*

Kali said, *"It's okay, Mr. Bean. Nobody picked up anybody today. Tiger Lily was just being mean."*

Ko said, *"Look. The detective table is back."*

Henrie arrived, a tray with little dishes in hand. They could smell bacon. He bent to place a dish in front of everyone.

He stood, however, with a dish in his hand and appeared to count heads before he realized Tiger Lily was the missing cat.

"Where is Tiger Lily?"

Everyone ignored him.

Henrie shrugged and walked back to the kitchen with the dish.

Looking around the room, Little Socks decided to take charge. *"So, who has a report?"*

Everyone ignored her. She stomped her foot on the ground. *"Who has a report?"*

"We duzn't has to report if we gots nuttin' to report."

"Trill!"

Kali and Ko translated at the same time. *"He says you aren't in charge."* *"He says he won't give you a report."*

Little Socks stomped her feet and turned her back, deciding it would be better to clean herself than talk to these idiots.

Eventually, Tiger Lily wandered in.

She walked past the cats and into the kitchen, pawed Henrie's leg from behind, and asked – politely – to have her snack in the kitchen.

Whether Henrie understood her or was too busy to walk to the other room, she didn't know. She was happy to eat under the kitchen table. She wanted nothing to do with the others, and she wasn't about to tell them what she knew.

When she finished her bacon, she jumped to the counter where Henrie worked.

She poked him on the shoulder. He said, "Hello, dear girl."

She poked him again. He looked around, saw the empty dish and asked, "Are you still hungry?"

Tiger Lily shook her head, side to side.

Henrie stopped what he was doing and looked at her closely. "You want something."

Tiger Lily blinked one time.

Henrie asked, "Is it about that cat? And her kittens?

Tiger Lily blinked one time.

"Oh, I see. You want to see them, to make sure they are safe?"

Tiger Lily blinked one time.

"Allow me to make a call." Henrie picked up a cellphone. Maggie answered.

"Miss Maggie, I must ask a favor."

Pete and Cyril were ready to go. It was Friday. Janet had been neglected for most of the week. He had put one case to bed – a large one, involving twelve out-of-staters – and once again, the State Police were in awe of his investigative abilities.

He intended to work most of the weekend, however, looking for Harper and doing what he could to put evidence together for the FBI for the murders and arsons as yet unsolved.

And he had another murder, one he thought he could connect to the murder of the vets. Ed, Hank's assistant, was found in an abandoned house at the end of Washington Street, one bullet through his head.

Pete had to wonder how he let himself be trapped there. Perhaps he had been doing the murders for Hank, or perhaps he had been scouting. Or perhaps, he only saw something he shouldn't have seen, wrong place, wrong time. Hank had to have lured him there to tie up a loose end.

Either way, he would collect evidence. Where were his crime-fighting cats when he needed them? When he accepted accolades from the State Police, in the back of his mind, he realized that for the first time, he was being given credit for work he had done himself. Not work that had been done – originally – by cats and dogs, his private "sixth sense."

Maybe he was just getting good at the job.

Maybe.

Cyril sat in the doorway, a smile on his big, happy face. "Time to go, boy. It's Friday night."

21

Friday evening was hopping at Sassy P's.

Jesus, sitting with Minnie at the hodgepodge of tables pulled together in the back dining room, looked at Annie. "Maybe we should get to work. . ."

"No! You took the evening off, and you will enjoy it. We're most of your customers, anyway, so we'll be gentle with your staff."

"Okay." Jesus looked at the faces around him. Their friend Jeff Bennett was in town for the weekend and was here with Annie, Chris and Henrie. Nancy and Sam sat with them. Carlos and Isabel sat with Jerry and Pastor Teresa. Boone and Hilly sat next to two younger men. Jesus recognized them as Gene, one of the vets, and Wyatt, a guest at the Inn.

Scattered around the gaggle of tables were others from town, most of the people who lived and worked on The Avenue. Notably absent were George and Candice. Jesus knew they were working tonight because they planned to be off work for the rest of the weekend.

Ray and Cheryl had come in from The Marina and sat with Pete and Janet. The dogs were not here, which meant they were at the Inn with the cats. All of the neighborhood cats were probably there, including Clara's cat and her boyfriend's dog, the pretty Bergamasco, because Clara and Ramon were here as well.

Jesus looked at Minnie again. "Let's relax!"

Percy and Sarah sat at the bar, talking to George whenever he was free. On a Friday night, that wasn't often. For the moment, though, he was available. He said, "So I haven't had much time to spend with the wedding couple, but I think it will be fun."

"It will be!" said Sarah. "This is such a great place, and can you believe, the Inn gave us a room for free!"

George looked at them. "Free?"

"Yes! For two nights."

"How'd that happen?"

Percy leaned in. "Did you meet the folks that were here for some kind of scavenger thing?"

"Yeah. Unfortunately."

"Well, our friends helped the police when they went in to arrest them. Played a little game, you know, and gave them a reason to get a warrant."

Sarah picked up the story. "So, when Henrie realized they had friends that would drive back and forth for the wedding, because we can't afford to stay, you know, he said, bring them on!"

"And here we are!"

Candice came up behind them. "I'm getting ready to bring out your food. Do you want to eat here, or back at your table?"

"Table's great," said Percy. "George, I'm looking forward to tomorrow!"

It was a strange evening at the KaliKo Inn. Of course, the neighborhood cats had come. It was a full Avenue party.

The doors were open, allowing the big dogs to get around as easily as the cats and Tillie. Usually, though, they played and talked together. Tonight, most of the cats were in one room and the dogs – with Tiger Lily, Honey Bear and Moriah – were in another.

Tiger Lily curled into Fiamma. Her soft dreadlocks cushioned her from the floor like nothing else could do. Fiamma licked her about the head and ears, taking care to get the insides. She said, *"Those cats are silly, Tiger Lily, not mean. They'll come around."*

"I don't care if they do. Anyway, I get to go to the shelter tomorrow, to meet that cat and her kittens."

"Really?" said Cyril. *"You have to tell her I said hello. Me, Cyril. I told her my name."*

"I'll do that. Henrie told me that three of the babies survived. The others were too sick."

"I was worried about them. I should have done more to help them." A tear started to run from his big eye.

"Don't cry, Cyril. Henrie said that the Maggie woman said they were doing very well. She said the momma must have been getting food from somewhere. She still has milk."

"Gene was taking food to her. And how is the momma? Is she okay?"

"She's healthy, but she doesn't want humans to touch her. They want to take her to a farm family or something. Somewhere she can get food and everything, but she doesn't have to talk to humans if she doesn't want to."

"That sounds like a good idea."

Jock interjected. *"We need to bring Cyril up to date on Harper."*

Cyril stood to attention. So did Tillie. *"What about Harper?"*

Jock sat up, puffing his chest just a little. Well, a lot.

"He's on The Escape. He went there to hide, and Ray hired him to work with us this weekend. He's going to help with the wedding, and then he's going to slip off in another town and hide."

Tiger Lily said, *"But the plans may not go like he wants. It seems like both Wyatt and Gene may be on the boat, too, with the wedding party."*

Moriah piped up. *"Gene? How did that happen?"*

"Remember Wyatt was invited? He asked if he could bring Gene. He thought Gene could use a break."

"When?"

"This evening, when Boone and Hilly and Gene came to pick Wyatt up. He asked Gene then, said he'd been given permission to bring a guest, and he thought Gene could use a nice afternoon and evening."

"Wow," said Moriah. *"This detective stuff is great! Can we go, too? And see it all happen?"*

Jock laughed. *"No, that's not gonna happen. But I'll tell you all about it the next time we get together."*

Tillie asked, *"Why haven't the other cats said anything?"*

Moriah sat up, puffing her chest as big as Jock had. *"Because they don't know anything. They've fallen down on the job. They're too busy being big baby bumper stickers to be good detectives."*

Cyril gently rebuked the little cat, on whom he had a minor crush. *"They'll get over it, and they'll be as good as new.*

Don't think badly about them. But while we're talking, let's stay up-to-date on Jeff Bennett. What do we all know about him and Hank?"

Moriah asked, *"Did he get that job?"*

Cyril nodded, and said, *"Oh, I forgot to tell you we found Ed, the guy who supposedly walked off the job. He walked off the job to get dead."*

"No!" said Tiger Lily. *"Did Hank do it?"*

"That's the working theory."

"So Jeff could get dead, too?"

"Probably not," said Cyril. *"As long as he doesn't let Hank know who he is."*

"How will he do that?" asked Fiamma.

Sis, who until now had listened to everyone else, said, *"He's got a disguise. He's wearing a beard, a hat, glasses, a suit, and he rubbed some kind of oil on his neck."*

"That's what he did? I knew I didn't recognize his scent. What did he use?"

"Some kind of pepper. He told Chris he didn't want to hide from the dogs, but he didn't want his dog friends to come up to him and be friendly."

"That makes sense. He was just protecting his six," said Cyril.

Tiger Lily asked, *"His six what?"*

Cyril looked at Tiger Lily. *"Sorry. I meant he's watching his own back. You have to do that if you go undercover."*

Tiger Lily realized she needed to give Honey Bear some information. *"Thanks for telling me about those guests, Honey Bear. Pete arrested all of them today."*

"He did? What for?"

Cyril answered. *"They had counterfeit money, fake jewels, lots of stolen stuff, and police departments all over the country are wrapping up cases."*

"Wow."

"Your instincts were right on," said Tiger Lily. *"It's good to have you as a detective."*

Candice took care of a rollicking table of six. Her friends Kara and Tank, Don and Suellen, the engaged couple, and their friends Percy and Sarah.

Sarah looked at Suellen and said, "This is going to be great! And there will be two more?"

"Yeah," said Suellen. "This is such a fun town. Don, we have to do our first anniversary here. Anyway, a guy at the Inn has been here for several days looking for his dad, who's a homeless vet, and he came to Chelsea with a bunch of other homeless vets, and then they all started getting killed off, and burned, and shot, and – did I tell you we found a body? – anyway, it's so cool, but it's not, really, and this guy's dad wasn't one of them, so he's still out there, and he's still looking, but we thought he needed a break! And he asked the one young vet – they don't think anyone is trying to kill him, because he wasn't one of those Gulf ones – and anyway, they're coming! And these cats? Aren't these cats adorable? Don, we have to get cats. Lots of cats. Ten cats. Can we get ten cats?"

Sarah's face had turned to a look of polite confusion.

Candice walked back to the bar and told George, "I'm considering cutting Suellen off. But she's walking. . .and she's with friends and her fiancé. . . . I still may cut her off."

Annie was on her second glass of wine but felt like she was just beginning. "You're driving, right Chris?"

"Sure. With my very own two feet, I'm driving you home. Next door."

"Great. Then don't let them cut me off. Hey, Geraldine! Over here!"

"What's she doing here?"

"Get over it, Chris. She's a good friend now."

"I will never understand. . ."

"You don't need to. Geraldine, hi! Pull up a chair. I'm not used to seeing you out in the evening."

"I'm trying to make a new life. You know that. Even though we didn't spend time together, I remember you all coming out here on Fridays, and I thought. . .well. . ."

"It's great to see you." Annie waved her hand for a server, who may not have seen a new person join the table. "How was your week?"

"Pretty good. I was out of town for a couple of days after our meeting. They sent me to a show in New York."

"Did you see anything good?"

"As a matter of fact, I saw a dress that was just you. It was every color of the rainbow, belted, with a skirt that just begged to be twirled."

"How much?"

"A lot. Tell Chris to save his pennies if he wants to get you a great birthday present."

"I heard that."

Geraldine leaned in to look past Annie at Chris. "I intended for you to hear it." She pushed a card across the table to him. "Here's the order information."

"Ouch!"

Geraldine accepted a glass of wine from the server and, surprising even Annie, said, "Thank you."

Annie looked at Chris and mouthed the word, "See?"

Geraldine said, "Oh for goodness sakes."

"What?"

"That. . .Hank. He's here. At least he's here without that dreadful Ed."

Annie said, "Didn't you hear?"

"Hear what?"

"Ed's dead."

"What?"

"Hank was trolling The Avenue today, telling my staff and everyone that Ed walked out on him and he was looking for a business manager. And this afternoon, Ed's body was found."

"You don't say! What happened?"

"Pete isn't really talking about it, but, Chris, didn't he say Ed was shot?"

"Yeah."

Annie looked at Chris, expecting him to say more. "And? What else do you know?"

Chris shook his head with a look on his face that said, "I. Know. Nothing."

Annie, exasperated, turned back to Geraldine. "He was found in a vacant house somewhere. Some kids were walking by wondering why the neighborhood dogs were trying to get in, so they looked in the window, and there he was. Dead. Shot in the head."

"Ed?"

Annie couldn't help it. Two glasses of wine must have done the trick. She laughed so hard tears rolled down her face. That got Geraldine going, and before long, Annie realized Chris had moved away to talk to Ray and Cheryl. That got her going again.

Jeff moved to the other side of the table, so he could face Annie. "Hey. I see we're playing musical chairs here, so I thought I would come get another view of the room."

"What view, Jeff? Now all you can see is the back wall."

"It's a view, and I haven't had time to talk to you. Introduce me to your friend."

"Sure. Geraldine, this is our friend Jeff. He's staying at the Inn for the weekend." She turned to Jeff. "I didn't see you all day today."

"I was busy. You know. Doing stuff. So, Geraldine, tell me all about yourself."

Annie realized, even with two glasses of wine, that she needed to let Jeff carry on. She glanced around the room, wondering from whom he was hiding. And she bet Chris knew all about it. That little skunk.

Nancy came up behind Jeff. She whispered, "I'm sorry."

"What?"

"About this morning. I'm sorry. I shouldn't have. . .you know."

"It's okay, Nancy. Don't worry about it."

"What, Mom?" asked Annie. "What did you do?"

"Oh. . .I just ran into Jeff today. . .I mean. . .oh, I really ran into him. I wasn't looking where I was going and. . .well, I might have stepped on his feet. That's all."

Trudie and Felicity came up behind Annie's chair. Felicity said, "Hi, Jeff! When did you get to town?"

"Today. Spending the weekend."

"It's good to see you. Lunch is on us tomorrow, okay? Annie, did you hear Hank hired a new business manager already?"

"He did?"

"Yeah. Some guy came into the Café this morning looking for work, and it was just after Hank said he was looking for someone."

"Really? Who is he?"

"Don't know. Some guy got downsized, was just looking in the area. He got lucky. So did Hank, I guess."

"Did you hear about Ed?"

"The guy that walked off? What about him?"

Annie was sober now. "He's dead."

Nancy had moved away. Trudie leaned in. "You might want to check her meds, Annie. She sat down today with a perfect stranger and just started talking."

"What?"

"Well, Sam was with her, so she was perfectly safe, but if she had been by herself. . .well. . .I'm just sayin'. Check her meds. Or make sure she's taking them."

Jeff excused himself and wandered down the table to talk to someone else.

Tank leaned in and whispered to Kara. "What do you say? Want to come over to my place?"

Kara flinched. Tank noticed.

"I'm sorry. I didn't mean. . ."

"No. . .no. I'm sorry. I just wanted to spend as much time as I could with Candice, and she's working, so that means staying here to catch a word here or there."

"How about later?"

"Maybe. Let's see how the evening goes. We'll be together all day tomorrow. . . ."

Boone saw Hank walk in. Not even thinking about it, he raised his hand, went full-bore-Appalachian, and said, "Hey, Hank, how ya'll doin'? Goodtaseeya."

Hank stared. Then he walked closer. "Hey, Boone. Not used to seeing you with these folks."

"They sometimes lets me an' my lovely wife come out. You know my Hilly?"

"Yes. Nice to see you, Hilly. Well, I have friends waiting."

"Jus wantin' to say howdy, is all."

"Well, howdy, then."

Hank walked on with a perplexed look on his face.

After several seconds, Boone leaned in to Wyatt and Gene. He whispered, "Now you know what to look for. You see him, you go the other way."

Laila moved to the chair Chris had vacated. She got Annie's attention. "What's up with Chris?"

"He doesn't like Geraldine."

"That's not it."

"It is. And Geraldine found a great dress for me, and he thinks it's too expensive."

"He said that?"

"He said 'ouch.'"

Laila wasn't Annie's best friend for nothing. "You're trying to mind-read him again. You know that always ends badly."

"Not always. Sometimes."

"Okay. Let's start again. What's up with Chris?"

"Okay. He, Pete and Jeff are working on something and they won't tell me what it is."

"But it's probably something to do with a case. Really, do you have a right to know?"

Annie looked at her best friend. She hated it when Laila was right. "Not really, but they were talking about it in my house."

"Because you invited them."

Annie waggled her head.

"I know what you need to do."

"What's that?"

"Get away for a romantic weekend, somewhere you can find a quiet place to eat, drink and dance."

"Dance?"

"You know. That dance you do, where you hold on to one another, touch foreheads, and neither one of you leads."

"Neither one of us has to lead. We just know where the other is headed."

"I understand that when you're just holding each other, swaying back and forth. But what about those times when you move around the room or, you know, when he twirls you around?"

"I don't know. We just feel it. I know where he's going and he knows where I'm going."

"You don't even need music. Don't look at me like that. I've seen you. You come together and move to some kind of music that's in your heads. That doesn't mean you can always read his mind. Let go of it. Whatever it is, let go."

22

The Inn woke on Saturday to a beautiful June day. The weather would be clear all day with highs in the mid-to-high seventies.

Henrie was ecstatic – an emotion he rarely allowed himself – to have the detective table back in its usual place. With a smile on his face and a samba on his feet, he placed seven little dishes on the floor beside it. Kali dipped love hairs on the ankles of his black pants before she indulged.

Henrie noticed Tiger Lily. She stayed at the doorway, not coming close to the dishes. Every now and then, one of the others would raise a head and hiss in her direction. Not knowing if it was the right thing to do, he picked up the only dish not in use and walked with it to the kitchen. He held it out, beckoning her to come. She did.

"Having trouble with the sibs, big girl?"

She looked up from her dish to blink one time.

"They will get over it. Whatever it is. I am certain. And remember, you and I have a task today. After breakfast, we will go to the shelter to meet the momma and her babies."

Mr. Bean came into the kitchen. He reached up to pat Henrie on his hip. He hissed at Tiger Lily.

"Mr. Bean! Shame!"

Mr. Bean, hurt, left the kitchen.

Mr. Bean went back into the dining room and under the detective table with the rest of the cats. *"Did you hear that? Henrie's taking Tiger Lily to meet that cat."*

"What?" "Huh?" "He duz wots?"

"He's taking her — and not us — to see that momma kitty and her kittens."

"The ones she made us pretend to be?"

Mo trilled. Kali hissed.

Sassy Pants translated. *"He sez she was jus' tryin' to tell Henrie dose cats needed to be saved."*

Little Socks said, *"She didn't have to do it the way she did."*

Mo trilled several times. Ko hissed.

Sassy Pants translated. *"He sez wot would we has her do. She had to tell Henrie an' we can't talk or nuttin', an' we'ze bein' mean to her."*

"She was mean to us!"

Mo trilled again. This time Sassy Pants hissed. Ko translated.

"He says we're being really mean. All of us."

Mo waited until Ko was finished and trilled again, this time for even longer.

Kali and Ko sat up straight, staring at their brother. Sassy Pants was sitting straight also. She drooped and hung her head as she translated. *"He say we so silly we falls down on da job an' we izn't bein' good detectives, an' he tinks Tiger Lily keeps workin' on da cases an' we duzn't know wot's happnin' an' we'ze stupid."* A tear fell from her eye to the floor. Her lower lip quivered.

Henrie poured coffee as the guests arrived for breakfast. They arrived at about the same time; Jeff was the last to enter the dining room. Generally, he would introduce himself to the other guests, but this morning, he said, "Henrie, it looks like I'm going to miss another great meal, but I promised Chris I'd eat with him. We might go somewhere else for breakfast."

Chris came downstairs, having spent the night in the apartment. Sis was close behind. "Morning, Henrie. Annie will be down directly. Jeff and I need to talk. Mind if we take breakfast out to the back porch?"

"Please do. You'll find trays in the corner over there."

As they helped themselves, Henrie fixed a carafe of coffee and took it to the porch with condiments.

He met them in the hallway on the way back. Softly, he said, "You do realize, Jeff, that one of our guests is involved."

"Yes. I picked him out. He's the son, right? I don't want to spend any more time than possible around him. No sense letting him know who I am."

"Certainly. And Chris, please tell Annie what is happening. She will trip over herself without realizing what she is doing."

"Right. I wanted to talk to Jeff first, but you're right."

Henrie, back in the kitchen, listened to the talk in the dining room with one ear. Kara was talking to Wyatt. "So did you talk to Gene? Is he coming?"

"He's a little shy about it. He's been. . .um. . .on the streets for a while. He doesn't know quite how to act."

"What do you think? Do you think it's a good idea, or a bad one?"

"The problem will be, at least this is what he said, is that if he gets out there on the boat, and if he gets anxious, there won't be anywhere for him to go."

"He could always go to another part of the boat. We could leave him alone if he needs us to."

"Or maybe he could meet all of you first. Maybe we could have, like, a picnic or something before we go."

Suellen and Don spoke at once. "Or we could go to that Bean place." "We could eat at Mr. Bean's."

Don continued, "It's small. Not a lot of people. We could meet, have something to eat, no pressure."

Suellen added, "And then we can go right to The Escape. We're supposed to leave around two."

"I can call Candice, have her, George and Tank meet us."

Wyatt nodded. "Okay. I'll call the house where he's staying and check with him."

Henrie preferred to think of himself as "not the type" to insert himself. Well. . .he inserted himself. He went to the dining room and said, "Allow me to suggest lunch here at the Inn. I will be happy to provide a light repast, sandwiches, salads. Around noon? Serving ten?"

Four faces looked quietly around at one another. Kara did the honors. "Thank you!"

Annie reached the dining room to find it empty. She walked through to the kitchen to find Tiger Lily wide-awake napping under the table.

"Henrie, did Jeff and Chris go somewhere else to eat?"

"They took breakfast to the back porch. Allow me to help you make a tray."

"I don't know. . ."

"Allow me to help you make a tray."

Henrie went back to the dining room, followed by Annie and Tiger Lily.

Annie helped herself to hazelnut French toast and a bacon and egg sandwich on an English muffin. "Smells great, Henrie."

"It is, trust me."

"Are you sure. . ."

Henrie put a cup of coffee on a tray. "Allow me to carry your tray to the porch."

"Okay." Annie followed, hesitant, but obedient. She almost stepped on Tiger Lily, who seemed to stay on Henrie's heels.

Henrie placed Annie's tray on the table as Jeff rose. "Annie, good morning. Sorry we didn't wait for you."

"No problem, Jeff. I know you have things to do."

Henrie turned to leave, not before Annie caught a look between him and Chris. Chris turned to Annie.

"Sit. Have some coffee. Let's talk."

Tiger Lily, torn, looked to Henrie. "You may stay here, big girl. I will let you know when it is time to go."

Tiger Lily stuck close to Henrie, following him from the kitchen to the dining room, back to the kitchen, to the dining room, to the kitchen, dining room, back porch. She stopped at the back porch. It seemed she would get good information here. And none of the cats had followed. Good. Let them stay under the detective table and pretend to detect. Big baby burpy brats.

Tiger Lily joined Sis under the table. *"What have they been talking about?"*

"Mostly about Jeff working for Hank and how dangerous that could be. They also talked about Annie."

"What about her?"

"That Chris isn't used to not talking to her, and that she could have said something without meaning to last night."

"What does that mean?"

"I'm not sure. Let's listen."

Listen, they did. Soon, Tiger Lily said, *"So, it's nothing new for us, but apparently they didn't tell Mommy everything. Now she knows what we know."*

"We did learn one thing new. Jeff starts his new job Monday, as Wally Krause."

"We also learned that his disguise is pretty good."

"Yeah. Otherwise, Trudie and Felicity would have recognized him. Hey, is Henrie taking you to see the cats?"

"Yeah. He remembers. Maybe Mommy will come. Maybe we can get a kitten. Or three."

Annie took the dishes to the kitchen with a lighter heart. "How is it, Henrie, that you always seem to know what to do?"

"I am a connoisseur of the human heart."

"And obviously a poet. Why is Tiger Lily sticking so close to you today?"

"I believe her siblings are ostracizing her."

"What?"

"Thursday. . .yes, I believe it was Thursday, they came to me with a problem. They wanted me to find, no, they wanted me to rescue, a feral cat and her kittens."

Annie sat at the kitchen table, eyes and mouth wide open. "What?"

"They must have learned about a cat that Gene found at that old marina, and, well, Tiger Lily, in her attempt to tell me what she needed, bullied some of her siblings."

Annie looked at Tiger Lily, sitting under the table, head and eyes facing up toward her. "Come up here, big girl. Come on."

After a moment of hesitation, the big girl jumped to the table.

"Did you do that? Bully your sibs?"

Tiger Lily blinked once.

"Was it for a good cause?"

She blinked once again.

"They'll get over it. They know, deep inside, that you had a reason."

Mo came into the kitchen and gave a soft trill. He jumped to the table. Tiger Lily reared back, but he stood firm. He trilled a few times and closed his eyes, a cat's notice of submission. Tiger Lily softened her stance. A little.

"See?" said Annie. "They know."

Annie reached over to caress Mo.

"So, Henrie, tell me about this cat."

"Maggie went to the marina and got the cat and her kittens. Three are still living. Tiger Lily wanted to see them with her own two eyes. Maggie expects us this morning."

"Well, then, let's go. I'll get your harness, big girl."

Henrie said, "We will leave as soon as I prepare lunch. I must return by eleven thirty."

"You can tell me about that on the way. I'll change, get her harness and be back down in a few minutes."

Mo left Tiger Lily on top of the kitchen table. He joined the rest of the cats under the detective table and trilled. Kali translated. It was sullen, but it was a translation.

"He says we all have to apologize to her."

"Who?" asked Little Socks.

"You know who."

"Never."

Mo trilled again. Sassy Pants sat up straight. *"She's goin'? Witout us?"*

Mo nodded.

"Where?" asked Mr. Bean.

"She goes witout us to seeze da baby kittens an' da mommy."

"But we helped her tell Henrie!"

"We laffted at her an' we wuz mean."

"Trill, trill, trill."

Sassy Pants hung her head. Ko finally translated. *"Mo says Henrie knows we've been mean to her, and he told Mommy, so Mommy knows, too."*

Dejected, six cats lay on the cushions, wondering to themselves what to do next.

Moriah trotted in and stuck her head beneath the covers. *"Where's Tiger Lily?"*

Sassy Pants pointed with her head to the kitchen. Moriah went there next. Tiger Lily was still on the table. She jumped up next to her.

"Are you going to see the cat?"

"Yes. Henrie's going to take me. Mommy's coming, too."

"Can I come?"

"Sure. If I can figure out how to tell Henrie."

Henrie, croissant in one hand and a dish of ham salad in the other, came to the table. "Good morning, precious girl. What brings you to the Inn this morning?"

Tiger Lily put a leg – or her front arm, depending on your view of it – around Moriah and looked up, eyes wide.

Henrie looked at them for a moment and ventured a guess. "You want her to come with us?"

Tiger Lily blinked once.

Annie was back, sooner than Henrie expected, Tiger Lily's harness in hand.

Henrie said, "We will need two."

"I'll call Clara to make sure it's okay."

23

Don opened a bottle of wine and poured for Suellen and Sarah. "This is a great B&B. This all-season porch alone makes it unique."

Sarah said, "I know! We stayed out here until nearly two this morning. It was so nice, with all the windows open."

Percy asked, "Is this a private beach?"

"Yeah," said Suellen. "And there are a couple of cabanas, and that shed over there has chairs, tables, all kinds of things we can take out closer to the water."

"What's that over there?"

"Henrie said it's a marina, a really nice one. All those boats, some of them belong to people who live here, but lots of them are out-of-towners. They stay out here weekends, or longer, living on their boats. That's why there's so much foot traffic in town. Chelsea has motels and B&Bs, but a lot of folks live out there in the summer."

"Which boat will we be on?"

"That big rainbow-colored one. See it?"

"Wow. This will be fun! Is it true what you said last night? That Wyatt is somehow connected with the vets?"

"Did I say that?"

"You did. You were pretty toasted, though."

"Me?"

"Yeah," said Don. "Candice cut you off."

"Our wedding guest Candice?"

"The one and only."

"She must have had good cause."

"She did, indeed. Anyway, tell them about Wyatt."

"Okay. He's been looking for his dad, a vet who left home several years ago. He's been living on the street, and something that he left at the house led him here, to Chelsea."

"Because of those arsons and murders? It's been all over the news. Chelsea is famous!"

"You told us it was already famous."

"It is, and this place, too. Lots of exciting things happen around here. Get me loaded tonight and I'll tell you everything."

Jeff and Chris wandered The Avenue. While appearing aimless, they actually had an ulterior motive. Information.

Jeff said, "Let's try CyberHealth."

"What? I don't think Hank drinks tea."

"No, but he may stop in from time to time."

"Okay."

Jeff looked back toward the lake as they walked. "I was looking forward to getting out on The Escape this weekend. Bad luck for me there's a wedding."

"And everybody got invited but us."

"No kidding?"

"The couple has a pair of friends coming down from Marsh Haven, but that was going to be it. Until they ran into the tornado named Kara."

"Kara? That friend of George and Candice?"

"Yep. She never met anyone she didn't know. She practically invited herself, then George and Candice, then Tank, then Wyatt, then Gene."

"Is she a wedding planner?"

"You know what? I don't know what she does. But that would be a good profession for her."

As they went through the door, Chris caught sight of Mem. He waved and pointed to a table. Mem nodded and indicated she would be right there.

"So," said Chris. "How does this work?"

"I'm out from under cover on the undercover assignment, and I can ask questions straight up, to people we trust not to talk."

"Okay."

When Mem got to the table, Chris pulled out a chair. "Sit. Visit a while."

"I will, but let me bring tea first. What's your pleasure?"

"What do you recommend?" asked Jeff.

"I have a dandy early summer tea. Kona pineapple, served on ice."

"Sounds good," said Chris. "Do you have fresh scones?"

"I made a batch today with fresh berries. Raspberry, blueberry, blackberry."

"Perfect. Do you really have time to join us?"

"I'll make time. I'll be right back."

Mem was an Avenue enigma. She was more mature than every other business owner on the street – at least that is how she described herself – a product of the sixties, as noted by her generally eclectic mode of dressing, and the woman most other women in town came to if they were in need of advice.

Apparently, men desired her advice as well.

Jeff looked around. "Have you ever been on those computers, Chris?"

"No. But I see other people here all the time."

"Hank?"

"I don't recall, but we can ask Mem. What are you thinking?"

"I'm thinking it would be a great resource to look around the web, and it would keep those searches from showing up on your own computer."

"Some of that stuff costs money, and it would have to be tied to a credit card. An email."

"You can get a second email address, connect a credit card to that address."

Mem returned with a tray, three glasses of iced tea, a pitcher of more, and a plate of scones.

"To what do I owe the pleasure, guys?"

Jeff asked, "How good are you with secrets?"

"The best. But I'm also a horrible gossip when no one has asked me to keep a secret."

"Go on with the gossip," suggested Jeff, "and then we can push on."

"Okay. Well, here's the latest. Just as you came to town, Jeff, a new fella, a bearded fella, about your size, comes to town looking for work. Interesting, a job is available, and it happens to be a position as Hank's business manager. The original showed up dead yesterday. Imagine that!"

Mem took a sip of tea and broke into a scone. "Now I'm pretty astute about these things. And I believe a couple of other folks in town are as well. Am I right, Jeff?"

Jeff nodded and took a drink of tea.

Mem continued. "I'm sitting here where I can see everything going on, on the other side of The Avenue. Those girls at the Café don't have my age, my insight or my line of sight. How am I doing so far?"

Jeff chuckled. "Remind me not to commit a crime in Chelsea. At least not on the other side of The Avenue."

"Right," said Mem. "Why'd it take you so long to come see me?"

"Obviously, I need to go back to training. So Mem, what else can you tell us?"

"I think Hank has always been up to no good. I don't know why you're here, and I don't know why you want to work for him, but I'm positive you didn't murder Ed to get the job. Which means that, probably, Hank murdered him and you just got lucky on your timing."

Jeff and Chris could only stare.

"So, I've been thinking about Hank this morning. By the way, it was great to see you last night, Jeff. I didn't really put two and two together until I woke up. Isn't it wonderful, how waking up with a thought in your head means you're absolutely correct about something?"

"Amazing."

"So, I've been thinking, and I try to keep from wondering just what it is you're digging into. That line of thinking would only confuse me. So I thought back to what I know of Hank. He comes in here every now and then, you know, to use the computers. He's not much of a tea drinker."

"Any idea what he does on the computers?" asked Jeff.

"No, but I looked up his records. He puts things on a tab and pays at the end of the month, so I have all of the records for this year. If you need them, I could go back a few years. But here," she reached into the pocket of her apron, "are copies of the times he has been on this year."

"Any way we can find out what he did?"

"I suppose, but it might be a mess. He's supposed to say which computer he's on, but look, he leaves that off most of the time. That means we'll have to look at all of them for these time periods and try to figure it out."

"Is it possible?"

"It is, but you'd have to bring in your forensic experts. It seems as if he's usually at one of those three, when I notice him at least, but I may not see him every time he's here."

"It's a start. Tell me about Ed. What did he do for Hank?"

"A little bit of everything. Hank walked around town all day, every day. He went to see rich folks, poor folks, debtors, sinners, top of the heap, bottom. . ."

". . .I get it. And Ed?"

"He managed all of his businesses, which are myriad. Hank owns properties, mostly dumps, and makes investments you don't want to dig into. Oh, excuse me.

You might want to dig into them. I forgot for a minute who you are."

"And Ed was always in the office?"

"Not always. He forwarded the office phone to his cell, so he could handle things from almost anywhere."

"Do you happen to know where he went? What he did?"

"No, sorry."

"Know who might?"

"No, not really. I think I've given you everything I have that is Hank-related. Are you going to share what you're doing?"

"Um, no," said Jeff. "You'll get the full scoop as soon as I can give it."

"I should work for a newspaper. I'm gonna get an exclusive."

Pete and Marco called in all of the full-time, part-time and reserve officers. They combed the old marina, the town park, the state park, abandoned buildings, cars trucks and boats that had been hanging around for several days or weeks.

Marco finally said it. "We're done, Pete. He's gone. He left town, one way or another."

"Or he's dead."

"No, we woulda found him if he was dead."

"Probably. Well, I hate it, but you're right. We're done. Pull everyone in; send them home if they're supposed to be off-duty."

Pete sat in his office, dejected. Cyril tried to help by putting his head in his lap. He desperately wanted to tell Pete where to find Harper, but he didn't know how to do it. He had tried to get Pete to the Inn a few times, hoping Tiger Lily could help. The furthest he could get him was to the Café. And Tiger Lily didn't usually work on Saturdays.

Pete finally said, "Let's go home, Cyril. Let's enjoy the rest of the weekend."

Cyril whined.

"Perk up, Cyril. We had a good week. We arrested a dozen multi-state felons. We brought Jeff in to make an arrest. We got one of the young guys off the street. It was a good week."

He didn't say it with meaning.

Annie and Tiger Lily walked Moriah back to Bloomin' Crazy. Clara was in the shop by herself, arranging a vase of pink and white roses. "Did you enjoy your trip to the shelter, little girl? I'll bet you're glad you already have a home."

Moriah purred and jumped to her bed on top of the counter. Three turns, and she settled down to sleep.

"Tell me how it went."

"First of all, let me tell you about your little beauty there. She. Does. Not. Like. A. Harness."

"I've never tried. What did she do?"

"She squirmed, jumped, bit, scratched, screamed like a banshee and turned rigid."

"All at once?"

"All at once. But when I told her that was the only way she could go to the shelter, she stopped. Just like that. And let me put it on her."

"She's a pip. Did you find that momma kitty?"

"We did. She stayed in the back of her cage, but it seemed like she communicated with Tiger Lily. She's a pretty one, but she's got some battle scars. Her kittens are beauties. Two girls and a boy."

"What color?"

"The momma is black as night. Her girl babies are classic calico, black and orange and white. One has a perfectly black eye and the other has an exact half black face."

"And the boy?"

"Orange."

"What will happen with them?"

Tiger Lily pawed at Annie. Annie said, "Maggie hopes to find a place in the country for momma, after the babies are weaned. I told her I'd check with Brian and Janet, see if they want an outdoor mouser for their winery."

"That would be perfect. They have several buildings she could use for shelter, and they probably all have mice. What about those babies?"

"Do you want one?"

"Honey, I have one that is as demanding as four, and a big dog to boot several days a month."

"So, that's a no?"

"That's a no."

Tiger Lily pawed at Annie again.

"I wonder if Mem. . ."

"Stop it! No cat would ever mix with Frank's Claire, so don't even go there. You would save everything on four legs if you could. Why don't you see if Brian and Janet want the full set?"

"I could ask. Yeah, I should do that before asking anyone else."

Tiger Lily pawed at Annie one more time. "Tell you what, big girl, you go on home. I'll be along after I check in with folks."

Henrie finished putting food on the buffet just as the dining room burst to life. The wedding party arrived, all but Gene. Henrie made eye contact with Wyatt, who shrugged.

As Henrie poured coffee and lemonade, refilled sandwich platters and brought out a new bowl of cole slaw, they talked, laughed, got to know one another, and made suggestions for wedding vows.

George had just given his, "Just say 'may we grow old together,'" when they heard Boone come in the door.

He came to the dining room with Gene in tow. "Hi y'all! Hope we ain't too late."

"No!" came the chorus.

Wyatt stood to introduce Gene. He did it with what Henrie considered to be the right touch of sincerity. "This is Gene. He spent the last few years with a group of friends that are no longer together. This is the first time he's met a bunch of new folks. Gene, this is the wedding party, Suellen and Don; their friends, Percy and Sarah.

This young lady here is Kara. If you want to spend quiet time, make sure she's as far away from you as possible. These last folks all live here in Chelsea. If you stick around here for a while, you'll get to know them. George and Candice work at Mo's Tap, a great place for a beer, and Tank is the fire chief."

Gene held the eyes of Tank for several seconds. Tank finally said, "I'm real sorry for the losses you've suffered this week. Real sorry."

Gene shook his hand, looked at Boone and nodded. He would be okay.

Tiger Lily said good-bye to her mommy and Clara and walked home. She stopped in the foyer.

She didn't want go through to the dining room. Most of the cats were probably in there.

She thought about the library. No, Kali and Ko were probably sunning on the windowsill. They probably watched her walk down the sidewalk.

How about the apartment? No. Sometimes Mo preferred the windowsill in the apartment's dining room. Well, that wouldn't be so bad. Mo seemed to apologize to her this morning, but she couldn't understand what he was saying.

She could stay here, in the foyer. The house felt empty. All of the guests were either in the county jail or on The Escape. She peeked around the corner to the dining room. Yep. The table was filled with dirty dishes and Henrie was cleaning up. The house was empty. Except for Henrie.

And those dratted cats.

A tear escaped her eye. Darn it! She wanted to be mad, not sad.

When her lower lip quivered, she realized she had to go somewhere to hide. But where?

She turned her head away quickly when Mo came down the stairs. He walked straight to her and gave her a full body hug. She tried to keep her back to him, but she couldn't. She dropped to the floor and allowed him to cover her in a hug. He licked her cheeks, catching the tears that now flowed freely from her eyes.

It didn't take long for the other cats to appear. Tentative, they came from the dining room and the library. Sassy Pants first, then everyone but Little Socks found a foot, a haunch, or the top of her head to lick.

Eventually, they stopped, lying together in one big pile. Except for Little Socks. Finally, Little Socks put a paw on Tiger Lily's tail, with just enough pressure that she could tell another cat was there.

24

Hank sat in a blacked-out SUV in the town parking lot. It hadn't been planned, but his spot gave him a perfect view to the vehicle that pulled into the Inn.

It was Boone. And he had the young vet with him. So that was where he had gotten to.

He had been sitting with Boone the night before. And what had Boone been up to? All that hi-y'all and glad-ta-see-ya stuff. Did Boone know more than he should?

The circle was getting wider. It had been a mistake to bring the vets here. He hadn't been thinking clearly.

He thought, on his home turf, he would be able to get them all at one time.

It was just bad luck.

Ed had located them easily enough. Hank thought it would be easy.

First, he thought they were all asleep in that group of boats, but some of them had gone off to drink. He only got one. The big fish. The only eye witness. But they all knew too much. At least the Gulf vets did. The young ones probably knew everything now, too.

So he tried again.

Once again, Ed found them, and once again, Hank tried to get them. Most of them were somewhere else, leaving that one hapless guy. Someone pulled him out of the fire. He wasn't sure who had done that. Maybe one of the vets. At least the guy died without talking.

Ed put bullets in two more; Hank started another fire. Now they were down to one young vet and one Gulf vet.

And now, he had found the young one. The young one had to know where the old one was.

Halfway across the parking lot, George turned to walk backwards. Yes, everyone was still coming. They stretched from his position almost to the Inn.

He caught Candice's eye. She trotted to catch up.

Candice said, "They're already two sheets to the wind. Isn't that more than Ray allows on the boat?"

"Yacht."

Candice laughed and threw her mane of dark brown hair from one side to the other.

George said, "He'll see the way they stumble before we get there. He's watching from the deck."

"You still have the vows? And the rings?"

"In my pocket. At least I won't lose them before the wedding."

Candice nodded. "I'm thinking both of us should stay sober."

"Very. I'm gonna keep an eye on Gene, too. He still seems a bit skittish."

"Do you think this was a good idea?"

"Can't tell yet."

Ray stood on deck with Jock. "Oh, boy." He said. Jock gave a happy yip. "This is going to be fun. Not." Jock's yip was still happy.

Ray reached down to take Sarah's hand. Helping her up didn't seem to be happening. "George, uh, Candice, how about giving her a push."

Candice laughed and gave Sarah a shove while Ray pulled and steadied her. Jock gave a happy yip.

George was the last to board. "We're ready, big guy. Are you gonna give 'the talk'?"

Ray turned to give 'the talk.'"

"Welcome aboard! We're proud to be your wedding hosts today. Let me tell you what to expect."

Ray went through the high points, pointing out the life boat and life jackets. "No horseplay, no sitting or standing on the railing. No smoking. No drinking to excess, but I guess I may have been a little late on that one." Jock gave a happy yip.

"We'll be stopping in the middle of the lake and you'll have plenty of time to swim, but only if I think you're capable of getting in without getting dead. Jock here will be your lifeguard." Jock gave a couple of happy yips.

George zoned out. He had heard "the talk" before. Several times. He leaned back, eyes closed, face to the sun, drinking in what he referred to as Juneshine. This was going to be a great day.

Candice moved to his side and whispered, "What's Hank doing here?"

George snapped to and looked where she pointed. There he was, standing at the end of the dock, looking hard at The Escape.

George looked at Ray, who had just seen Hank. This wasn't good. Ray had banned Hank from The Marina for life. "I'll get it, buddy, don't worry."

Before George could get down, however, Jock jumped to the dock and rushed toward Hank.

Everything turned to a slow motion widescreen shot. George watched as Jock's big, black body jumped from the deck to the railing to the dock. He turned to see Ray, yelling something to Jock. His turn continued, and he saw a man emerge from the galley.

The man registered shock at. . .in the slow motion of his mind, George thought it was Gene, Wyatt or both. Then the man looked over George's shoulder, grabbed at Ray, pointed, yelled, turned and ran back into the galley. In slow motion.

George jerked back to real time. Ray yelled something. What was it? Oh, yeah. "Get us loose!"

George yelled, "Candice! Get down! Get everyone down!" while he ran forward to untie. He got the front loose, turned to run to the back, and saw it.

Hank ran toward the dock while he reached into his pocket for something. Jock barreled toward him. They met. Hard. Jock pushed off the dock with both hind legs and hit Hank in the chest, propelling him into the water. Turning in midair, launching himself from Hank's chest, Jock returned to the yacht at a full run. One mighty jump, and he was on deck. As soon as he landed, George let go of the rope.

George grabbed the rail to keep himself upright as Ray kicked The Escape into gear. They left the harbor as quickly as the yacht could manage.

The cats eventually moved back to the detective table. It had been a while since they had all been there together. Tiger Lily didn't speak at first.

Mo gave a soft trill.

Sassy Pants translated. *"He wants to know duz you want to ask for reports."*

"Really? You still want me to do that?"

Kali and Ko spoke together. *"Sure." "Yeah."*

Mo trilled again, and Kali translated. *"He says you're the only one that has kept going. The rest of us fell down on the job."*

"I'm sure you didn't. But okay. Does anyone have a report?"

Cats looked around at one another. Finally, Little Socks spoke. *"I think we were all here when Pete arrested the scavenger people, so we know where they are."*

Tiger Lily nodded. *"Okay. Does anyone else have anything? No? Then I'll give mine. What do you want to hear about first? Harper? Hank? Jeff Bennett? The momma kitty?"*

Mr. Bean said, *"Tell us about the kitty."*

"Okay. Well, she's been lost for a long time. Her name used to be Scooter, but no one's called her that in forever. She had several babies, but some died. Three are still living. She's real scared of humans, but she liked that man Gene. He was taking care of her, and she had nice things to say about Cyril, too. She was going to try to hide from everybody, but she decided she needed to let herself be rescued so her babies would live."

"Wow!" said Mr. Bean. *"That's scary!"*

"What will happen to her now?" asked Kali.

"The shelter lady, Maggie is her name, she said she will try to find a farm for her to go to, someplace she can hunt for mice. It has to have a place where she can get out of the weather. Scooter doesn't want to live in a house. She doesn't want to talk to people."

"Where will they find a place like that?" asked Ko.

"Mommy says she'll ask those people that have the new winery, Chateau Simon. You know, where that cat Simon lives."

"That would be a nice place."

"We's been dere. Dey has lots of buildings an' such."

"What about the kitties? Will they go, too?"

"Mommy will ask if they want all of them, but they might be able to find homes, too. I tried to tell Mommy we'd take them, but she didn't understand."

Mo trilled.

Kali said, *"He wants to know what they look like."*

"Scooter, the mommy, is your color, Little Socks, but she's all black. She doesn't have any white."

"None?" asked Little Socks.

"None. She has two baby girls and one baby boy. The baby girls are calico. Not dilute calico like you guys," she said to Kali and Ko. *"Instead of gray and peach, they're black and orange, with some white. One has a black eye, and the other, she has a face that is exactly half black. Even down the middle of her nose."*

Mr. Bean asked, *"And the little boy? What color is he?"*

"Orange."

"Orange? Like Uncle Honey Bear?"

"*Kinda. But not long haired like him, and he doesn't have exactly the same color of orange. He's brighter.*"

"*It would be nice to have another boy in the house,*" said Mr. Bean. "*Me and Mo are outnumbered.*"

Kali and Ko said at the same time, "*Mommy won't do it.*" "*Mommy thinks we're too many kitties as we are.*"

Tiger Lily agreed. "*She asked Clara if she wanted one, and Clara said Moriah is too many kitties.*"

"*She's a diva,*" spat Little Socks.

Tiger Lily said, "*She may be a diva, but she's a darned good detective.*"

They got quiet for several seconds. Then Mo trilled again. Sassy Pants said, "*He wants to know about Jeff Bennett.*"

"*Oh. That's pretty exciting. He's undercover sometimes. He wears a beard and a hat and glasses, and he puts pepper oil on himself so the dogs he knows won't be friendly.*"

A chorus ensued. "*Why?*" "*What for?*" "*Pepper?*"

"*He's here to figure out how Hank killed those vets.*"

"*Hank?*"

"*Hank. And then he killed his business manager, Ed…*"

"*What?*" "*How?*" "*Really?*"

"*Well, that's the working theory, anyway. And it happened at just the right time, when Jeff needed to get close to him, so in disguise, he's going to go to work for him.*"

"*Slow down!*" "*What?*" "*I can't keep up!*"

Tiger Lily took a deep breath. "*Okay. Sometimes, Jeff will be here at the Inn, and he'll be Jeff. Sometimes, he'll be undercover as Wally Krause. When he's Wally, he's going to work for Hank, and he's going to try to prove that Hank killed the vets, and now, he'll probably try to prove that he killed Ed."*

"And the dogs can't like him?"

"Right. The dogs can't be friendly to him when he's Wally."

"But dey duzn't has to be mean to him, right?"

"Right. Just not friendly."

"Okay," said Little Socks. *"I think we're all on board with that. What else is happening?"*

"Well, Harper is on The Escape."

"What?" "Huh?" "How did that happen?" "Trill!"

"Right. And you probably all know that Wyatt and Gene are on The Escape by now, too. The plan was for him to help Ray with the wedding and then get off at some town or another, but I imagine things will change when Harper meets his son."

Ko asked, *"Gene?"*

Tiger Lily replied, *"Wyatt."*

Kali spat at her litter mate, *"Keep up."*

"Shut up."

"You shut up."

"Fat baby."

"Big baby buggy bumper cars."

"You're mean!"

"No, you are!"

Before the girls could dissolve into a full body scratching hissing fight, Mo sat on Kali's butt. Tiger Lily did the same to Ko.

Little Socks said, *"Are you done now?"*

The big girls spit a little, but they didn't say anything.

The kids heard Annie come in. She stopped at the table, lifted the cover a bit and looked in. "I see everyone is here. It looks like you're all getting along now. That's great."

Hank pulled himself out of the water and cursed. He pulled the grenade from his pocket and tossed it into the harbor. It would be worthless now, anyway.

He looked after The Escape, then ran toward his SUV. He had a lot of miles to put on and not a lot of time to do it. He probably wouldn't make it up The Avenue before the police started down.

No. Scratch that. They may already be on the way. He should have brought his emergency pack with him. Too late for that now.

Hank doubled back to the dock and ran past the office, keeping low. He ran down the series of docks with smaller boats until he saw a possibility.

A woman was on the deck of a medium-sized boat. It wasn't big enough to be a yacht, but it was big enough to have a couple of staterooms. It would be faster than The Escape, at least in the short run.

Hank slowed and walked down the access dock, hand in his pocket. He waved with his other hand and called out, "Hey, hello! Is this the right boat?"

"I'm sorry?"

"Is this where I'm supposed to be? To meet Harry and George?"

"Sorry. No Harry or George here. I know just about everyone on this dock. Nobody by that name. Hey, you're all wet. Did you fall in?"

Hank pulled the gun and jumped on deck at the same time. "Just be calm. You're gonna get me out of here."

As the boat pulled out of the harbor, Hank watched the activity in the municipal parking lot. Poor Pete. Too slow again.

Hank could also see The Escape in the distance. It was headed in a northwesterly direction. "Go out a ways, then head south."

25

Pete and Janet had not left the house before Cheryl reached them by phone. Pete raced for the door. "I'm going to pick up Cheryl, get her out of there. Follow me, but don't drive past the Inn."

Janet was well used to jumping when Pete said to do so. Not in their personal lives. He would be met with the fine end of a pool cue had that happened. But they both knew how to differentiate between personal and professional.

Pete swung into the parking lot, multi-tasking as usual. He had Ray on his phone, patched through via radio, one eye out for Hank and his black SUV, and the other on his driving. Cyril stood guard in the passenger seat, nose pressed against first the front window, then the side.

While he took care of business, he talked to Ray. "He's unhinged. Completely. Was he reaching for a pistol?"

"George thinks it could have been a grenade or something like that. Even unhinged, he could see how many people were with us. One pistol wouldn't have made a dent."

"Was anyone hurt?"

"No, but hey, one more thing, George saw a boat leave the harbor not too long after we did. He wondered if it could have been Hank."

"I'll have Cheryl notify the Coast Guard as soon as we clear The Marina. Tell me again who's with you."

"Ten guests."

"And?"

"What?"

"You said Harold told you Hank was killing the vets. Who's Harold?"

"Okay. You got me. I have that last vet. All he wanted to do was get away. I swear, Pete, I was only trying to help him."

"You knew I was looking for him."

"I didn't. I swear. He. . .I found him on board, and I promised to help him get out of town. He recognized Hank."

"Had he told you about Hank before today?"

"No. I swear. Pete, you're my best friend! I would have said something."

"Right. We'll discuss this later. For now, let's focus on getting you out of there."

"Good plan. By the way, what's the plan?"

"Chris is on the way. He's got a couple of boats headed in your direction. They'll escort you back."

"And then what?"

"We need to get Harper somewhere safe."

"What about the rest of us?"

"Hank's running now. He has to be."

"If he's running, why do we have to keep Harper safe?"

"Lots of people want to hear his story."

"Okay. Hey, I'd better clear this channel. Thanks for the help, Pete. Oh, hey, looks like I've got a family reunion on my hands."

"Let me know how that goes."

Marco radioed in. "Boss, we have Hank's SUV. It's here in the lot."

On The Escape, the bubbly ran freely. Ray had relaxed one of his rules, the one about not drinking to excess. Heck, he felt like having one himself. He was happy to see that George and Candice abstained, and, for the most part, Kara and Tank.

As he powered The Escape toward the two Coast Guard cutters, he noticed one turning away. That was probably Chris, headed off in search of Hank, who was probably on that boat after all.

Ray looked back at his guests. Tank was making an effort to get close to Kara. The effort was not quite reciprocated. He wondered what was up with that. They seemed to be a good fit.

He looked around, finally finding Harper with Wyatt and Gene on the foredeck. Gene had been looking a little jumpy. Being with his friend Harper seemed to calm him a bit. He had almost relaxed, allowing himself to drink a beer.

He realized he should probably perform the wedding ceremony before The Escape hit the harbor. Maybe George could take over the wheel. All he had to do was follow the Coast Guard in.

Annie went to Chateau Simon for a mid-afternoon meal minus many of the people she would have joined. Jeff Bennett rode with Marco on the hunt for Hank. Pete was at the office coordinating state and federal resources. Chris was still on the lake. Janet and Cheryl had returned to The Marina to call the Coast Guard and were now checking in with clients. Until everyone was located, Cheryl wouldn't know which boat was missing, if any.

Henrie ordered a bottle of merlot to share and tenderloin medallions with cabernet mushroom sauce; Annie shared the bottle and had the Cornish hen with herb bouquet. Nancy and Sam ordered a bottle of unoaked chardonnay and shared a plate of salmon patties with remoulade sauce.

Annie said, "So what do you think, Henrie? Have we had a week, or not?"

"We have had a week. A profitable one."

"That was a neat trick you pulled. We're making money through tomorrow on that group. Will we get the money before their cards are stopped?"

"Yes. The money has already been deposited in our accounts. And did I tell you dinner tonight is on Frank and Gema?"

"No. When did that happen?"

"They were grateful we alerted Pete to the situation."

"They could have lost thousands."

Nancy asked, "Are you talking about those scavenger hunters? I had a really bad feeling about them. I was at the shop when they made arrangements to 'hunt' in there."

"Really? At the antique shop?"

"Yes. They had an outlandish proposal about getting things out of the cases, taking photos. It just sounded so hinky."

Sam added, "She told me all about it when she got home. It sounded hinky to me, too, so I called Frank."

"What did Frank have to say about it?"

"He appreciated the take on it, said he would talk to Gema about their options. So what happened?"

Annie said, "They were all arrested. Pete found fake jewelry, counterfeit money. . .it would have been awful. Oh, here comes Janet. I asked her to join us."

Janet joined them at the table. "Hi, thanks for coming. It's so good to see you again."

Nancy said, "We don't get here often enough, but now that you're serving these wonderful meals on the weekends, we'll be here more often."

"You're our first customers of the day, and this is our first weekend with these dishes. How are they?"

"The meal is delectable," said Henrie, "as is the wine."

"Great! Annie, did you want to talk to me about something?"

"Yes." Annie pulled out her phone and showed Janet two pictures, one of the jet black momma kitty and the other of three babies.

"She's feral. Isn't she a beauty? She needs a home where she can live outside, mouse to her heart's content, maybe get some extra food and water, and have places for shelter."

"She's beautiful. We've been talking about an outside cat. We weren't thinking feral. We were thinking maybe a cat that could be both inside and outside, but we worried about Simon. We didn't want a bad influence."

Simon appeared, as if by magic, on the windowsill beside the table. Annie turned the phone toward him so he could see. Simon appeared to study the photo, then looked to Janet.

"So maybe you should consider a cat that won't try to influence Simon at all. Simon could watch her through the window, but she wouldn't come close to the house, probably."

"We would need to have her fixed."

"The shelter will take care of that when the babies are weaned. That will give her several days more with the kids while they get used to solid food."

"What about the kids? Do they have homes?"

"No. Are you interested?"

"Oh, I don't know. I would almost want to give them indoor homes."

"They would be safe here, with her to teach them how to live outdoors."

"Oh, I don't know. I'll have to ask Brian."

"Ask Brian what?" said Brian.

"You know how we talked about an outside cat? The shelter has this black beauty. She needs a safe outside home. And she has three babies."

"Three?"

"Aren't they beautiful?"

"Two calicos and an orange tabby?"

Annie said, "The tabby is a boy."

"Can they be fixed?"

"You'll have to promise to do that if you take them out of the shelter before they're old enough."

"Brian, let's go meet them."

"Four cats? How did we go from maybe one cat to definitely four?"

Annie laughed. "You live in Chelsea now."

Sis was happy to be able to stay with all the cats. Not just Tiger Lily. She noticed things were still tentative, but definitely on the mend.

Little Socks asked, *"Where's Chris?"*

"Chris is on the lake."

Mr. Bean asked, *"Why?"*

"That Hank guy went crazy and tried to do something. I don't know what. Get on the boat, shoot people, I don't know."

"He was trying to get Harper."

"Maybe. Chris didn't say. He just had one of his officers drop me off here."

"Will it be dangerous for Chris?"

"He didn't think so. He said he'd see me tonight."

"What about Jeff Bennett? Do you know where he went? He left here in a hurry."

Kali said, *"I watched from the dining room window upstairs. He went pretty fast to the town parking lot. There were police guys out there, and Pete got there, too."*

Ko added, *"He got Cheryl and dropped her off outside the Inn. Janet was waiting for her."*

Tiger Lily said, *"They must have thought it wasn't safe for her to stay at The Marina."*

Sis added, *"I hope Jock's alright."*

"*He'ze prob'ly fine,*" said Sassy Pants. "*He'ze a smart dog. He knows how to duck.*"

"*That's always a good skill,*" said Sis.

Tiger Lily said, "*If they're hunting for Hank, he has to know it. I'll bet Jeff doesn't have to go to work for him now. He won't have to put that beard on.*"

"*Or the pepper oil,*" added Sis. "*That's a good thing.*"

"*So he came here for nothing,*" said Mr. Bean.

Little Socks said, "*No, not really. He'll be able to help with the arrest and stuff.*"

"*That will give the FBI a reason to keep sending him here,*" said Tiger Lily. "*That's good.*"

Mo trilled several times.

Sassy Pants translated. "*He sez he hopes dat Wyatt an' his daddy gots along good.*"

Honey Bear displayed an astuteness that gave the others pause. "*That will be a touchy situation. Harper won't want to get close to him. He might not be angry, but he won't want to go back. Sometimes, you can't go home.*"

Harper recovered from the shock of seeing Gene, seeing a man he knew had been hunting the group of vets, seeing Hank, and the quick get-away.

Now he sat on the foredeck with Gene and Wyatt, catching up with all of the news. Most of it was not good.

"They's all gone?"

"All of them," said Gene. "Even Perry."

"Oh my, oh my. An' I know you say you're my son, but I don't recognize you. You sure he's okay, Gene?"

"Positive. Just like he said, he has something you wrote. He came to town after he heard about the first fire. He was looking for us, but he's been working with the police, trying to find all of us to get us to safety. You, especially."

Harper turned to Wyatt. "How would I know you's my son?"

"You wrote about the murder of that reporter, left it at the house. Mom died. . ."

"She's dead? How?"

"Cancer. Died about a year ago. I went through her things, found what you wrote, and when I heard about the fire, I came right here."

"I'm real sorry to hear she died. Real sorry. She was a good woman." Harper stared at the lake for a while. "So, you found somethin' but that don't make you my son."

"You're right. I can tell you about the swing you made for me, the times you took me to the ballpark. I can tell you what you used to call me. You never liked the name Mom picked for me. You used to call me Why. Sometimes you'd say Why Not, or Why Him or Why Dat."

Harper smiled to himself and nodded. "I'd forgot all about that. I'd forgot a lot of things."

It was Wyatt's turn to nod. "Gene here explained some things to me, like how there's probably no going back for you. That 'home' doesn't mean the same to you as it does to me."

"I guess that'd be right. There's still a chance for you, Gene. You can still go home."

"Nah. I can't go home. I can prob'ly make a home for myself. Go somewhere else. Get a little place, a job. Might be able to hang on to 'em for a while. Maybe."

"I think you ought to give it a shot."

"I think I will. That Boone fella, he said he'd help. He said he'd take me to the state capital, find me a small place and set me up with a friend of his for a job. If I want, anyway."

"I'm thinkin' you oughta do it."

The three were silent for a while.

"What about you, pop? What are you gonna do?"

"I dunno. I need to get back to a city. New York. I had a home there. Had my own bridge. My own crib. You know. It was just boxes, but they was mine."

"It won't be the same without Mal," said Gene. "And Tempo, Ben, Farrell. . ."

"Heck, it won't even be the same without you, kid. You was good to have around, 'specially when my ole back wouldn't work."

"I could come with you. . ."

"No. You got your life to live. Go live it, the best you can." Harper looked at Wyatt. "Hey, Why Dat. What about you?"

Wyatt gave a sad smile. "Well, pop, after I drop you off in the middle of New York City, I'll go on home. I have a life. A job. They were good to give me some time off. I have a girlfriend. She'll be waiting for me."

"You don't have to take me to New York City."

"I want to. It will give us time to talk, and it will probably be the last time, right?"

Harper nodded. "I guess I can live with ya for that long."

It was late afternoon. Mommy and Henrie were home from the winery, but they were downstairs. So were the other cats and Sis. Tiger Lily was alone.

She walked along the shelves in the apartment, reading the titles of Annie's books. She stopped when she found the one she sought.

Carefully, so as not to damage the spine, she pulled at the top until it came away from the other books. She worked at it until the book was free and fell to the floor.

Once on the floor, it was easy. She opened it and used her paws to turn through the pages. Finally, she found the picture.

It was glossy with a black background. The picture itself was bright reds, oranges and yellows.

She sat in front of the picture and gazed at it, fascinated.

That's how Annie found her when she returned from Chateau Simon.

"What's this, big girl?"

Tiger Lily looked up, eyes wide, and pawed the picture.

Annie sat on the floor. "It's a fire dragon. Pretty, isn't it?"

Tiger Lily settled herself between Annie's legs, giving her time to think about the picture. At least, she hoped

Annie was thinking about the picture. Tiger Lily wanted information.

"You know, big girl, it's strange. I talked to Clara, and she said she received some kind of message to order fresh flowers related to dragons. And we've had a few fires this week, haven't we? What do you suppose? Could we call them dragon fires?"

Tiger Lily purred and kneaded Annie's leg. She reached around to pick up the book.

"Let's see. Did you know I'm a fire dragon?"

Tiger Lily blinked twice.

"You didn't? Well, I am. And since you and I belong together, you could probably be a fire dragon also. Do you want me to read about your personality?"

Tiger Lily purred.

"Okay. I'll just hit the high points. Let's see. You're proud, and you have a never-ending supply of self-confidence. You're highly intellectual. I imagine that's why you've been able to learn to read and write. You're determined, you're strong-minded, and you set very high standards for yourself."

Tiger Lily purred louder.

Annie read a little further. "Uh oh. With every positive comes a negative. You're quick to criticize people – I guess that includes cats – who try to make a fool out of you. Is that what happened this week? It says here that you can be straight-to-the point, not very diplomatic, and if you think you've been insulted, it will take a long time for you to trust those people or cats again."

Tiger Lily looked down at the floor. This was so true.

"Look, it says here your views are highly valued, and you're prepared to work long hours to get what you need. It also says you hate to be kept waiting. You're impatient."

Tiger Lily waggled her head from side to side. Maybe.

"Last thing, then we're done for a while, okay? This says you have a lot of faith in your own abilities. You can be a winner, but if you don't win, you'll bounce back and pick up the pieces again."

Tiger Lily purred and settled into Annie's lap. Annie settled in, too. She loved having the big girl in her lap. And she had more to say.

"No matter what you think about the fires, and bad things that might happen, fire dragons are on this world for good. We protect those who can't protect themselves. You remember that."

26

Ray didn't have an option to stop and conduct a wedding ceremony in the middle of the lake. Instead, he made do with that he had. George.

George took the wheel, keeping pace with the Coast Guard escort, while Ray gathered the wedding party on deck.

"Let's at least get this part right," he said.

Don and Suellen, now two and a half sheets to the wind, stood in front of him.

"Hey," said Don, "George has the vows and the rings."

"Jock, go get the stuff from George."

Jock went up, barked happily, pawed George's pocket, and to the surprise of no one, returned with rings and the vows. The vows were a little slobbery. Thank goodness, the rings were in a box.

Ray said, "Dear people on a boat, we're gathered here today in the sight of lots of folks who don't know this couple at all, and they wish to say their vows. Let's hear them."

Don faced Suellen, rocking back and forth just a bit, "I promise to love you, um," he looked at the notes. They swam in front of his eyes. "That's it. I promise to love you, baby." He smiled, a drunk, happy smile.

Suellen leaned into him and said, "I know."

She turned back to Ray, who said, "Without further ado, I declare you man and woman. Um, husband and wife. Um, yeah. We'll go with that last one. The two of you may kiss one another if you want."

They wanted, and the deed was done.

Candice served champagne, and the party continued.

Harper, Wyatt and Gene watched from the foredeck. They clinked beer bottles at the end of the nuptials.

Pete answered his cell. "Hey, Scott, what do you have for me?"

Scott, a dispatcher at the Coast Guard station, said, "A fishing boat pulled a woman from the lake. She's got guts. Swam for what she thinks was at least forty five minutes before they saw her."

"Is she the woman Cheryl identified as the missing boat owner?"

"She is. She identified Hank, too. At the time he threw her overboard, he was headed south. He was out, maybe a couple miles, into the lake."

"He could be anywhere. Is the woman alright?"

"She's great, considering. Scared. Mad. Tired. Said she was just about done, until she saw that fishing boat."

"Have you told Chris?"

"Yeah. He's headed that way, but he doesn't think he'll find him."

Candice ran up the steps to their apartment. She had bags of carry-out from Sassy P's. Inside, she heard George and Tank yelling at one another.

"What game is it?" she asked Kara.

"Fortnight. What else?"

"Well, we may as well go ahead and eat. They'll be at this for hours. So, what did you think about the boat trip?"

"Besides the fact that it was too short? That we didn't get to the middle of the lake? That we couldn't swim? That we were nearly killed?"

"Yeah. Besides all that."

"I can't wait to come back!"

Suellen was sound asleep. That was how Don put it. Sarah laughed. "She's passed out, Don. Why don't we take her upstairs?"

"It's so nice here on the porch. It won't hurt. She's comfortable."

Percy laughed. "You're going to have stories to tell your children, but first, you'll have to remind Suellen."

Sis took Chris's spot in the bed. Annie woke when she jumped down and trotted to the kitchen.

Chris followed Sis back to the bedroom. "Sorry I'm so late."

"Did you get him?"

"No. He got away. He could be anywhere."

"At least he won't be here."

"We can hope."

"Everyone knows him here."

"Think about Jeff. A lot of people know him, too, but they didn't recognize him. Well, at least not everybody."

"Not at first, but today, I kept hearing people say how much that Wally guy looked like him, and wasn't it funny they came to town the same weekend."

"Well, he would have fooled Hank."

"For a minute."

"Don't tell Jeff."

"Wouldn't dream of it. Are you sleeping in tomorrow or going to church?"

"Ask me tomorrow."

"Actually, it's already tomorrow."

"I'm sleeping now. . . ."

Nancy and Sam popped through the kitchen door. "Good morning, Henrie," said Nancy. "Can I help with breakfast?"

"I do not need your help, but I am happy for your company. Please help yourselves to coffee while I finish in the dining room."

"What's the eats?" asked Sam.

"The usual meats and breads – too much of everything – and asiago and spinach quiche tartlets. I also have a wonderful quinoa creation. You will love it, Nancy."

Seven cats and a giant schnauzer appeared in the kitchen, ready for morning bacon. "Nancy, if you do not mind. . ."

"Of course, Henrie. Come on, kids. Grammy will get your bacon. You, too, Honey Bear."

Annie yawned on her way in. "I've even had a shower and I still want to go back to bed. I don't know how you do it, Henrie."

"Power naps in the afternoon."

"Really? When do you find time?"

"That is why they are called power naps. They take relatively little time."

"I'll have to try that."

Sam said, "What did Chris have to say? Did he get Hank?"

"No. Hank got away. He could be anywhere."

Henrie sighed. "At least we had good news this weekend. We will see our wedding guests off to their honeymoon.

Nancy asked, "Where are they going?"

Annie answered. "I think someplace safe. Niagara Falls? Las Vegas?"

"Those places aren't safe," said Sam.

Henrie said. "Apparently, they are safer than Chelsea."

"Well, that could be the case."

Nancy asked, "Will there be a picnic after church today?"

"Yeah," said Annie. "Laila is making most of the food. We helped her with money. I think Felicity and Trudie are bringing fried chicken, and Jerry made pies."

Nancy said, "I just love Chelsea on a Sunday afternoon."

Don and Suellen brought their luggage to the foyer and headed to the dining room for breakfast. Percy and Sarah were already eating.

"You have to try these tartlet quiches. They are to die for!"

"Don't say that!" said Suellen. "You might be calling some bad luck our way."

Kara was also at the table. "So, are you ready to go? Niagara Falls! Wow!"

"We booked it because it has an element of danger, and we wanted excitement," said Suellen.

Don added, "So this morning we changed our reservations. We're going to Fort Wayne, Indiana."

Honey Bear finished his bacon and sat back, cleaning his paws and ears. He looked over at Tiger Lily. *"Did you hear anything? About the boat? What happened?"*

"Hank got away, but we haven't heard how it went. We should go listen to the guests, but in my experience, they don't usually talk about it. We'll probably have to wait for Jock."

Kali and Ko said at the same time, *"Wyatt just came in."* *"Wyatt's in the dining room."*

Eight cats and a dog sneaked from the kitchen to underneath the detective table. To be honest, Sis's nose was under the table. Not so much the rest of her body. They were rewarded with a conversation.

Kara asked, "So, Wyatt, how did it go?"

"Oh, it went okay." Wyatt helped his plate before expounding. "Gene pretty much told me what to expect. He was right. Dad, at first, didn't recognize me. He kind of wanted me to prove I was me. Then he didn't really want anything to do with me."

"So. . .is that how you left it? You just. . .left?"

"If he shows up here this morning, I'm going to drive him back to New York. Drop him off. It will probably be the last time we talk."

"What do you mean?" asked Sarah. "If he shows up."

"He said that would be okay, but when we got off the boat, Gene told me not to be disappointed if he doesn't show. Now that he's not hiding from a maniac, he'll be able to get a ride back, one way or another. Probably hitching with a truck driver."

"So you're just going to wait?"

"Yeah. I'll hang out here until two o'clock or so, then I'll take off. I hope he shows. But at least, you know, I got to see him. I know he's as happy as he's ever going to be. That has to be it for me."

"Did he stay on The Escape last night? You could go over there and pick him up."

"He did, but I won't go there. This has to be his decision."

Don said, "I'm glad it all worked out for you. It made the wedding kind of special, you know, to have a reunion of sorts."

Percy laughed. "Your wedding was all kinds of special for lots of reasons. We'll all have stories to tell our kids and grandkids."

Sis pulled her head out from under the table. She heard Chris on the second floor. She went upstairs to find Chris and Jeff on the computer in the second floor's common area.

"Hey, girl. Did you get bacon?"

Sis nodded, sure that Chris understood her. All the times he said he wasn't going to learn to communicate with her, he was being silly. Or did he really not know? Oh, well. He was still a nice human.

"Henrie's pretty special, isn't he? Do you want to go out on The Escape today?"

Sis, sitting beside him, stood and hopped a bit, to let him know that yes, she wanted very much to do that. She could spend time with Jock!

Wyatt sat on the front porch of the Inn, his feet on the railing, soaking in the sun and the temperature in the high seventies. The week had been beautiful. Sunshine, for the most part, moderate early summer temperatures, a light breeze from the lake, and a town that was at turns quaint, cute and trendy.

He recalled his early days in town, not willing to trust anyone and, in turn, finding that people could not trust him. If it happened again, he would make a much different appearance. The problem was, he was unsure who was planning and executing the murders.

Now that he knew, it was clear that no one he had met could possibly have been involved.

He would have to plan another trip, a pleasure trip, with his girlfriend. Maybe, now that this was behind him, he would propose, she would say yes, and they could honeymoon here.

Not on The Escape.

He had enough of that to last a lifetime.

Now it remained to be seen if he would be able to spend time with his father or not. He had a lot to say. Things he wanted to thank him for. Things he was proud about. He didn't need to dwell on his father leaving.

When that happened, he was almost a teenager. He could take care of his mother. They managed. Had a good life. His mother remarried, and things were fine until she got sick. That was bad, but his father's presence wouldn't have fixed that. May have only added to the problems.

No, he wouldn't dwell on that.

He'd tell his father the good things. That he did well in school, played baseball and basketball. Got a partial scholarship to college. Had a good job, a great relationship.

If he could get an address – he'd ask about general mail delivery – he would send pictures from time to time. If that would be okay.

If his father asked questions, he would answer. He didn't expect questions to come, but they might.

If he wanted to talk about his friends, that would be great. Hearing what his father thought of his friends would tell him a lot about what his father, himself, was like.

He could tell him that he got to know Gene, and how glad Gene was to have Harper for a friend.

Well, that was all pie-in-the-sky. His father may not even show.

He was ready. His car was packed; his keys were turned in; Henrie gave him a cooler of sandwiches, salads and drinks for the road. Enough for two. Just in case.

He hoped his father would come before noon. Otherwise, he might shy away from the group of people that were apparently going to gather on the private beach behind the Inn.

Wyatt's eyes snapped open when he heard someone walk up the steps.

"Well, Why Dat, are we a'goin' or not?"

Gene sat with Boone, Hilly and their sons in the back pew at church. Normally, the family sat in the middle, but

Boone thought the back would be more comfortable for Gene.

They listened as Pastor Teresa went through the service. Gene participated, at least to the point of standing and sitting. Gene wasn't about to sing, and Boone, in solidarity, held the hymnal but didn't open his mouth through the songs.

Hilly and the boys, though, they sang. Gene enjoyed the harmonies. Soprano and two tenors. He figured Boone would have come in on those low notes.

Pastor Teresa picked an appropriate passage for the week. It seemed to strike him that way, at least. He looked in the printed bulletin. She was reading from Psalm 39.

[1] I said, "I will guard my ways,
Lest I sin with my tongue;
I will restrain my mouth with a muzzle,
While the wicked are before me."
[2] I was mute with silence,
I held my peace even from good;
And my sorrow was stirred up.
[3] My heart was hot within me;
While I was musing, the fire burned.
Then I spoke with my tongue:
[4] "Lord, make me to know my end,
And what is the measure of my days,
That I may know how frail I am.
[5] Indeed, You have made my days as handbreadths,
And my age is as nothing before You;
Certainly every man at his best state is but vapor. Selah
[6] Surely every man walks about like a shadow;
Surely they busy themselves in vain;
He heaps up riches,
And does not know who will gather them.

[7] *"And now, Lord, what do I wait for?*
My hope is in You.
[8] *Deliver me from all my transgressions;*
Do not make me the reproach of the foolish.
[9] *I was mute, I did not open my mouth,*
Because it was You who did it.
[10] *Remove Your plague from me;*
I am consumed by the blow of Your hand.
[11] *When with rebukes You correct man for iniquity,*
You make his beauty melt away like a moth;
Surely every man is vapor. Selah
[12] *"Hear my prayer, O Lord,*
And give ear to my cry;
Do not be silent at my tears;
For I am a stranger with You,
A sojourner, as all my fathers were.
[13] *Remove Your gaze from me, that I may regain strength,*
Before I go away and am no more."

This was new for Gene. Well, not new, so much as forgotten. In the recesses of his memory, he recalled going to another church, in another town, in another time, with a family that was no longer his. Would never be his again.

Maybe, some day, he would write a letter. Let them know he was alright. Maybe.

First things first. Tomorrow, Boone would drive him to a city in the middle of the state, introduce him to a friend. Get him a room, make sure a job was set.

He'd see how that went, first. Maybe he'd go somewhere to talk to people. Other vets. Maybe a counselor. Maybe. Maybe not. He'd see how it went.

Maybe he'd keep that Bible Boone put into his duffle. It was a new duffle, with new clothes, personal items, things he would need if he was going to make it in the city. He found some cash at the bottom of the duffle, hidden inside that Bible.

Maybe he'd keep it.

Maybe.

Chris, Pete, Jeff and Ray were on The Escape, out in the middle of the lake, enjoying a fine Sunday morning with a cooler of beer and some fishing gear.

Jock, Cyril and Sis were on the foredeck, getting some sun without human supervision. They had water, dog food and a thick blanket on which to lie.

Jeff said, "I'm thankin' my lucky stars I don't have to move into that cockroach and flea-infested dump tomorrow. I'll probably go to the office, though. He gave me keys on Friday. He might not realize who I am, and he might call in."

Pete said, "Are you going in disguise, as Wally?"

"I don't know. What do you think? I'm kind of out here on a limb. Have never been in this situation before."

Chris said, "Everyone in town knows who you are now. I think you can ditch the disguise. And besides, Hank will be calling in, not stopping in."

"You're right. Wally is officially dead."

Ray asked, "When is that forensic team coming in, to look at Mem's computers?"

"They're so high-tech these days they don't even have to come in. They're working on it already, from somewhere out west."

"How long will you stay in town, at the office?"

"I'll go in and look around, go through the files, a computer if there is one. I can forward the phone to my cell, so I can get the calls for an indeterminate period of time. I don't know when things will start to close down, you know, the phone, electricity, water. The Bureau has okayed my being here for the time being, to see what I can come up with."

Jock told the story of the Saturday afternoon boat trip. As Jock was wont to do, the story was embellished. But only a little.

"We were supposed to be out until after dark. You know, a trip to the middle of the lake, then swimming – I would have been the lifeguard – then the wedding and dinner. But that was derailed."

"By Hank," said Sis.

"Right. First, I had to save everybody. I saw Hank on the dock. You know Ray doesn't want him to be anywhere close to The Marina. So when I saw him, I knew he was up to no good."

"What did you do?" asked Sis.

"I jumped to the dock and ran toward him."

"You ran toward the danger?" Sis was impressed.

Cyril gagged.

"Yes. I ran toward him and pushed him into the water. He would have killed us for sure if I hadn't. Then I ran back to the boat. George had already cast off and Ray was gunning up. I had to jump, oh, it must have been ten feet, while they were moving."

"Oh, my!" said Sis.

Cyril rose to get a drink of water.

"Then, I had to watch our flank. Ray was doing a good job getting us out of there, and George was doing a good job keeping everyone down. I had to keep an eye on Hank. He got out of the water and then got confused."

"How was that?"

"First, he ran toward the parking lot, then he turned and came back toward the dock. I had to bark real loud to let George know — I was down by him, you see. Ray was up top."

"Did George understand?"

"I think so. He sat up and looked toward Hank. He could see him running toward us, then turning to go toward the other docks. He got binoculars out and watched a boat leave the harbor. He told Ray he thought it was Hank, and Ray told the Coast Guard."

"Did he chase you?"

"We thought he was going to, but then he went in another direction."

Sis said, *"He was probably scared of you."*

"I'm sure he was."

Cyril decided it was time to help Pete catch fish.

Kara threw her bags into her car. She turned to give Candice a bear hug. "This was the best vacation EVER! I can't wait to come again!"

"I hear Tank can't wait for you to come back, either. So…what did you think about him?"

"Fun guy. But he got a little 'bossy' yesterday. Tried to shame me into staying an extra day. I want to see him again, but we'll see. What's for certain is that I want to come back. Soon! This is a great town!"

Tank joined George and Candice at the Sunday afternoon beach picnic on the KaliKo Inn's private beach. "I still don't understand why Kara couldn't stay a little longer."

"She has to go to work tomorrow. It will be nearly ten before she gets home as it is."

"She could have taken an extra day from work."

"Tank," said Candice, "this is exactly the way to ruin a relationship with a strong woman."

"What?"

"It's probably a good thing she had to leave. It will give you time to think about it. Think about her. Decide what you want from a relationship."

"I don't understand…"

George intervened. "Stick with me, buddy. I'll try to 'splain it to you over time."

Candice said, "Let's just hope it doesn't take you as long to learn as it did George."

Sassy Pants and Mr. Bean loved the Sunday afternoon beach picnics. Plenty of food dropped onto the ground in front of them – certainly by accident – and they were able to play at the edge of the water. Tiger Lily and Little Socks turned into little parents when they did that, sitting in the sand close to the edge of the water, making sure the young ones didn't go too far.

As they watched, Little Socks cleared her throat.

"Yes?" asked Tiger Lily.

"I just wanted to say I'm sorry. I should have understood what you wanted to do. We have to work hard for humans to understand us."

"Thanks. I appreciate the apology. At the time, I didn't know what else to do."

"It worked."

"To be honest, it didn't. Henrie had already taken care of it."

"But you didn't know that."

"I didn't, but I'll probably not do anything like that again."

They remained silent for a while. Eventually, Little Socks said, *"I'm also sorry we stopped detecting. We left all of that to you."*

"Moriah helped. And Honey Bear."

"I know. We — you know, the experienced ones — we should have been with you every step of the way. And because we weren't, we didn't get to meet the momma kitty and her babies."

"You may be able to. They'll go to Chateau Simon, and sometimes Mommy takes us there."

"Not very often."

"It will happen."

Mo and Moriah trotted up to sit beside them. Mo trilled.

Tiger Lily looked around. None of his translators were nearby.

Moriah said, *"He wanted me to come with him, but I don't know what he's trying to say."*

"Try it again, Mo. I'll try to understand what you're saying."

Mo took a different approach. He got low to the ground and crawled on his stomach for several feet, turning his head from side to side. Then he went to Little Socks, touching her with a front paw, and did the same with Moriah. Finally, he looked at Tiger Lily, face expectant.

Tiger Lily put her thinking cap on. Finally, she said, *"I think you're saying you want to train to be a cat burglar. Did I get it?"*

Mo smiled. She got it.

"Okay. We all need to be able to multi-task, and there are times we need more than one burglar. Or two. What do you think, Little Socks?"

Little Socks looked at the sand. Her special skill had already been usurped by Moriah, and now Mo? *"I suppose it would be okay. If I train him."*

Tiger Lily sighed. She was glad she hadn't decided to quit. This detecting business was fun, and it was only going to get better.

Nancy and Sam shared a table with Frank and Mem. "What a week!" said Nancy. "I can't remember when there has been so much going on."

"Not all at once," said Mem. "I will never get over the ignorance of some people."

"Which people?" asked Sam.

"Those scavenger hunters, for twelve. Hank. I can't believe how often people think they can get away with audacious acts."

"Especially here," said Frank. "A small town like this sticks together. We talk. We see things."

"Hank, of all people, should know that."

Nancy shook her head. "Hank has always put himself above the law, so to speak. He's often done outrageous, even illegal things, and he never faced a consequence."

Mem said, "He will now. Even Hank can't get away with murder."

"It will have to be proven," said Frank. "I wonder if Pete has the evidence."

"He probably does, and with what the FBI can find from the web searches, they should get what they need."

"There's also the matter of the murder of that reporter."

Sam shook his head. "I'll bet that one will go unsolved. Remember, the one who could actually put Hank in that alley is dead now. He should have stopped while he was ahead. He got the important one first."

"Hank's too stupid to know when he's ahead," said Nancy. "At least he's gone now."

Frank said, "Don't put all your eggs in that basket. He could come back."

"To do what?"

"Who knows."

Geraldine sat with Henrie and Annie. She sipped a wine cooler and looked out at the lake. "Is that The Escape? Headed back in?"

Annie looked. Sure enough, the rainbow-colored yacht was nearing the harbor.

"Great! They might get here before the food is gone."

"They might," said Geraldine. "I just remembered the first time I came to your private beach. Do you remember that?"

Henrie chuckled. "That was quite a day, Geraldine."

"It was. I was haughty, angry, nasty. It feels better today."

"Yes, it does," said Annie. "It surely does."

Geraldine smiled. "I learned one very important thing that day."

"What's that?"

"Never, never, ever take your mother on in a fight."

"You learned that? That day?"

"Let me clarify. That is the first time I had a thought that perhaps I should not take her on. I recall, however, that it took a time or two for that to sink in."

"My mother has the great ability to make people think she's an idiot. Then, lo and behold, she's got her hands around your neck at just the right moment."

"You're a lot like her, you know."

"I don't understand why people keep saying that."

Henrie had one of his rare, superlative laughs.

28

Monday morning ended the weather's good streak. The Avenue was flooded. Literally.

Rain fell at a rate of half an inch an hour. Storm sewers were overtaxed, backing water up in the streets and flooding the sidewalks.

Hilly ran into the Inn from her car without using an umbrella. Inside, she shook her clothes and hair with both hands. "I declare! We haven't had rain like this in months!"

Henrie asked, "Do you need a towel?"

"No. I'll dry out. I will take coffee, though."

As they walked through to the kitchen, Hilly asked, "Who's still here, Henrie?"

"Jeff Bennett is the sole remaining guest. I will attend his room."

"Do you have guests coming today?"

"Not today. Most of the rooms will be in use by tomorrow and Wednesday. Tell me, did Boone take Gene to the city?"

"They left this morning."

"Was Gene still receptive?"

"Receptive, yes, but I think a little scared. He hasn't had a job or a place to live in a long time."

"My hope is that it goes well."

"Boone intends to stay in touch. Hey, Henrie, what do you think about the situation with veterans in general here in Chelsea?"

"I do not know, Hilly. I do not believe we have homeless veterans in town. At least, not now. But I have talked to several people about our lack of services. Many people, including Boone, as you know, George and others, seem to believe there are hidden issues. Physical injuries, emotional injuries. We have not done what we need to do to provide support to veterans or their families. Or the families of those on active duty."

"What can we do about that?"

"I believe it will be a larger issue. Local groups will have to consider the issues, come up with plans, perhaps approach the town council or county government. Frankly, I do not know where to start."

Chris and Jeff were real men. They didn't need no umbrellas. Chris parked as close to the door as he could. It abutted the sidewalk, straight in from the concrete. The storm drain was filled; water ran freely on the street and covered the sidewalk.

Chris said, "It looks like the water will go right through the door when we open it."

"Great."

They waded through the water, rain running down their faces, and Jeff unlocked the office door. Sure enough, water rushed through the door, stopping about two feet in.

He walked in, Chris and Sis on his heels. The humans held their noses. Sis refused to come all the way in.

Jeff reached around until he found a light switch. "No wonder it's so dark in here. There are no windows."

Chris said, "Get in here, Sis. It's raining out there."

Sis whined. She backed out of the door, staying in the rain. Her dark gray coat was soaked.

"Okay. Jeff, I'm taking her to the truck."

When Chris returned, dripping, Jeff said, "Too bad it's raining so hard. This place needs to be aired out."

"What is that smell?"

"I don't know. It's not a body, but it could be a backed-up toilet or something like that."

Chris, holding his nose again, eased into the room and walked to a door at the back. He opened it and found the source. "This toilet has been backed up for...um...a while."

Jeff looked at the floor. "Mice droppings, too. Or rats. You know, it's a wonder no one ever smelled this on Hank. This is the kind of odor that sticks to clothing."

"I don't think Hank spent time here. Ed, his manager, didn't hang around town much, and he lived upstairs. He probably had a horrible odor about him, but no one noticed."

"Let's get what we need and get the heck out of here."

"What do we need?"

"I'll check these filing cabinets. Take a look through the desk."

"Okay. Do we need boxes?"

"We'll see."

Jeff opened file drawers and flipped through folders. "This is all old stuff. Musty, mildewed. We probably need to take it, but so far, I don't see anything pertinent to today."

Chris looked through the desk. "Whiskey, empty bottle of whiskey, empty bottle of whiskey, cards, porno magazines – lots of those – and I don't even want to think about what these rags were used for. Back to my question. Do we need boxes?"

"You want to go get boxes, Chris?"

"Yes! Please! I'll drive to the Café and get some from their Monday deliveries. You know, before they get thrown into the alley. Today, a box thrown into the alley becomes a useless box in a matter of minutes."

Jeff laughed. "And it will smell better, right?"

"Right! I'll be back as soon as I can. Well…I'll be back. I'll bring coffee."

Pete checked in with his source at the State Police. "No, Pete. We haven't seen him; haven't heard anything about him. It's possible he's in another state by now."

"And it's possible he's not. What's your best guess?"

"We've taken a look at his financials. He doesn't have much in the accounts we know about. So my best guess is that he has accounts at one or more other banks, out of our jurisdiction. As long as he has access to money, he can keep running or he could come back for…well…I don't know what. Maybe his money is all in cash, and maybe it's stashed in Chelsea. I wouldn't discount that possibility."

"That's what I was afraid of."

Pete hung up and called Marco. "Hey, let's call in a couple of reserves, put them on patrol. I'm afraid Hank may come back."

"Why? What could he possibly want?"

"He's crazy, man. Just plain bat-crap crazy."

Pete looked out the window. "Hey, Cyril, Chris and Sis just went into the Café. I thought they were with Jeff. I don't like leaving him out there alone."

Cyril, wise because Pete told him everything he was thinking, agreed.

Annie realized Chris and Jeff had said nothing about boxes. She got the Inn's SUV and drove to the back of the Café. There, she ran through puddles that threatened to turn into a pond, knocked on the back door and was let in by the cook. She shook off the water as she stepped over several empty boxes.

"Are you done with these?"

"Yep. I was waiting for a break in the rain to take them out back."

"If it's okay, I'll take a few."

"Be my guest."

Annie picked five that seemed to be the right shape and size for files and other office things, ran back and forth to the SUV, then took off, cursing her wet clothes.

She drove the short distance to Hank's office and noticed Chris's vehicle was missing. The front door was open, though. Jeff must be inside.

She picked up the box on the passenger seat and ran in, using the box as an umbrella. Inside, she nearly gagged. "Pee-yoo!" she said, directing the comment to Jeff. Wait a minute. That wasn't Jeff.

Cyril shook himself off inside the Café door. He was happy to see Sis without Jock. *"Hi. What are you doing here?"*

"We came to get boxes and coffee."

"What for? I mean, why boxes?"

"Chris said Jeff wants to take some files and things. I wasn't inside, so I'm not sure."

"Why not? Did Chris leave you in the car?"

"He did, but because I wanted him to. That place stinks!"

"Eew. And I probably have to go in there."

"Why?"

"The State Police think Hank might come back."

"Then we'd better go. We left Jeff by himself."

"There go Pete and Chris to the kitchen. They're probably getting the boxes now."

Pete knocked water off his uniform before he got to the coffee bar. Jeff leaned against it, talking to Trudie. "Is Jeff at the office?"

"Yep. Man, that place stinks to high heaven! I don't know how Hank – or Ed, actually – could stand it. Anyway, I needed fresh air and we need boxes for files and things. Thought I would take coffee back at the same time."

"Just so you know, the State Police think it's possible Hank is coming back here."

"Why? What could he hope to accomplish?"

"I don't know. Pick up a stash of cash or incriminating evidence, get another shot in at someone, do something stupid and get himself killed. . .who knows."

"Well, help me get boxes and we'll both go back. Trudie, please add a cup for Pete and put these in a carrier. I'll pick them up on the way out."

Pete held the door as Chris went into the kitchen. Chris said, "Hi, guys. Trudie said your deliveries came; I just wanted to get some boxes."

"Sorry, man. Annie took the best ones already."

"What?"

"Annie. She left a few minutes ago. Took the best ones."

"Huh. She's always been smarter than me. Okay. Thanks."

In the car, Pete took a call. It was the FBI forensics team.

"We found something really interesting. Have Agent Bennett give us a call as soon as he can."

"I will, but why didn't you just call him?"

"We tried a couple of times. It went to voice mail. We thought he would be very interested, so. . .anyway, have him call."

Pete hit the wipers, lights and siren, pulling out in front of Chris and hotfooting it to Hank's office.

Chris hit the gas, following Pete as closely as he could. Even in town, the spray from Pete's tires made it difficult for him to see. When they stopped at Hank's office, his heart sank. Annie's SUV was parked in front of the door. She had to be inside with Jeff, and whoever belonged to the other vehicle. The one pulled to the side of the building.

The door to the office was still open. Chris could see the outline of a man just inside. It was hard to say who it was. The rain wasn't lessening; it seemed to intensify.

The man turned. He recognized Annie. She was held at the neck in front of him, a pistol to her head.

Hank. Hank was here, and he had failed both Annie and Jeff.

Pete pointed to Chris. His meaning was clear. Stay in the car. No arguments.

He summoned Marco on the radio. "Get to Hank's office. Get everyone. Call the State Police. Tell them we have a hostage situation."

Pete opened the door and exited the car, letting Cyril out behind him. Cyril stayed low, ready to run, but knew better than to go forward now.

Pete crouched behind the open door, weapon pointed. The rain continued to pour. Pete was soaked; Cyril was soaked from the rain coming down and from the puddle he crouched in.

Pete raised his voice to be heard over the rain. "Hank, you don't want to do this."

Hank sneered and yelled, "Yes I do. I came back to get a few things, but if I can't do that, I'll go down fighting. And I'll take this perpetual thorn in my behind with me."

"She has nothing to do with this."

"She does. She just doesn't know it."

"Why don't you take this opportunity to tell her?"

"She needs to talk to that no good father of hers. He knows."

"He's dead, Hank, or did you forget that?"

"Then she can join him in Hades and ask."

"Okay, Hank. Tell me what you want. Let's deal."

Marco and two other cars, sirens blazing, screeched to a halt. Pete, from the rear view mirror, saw Marco direct officers around the building. A state trooper must have been on the interstate close to Chelsea. It, too, came quickly and braked behind Pete. The trooper mimicked Pete's stance.

Hank yelled, "You aren't helping by having all this firepower, Pete."

"Tell me what you want."

"I want to back up, get a thing or two from my office, and then I want to leave, quietly, and without being followed."

"I can't promise the second, but give me time to talk to some people. What do you need from the office?"

"I'm just going to back up and get it."

"Let Annie go, then get it."

Hank laughed. "I know how this works, Pete. She's gonna help me."

Hank disappeared, backing into the dark interior and closing the door. Pete took the opportunity to yell to the trooper. "See this guy here? In the SUV? He's not police. Get him out of the vehicle and behind the lines."

He watched from his other rear view mirror to make sure it happened. At least Chris didn't argue. He and Sis went quickly, not happily, behind the police cars and into the laundromat across the street.

Pete spoke softly to Cyril. "Watch for your opening. Don't wait for me."

Cyril, alert, and never taking his eyes off the door, huffed.

Pete spoke again to the state trooper. "There's another man in there, Jeff Bennett, with the FBI. I don't know his situation."

The trooper had opened Pete's passenger door and crouched there, getting every bit as wet as Pete. "You need to let me take over now. Stay here, but let me do the talking from here on out."

"Roger that." On the radio, he said, "Marco?"

"Boss."

"Where are we?"

"You can see an officer at each side. Two in the back."

"Can he get into that apartment from his office?"

"I don't think so. I think the only way in is those stairs up the side of the building. There's a back door. Nothing else on the outside. Not even a window."

"Basement?"

"Don't know."

Pete looked at the trooper. "How many troopers on their way in?"

"Several cars headed this way, but no one is close. The closest one is at least fifteen minutes out. Tell me the situation."

"Hank Jenson, that's who you'll be talking to, is a fugitive. He has us, you guys and the feds looking for him. Woman is a local, her name's Annie Mack. Current charges on Jenson include several murders, arson, kidnapping, a decades-old murder outside an Army base in another state. Feds have something on a forensic search, but I don't know what, yet."

"Any idea what he's after in the office?"

"No. The agent was getting ready to clean out the files. Doubt he's had a chance to look at anything."

"Money?"

"Maybe. Apparently, he doesn't have much in the accounts we were able to find."

"Anything else I need to know?"

"This Jenson, Hank, he hates Annie Mack with a vengeance. Not sure why."

"That can't be good."

"What about his request to leave?"

"Not gonna happen."

Pete cursed under his breath.

The trooper changed his position. He moved to the other side of Chris's SUV and opened the passenger door for coverage.

The door opened again. Annie appeared, again held by the neck and again with a gun to her head. Pete thought he could see the strap of a bag over Hank's shoulder, but he couldn't be certain.

Hank yelled, "Pete, we're leaving now. I'm taking her; she's driving; you will not follow."

The trooper, voice raised over the rain, said, "You're talking to me now. That's not gonna happen."

Hank's head turned to see the trooper. "No, it is. I got what I came for. I'm leaving."

While the trooper talked to Hank, Pete concentrated on Annie's face. Rain or not, stress or not, she seemed in control. She looked him in the eye, trying to tell him something. What?

Her eyes flitted down to Cyril, back up, down, up.

Pete realized that Hank, holding Annie with his right arm, was now facing left. Hank would have to rely on his peripheral vision to see him, and that was partially blocked by Annie's head. He whispered, "Cyril, can you get over there?"

Cyril huffed and moved. On his belly, he moved further to Hank's right, sloshing as quietly as he could, then moved slowly forward.

Pete forced himself to keep his eyes on Annie, who apparently forced herself to keep her eyes on him. When Cyril reached the best position, he rose quickly and lunged toward Hank, closing his teeth around Hank's right calf.

Hank screamed, Annie twisted and dropped to the ground, Cyril hung on, and two officers ran from each side of the building to cover Hank and take him into custody.

Pete ran to Annie, helped her up and pushed her to run toward the car. He continued into the building. "Jeff! Jeff! Are you here?"

Jeff didn't answer, but Pete found him.

Chris went through several feelings, what he referred to as the top arc of Annie's feeling rainbow. Sadness. Anger. Scare. He felt the colors, too. Blue. Red. Green. They meshed together, pulsing, vibrating, causing him to be dizzy and nauseated.

Fists clenched, he stood at the open door to the laundromat, Sis in front of him. She refused to come in out of the rain. Behind him, he intuited rather than saw ten or twelve people pushing into the windows, watching the action.

The scene rushed past. Nothing slow about it. Rain pouring down. Annie at the doorway, gun to her head. Pete in a crouched position, giving orders to his men. Rain pouring down. Annie at the doorway, gun to her head. Hank giving orders to Pete. Annie at the doorway, gun to her head.

Now gone. Annie was gone. The gun was probably still to her head. State Trooper moving, to get a better angle. How could he see? Rain pouring down. Annie still gone. Pete still crouched, Trooper still crouched. Annie back in the doorway, gun to her head. What was Annie doing? Signaling Pete?

Chris sensed rather than heard Sis whine.

He concentrated. Annie keeping eye contact with Pete. What were they doing? Cyril's head now in view. Good grief! What was he doing?

Cyril leaping, Annie spinning, Pete running, pushing Annie out of the way, Annie running. To him. Annie was running to him!

Chris didn't hesitate. He ran to her.

Sis couldn't see over the cars like Chris. She paced back and forth, in front of him, in front of the laundromat, in the rain, through the puddles. She could see Annie's face in the doorway, but nothing else.

She got low. Now she could see Cyril from underneath the cars.

Cyril was crouched, nearly but not quite on his belly. In the rain. In the puddles. Now he was moving. Slowly. He was moving slowly.

Oh, help him! Someone please help him!

She stayed low to watch his movements from underneath the cars. When he jumped, she jumped. What was he doing?

What a brave boy!

29

Annie couldn't believe it. They always had a rain-day location for the block party, but in the several years they had done it, they had only had to use that option one time.

This month, in the balmy month of June, the party was on the town park's beach. This was their annual Taste of Chelsea.

Always held on the last day of every other month – this month it was on a Saturday – perfect – the party was a way to bring the community together for a good cause. The cause for this party was veterans' issues.

True to her word, Geraldine had investigated options and found the National Veterans' Foundation. Ranking high on the scale for veterans organizations, it focused on helping veterans and their families enduring a crisis or having a critical need.

As always, food and non-alcoholic drinks were available at no charge to everyone who attended, assuring that most of Chelsea was here. On the beach, in the sun, enjoying the afternoon and evening.

Donation jars had been set all over town in June, and today, jars were available at every food and drink station in the event area.

Annie carried a cloth satchel. She walked through the event area emptying donation jars. She had several stops to make, and every tent was busy.

She waved at Felicity as she emptied the jar at the wrap tent. While she was at it, she picked up a chicken, mango and black bean wrap. She took a bite and said, "This is great!"

"That one was Trudie's idea. She wanted to add a little Jamaica to the party."

"What else do you have, I mean, besides the make-it-yourself bar?"

"Pre-made, we have the very good but too boring for me ham and cheese, turkey and cranberry, and chicken bacon ranch. I also made roasted sweet potato with pesto and lentil with tahini."

"This seems to be a popular tent."

"We've had to go back to the Café a couple of times for supplies. I think we'll have to close it before the evening is over. Well, we'll keep it open for the free drinks."

Annie left with the cash and headed for the next tent. As she emptied the jar, she took a deep breath, inhaling the aroma of grilled beef, pork, chicken and vegetables. Henrie stood at the grill, tending to the skewers passed to him by Hilly.

"This smells like heaven, Henrie. It looks like you have supervisors."

Henrie smiled. "As you know, Kali and Ko cannot resist a block party, but they are still most comfortable near the people they love. And you move too quickly."

"I'm happy they love you. You keep them safe."

Kali and Ko talked to her, both at the same time, with strident meows and ick icks. Annie looked first at one, then another, back and forth. She both enjoyed their signature talking over one another and wondered what they tried to tell her.

She took a stab. "I know it's hot. You stay here in the tent. Get in front of that fan if you have to, but you know this is the best place. Henrie has food here. There's nothing waiting for you at the Inn."

Kali and Ko looked at one another, turned and walked to the corner. They sat with their backs to the crowd, facing a fan, heads up to get a breeze on their necks and chests.

"Nail on the head," said Henrie.

At the next tent, Annie grabbed a ham salad sandwich on an onion croissant. It was Isabel's famous Mexican take on the picnic staple, with chopped onions and jalapenos and a touch of mango juice in the mayo.

""Marvelous. I'd ask for the recipe, but it's always easier to get the real thing from you."

"That's what Carlos says. Hey, have you seen Tillie or Mr. Bean out there?"

"Last time I saw them, they were on the bandstand, helping Ramon pick out music."

"Ramon picked this?"

Annie listened. It was definitely not Ramon's style. It was hardcore country.

"Yep. He promised to pick something for everyone. At least until his band starts to play."

Isabel laughed. She had finished refilling the cold fried chicken and now added paper containers of picnic deli salads to the refrigerated case.

"What do you have there?"

"American picnic salads, you know, pasta, fruit, potato, cole slaw, three bean."

"Cold fried chicken is all you need for a picnic."

"Again, that's what Carlos says."

"His tent is my next stop. I'm thinkin' truffles."

Annie dumped the donation jar from the dessert tent into her satchel and walked slowly in front of the counter. Carlos, noting her intense stare, said, "Want a tour?"

"Yes. What are these star-shaped things?"

"Hand pies. Like those. . .well I'll keep my opinions to myself. . .poptarts. These have more filling than crust, but it's the same principle. Easy to carry in your hand. I've got apple, blackberry, cherry and raspberry. And these paper cups have cheesecake. Key lime, raspberry and lemon."

"They look great, but I've already put on a couple of pounds. And you have fruit kabobs and cookies." Annie continued to peruse the counter. "Where are the truffles?"

"In that covered cooler in the corner. We're trying to keep them from melting."

"Did Jerry bring the Italian ones?"

"Not today. The featured truffles are these green ones."

"What are they?"

"Colored white chocolate, and look inside."

Carlos cut one open to reveal a pink filling. "Watermelon flavor, with chocolate chips as seeds."

Annie grimaced. "I know I should like everything Jerry makes, but, really? I have never taken to watermelon, and I can't imagine it with chocolate."

Carlos handed her one of the halves. "Try it."

Annie took a bite, managed to swallow it, and said, "Pass. What else do you have?"

"Dark chocolate cashew, milk chocolate raspberry, and dark and milk chocolate with peanut butter."

Annie sighed. "I can't. . .I can't. . .I can't. . .I shouldn't. . .I won't. . .Well. . .maybe one of the cashew ones."

Pete and Ray had the heavy duty of the day. They had to sit at the bar of the beer, wine and cocktails tent to make sure no one under the age of twenty one entered.

At least, that's what they told everyone who asked.

It seemed reasonable.

Ray told George, "Don't overserve me. We're going out on the lake tonight."

"Gonna watch the fireworks from there?"

"Yes, we are. We'll watch the fireworks, have a little wine, enjoy the breeze."

George had at least twenty types of IPAs on ice in the tent. He gave one to Ray and said, "Then all you'll get from me is beer. And not that much. I know what can happen when people get on that boat drunk."

"I'll have a designated pilot with me."

"Who?"

"Chris. He's not drinking today. Hey, have I said thank you?"

"For what?"

"For not drinking, for helping keep people safe, for getting us back to the harbor?"

"No, you haven't. At least, not since yesterday. I think you need. . ." George looked up and right, "at least five more days, and then you will have said it enough."

Pete said, "Hey, bartender. Dry over here! One of the same, please!"

George handed a beer over the counter. "Seen Jeff today?"

"Yep. We went to the hospital this morning. He'll be released Monday."

"Wow. Two weeks. He must have been beaten pretty badly."

"He was. Broken jaw, cracked ribs, punctured lung, ruptured spleen, broken fingers. And a nasty knock on the head. The doc said that came first. Jeff doesn't remember, but it appears he got hit on the head first, turned and tried to fight him off. Eventually the head wound took him down. And the rest of it was done when Hank thought he had kicked him to death."

"Somehow that information isn't getting out. This is the first I've heard it. I did hear, though, that Chris is beating himself up pretty badly."

"He is, but he shouldn't be. There's no way he could have known. I should be the one beating myself."

"Nobody knew. Hey, how much cash did he have? I've heard wild amounts, anywhere from one to one hundred million."

Pete laughed. "He had five million in cash, another ten in bearer bonds, passports and driver licenses in different names from several states. I wonder who pushed that rumor up to one hundred."

"I just said that now, to push you into giving me the real deal."

"You lied?"

"Bartender trick."

Janet found Annie at the bandstand. "I wanted to thank you for the info on the cats. I have pictures."

"Oooh! Show me!"

"Here's Spooky. She won't let me get close, but she eats the food I put out." Janet turned her cellphone around to show the black momma kitty from a distance in several shots. She was in the grape arbor, slipping into a barn, sitting in the sun and supervising her children as they ate.

"And the kittens are all over the place. Here are Bull's Eye and Half Track. They come to the deck all the time. I was afraid Simon would want them to come in, or that he would want to go out. So far, though, he's staying territorial."

"What about the boy?"

"Here he is. We named him Marmalade. He's a momma's boy. He came to the deck once that we know of. Usually, he sticks to the barns and the fields."

Annie felt a soft presence at her ankles. "Tiger Lily, do you want to see the pictures?"

Tiger Lily jumped to Annie's lap and watched as she scrolled through the photos again. She touched one showing the momma kitty.

"Janet named her Spooky. See? She looks pretty good, doesn't she? Let's look at the kittens again."

She stopped at the photo of the two girls. "This one, with the black eye, is named Bull's Eye. This one, with the striking face, is called Half Track."

Annie scrolled to one more picture. "This is the boy. His name is Marmalade."

Tiger Lily looked up at Annie, gave a soft mew and jumped down.

Janet laughed. "She wants to know everything, doesn't she?"

Boone dropped the two chairs to the sand by the water's edge. He sat in one, Pastor Teresa in the other. She said, "I kind of like babysitting duty. It's easier than serving food or drinks."

"Or playing kids games."

"Or helping with the surveys."

They settled into their duties, accepting a lick here or a giving a pet there. All part of the duty. The companions were given instructions to stay close.

While they watched the companions play, Teresa said, "The little ones aren't here yet, but the cats that belong to Georgia are going to come live with me. This is practice for me."

She got serious. "What do you hear from Gene?"

Boone was silent for a few seconds. "He left. Tried it for a full week, but that second Monday, he didn't show up for work. When they went to the apartment, he was gone."

"Where'd he go?"

"If I were to guess, I'd say he hitched a ride to New York."

"Did he take anything?"

"He took the duffel with the clothes and personal things we gave him, but he left the Bible and at least half the cash."

"He left the Bible?"

"Made his bed, cleaned up the bathroom and kitchenette, put the Bible, with the cash underneath, on the kitchen table."

"You gave it a shot."

"It's tough. I understand it. Kind of. I heard from Wyatt. You know, he planned to take Harper back to New York, drop him off, never see him again, if that's what Harper wanted."

"They didn't leave together? I thought Annie said she saw them get in the car."

"They did. Stopped outside Pittsburg for the night. When Wyatt got up, Harper was gone. No note."

"So he'll never see his dad again."

"But he knows his dad is at peace with his life."

Cyril raced Jock up the beach and back. They didn't go far. Their humans had been specific. They were not to leave the sight of Boone and Teresa.

It wasn't that the big dogs couldn't handle themselves, but the smaller cats needed a level of protection. A shark could appear at any moment.

This was one area in which Cyril wasn't wise. He was a land-locked Marine's dog. He didn't know sharks would not be found in a Great Lake.

Fiamma and Sis watched as the boys raced. Sis said, *"I like the water, but I've not gotten used to running in sand."*

"I try not to. It gets into my mats and locks and I can't get rid of it."

Tillie trotted over to join them. *"You aren't racing?"*

"No," said Sis. *"We're ladies."*

"Well, I guess I am, too. Good. I'd never be able to keep up."

"What were you doing over there?"

"That little Jones boy dug some gutters into the sand. He made it like a maze, and I was trying to find my way around without having to jump over a barrier."

"Did you find your way?"

"No. I kept running into barriers. If you want to know the truth, I think he cheated and put barriers everywhere."

Sis laughed. It felt good to laugh with the girls. She should try to do this more often. She looked over at the cats. The younger ones dabbled in the water, but the older ones stood watch. Except for Tiger Lily. She was just now trotting over to the group of older cats: Little Socks, Simon Finnegan and Oscar McMurphy.

Tiger Lily sat next to Little Socks, who couldn't contain her laughter. *"What's up?"*

"Look at Mo and Moriah. They're helping that kid build a sand castle."

"What's so funny about that?"

"With their long hair? They'll be dropping sand all over the place for a week!"

"Where's Honey Bear? He and Claire might have the same trouble."

"No. They found a towel. See? Over there by Teresa. They begged and begged until she finally put her towel down."

"At least she tried to communicate."

"She did pretty good, too."

Tiger Lily called out, *"Mr. Bean! Sassy Pants! Get out of the water!"*

They stuck out their tongues, but they got out of the water. Until Speckles and Daryll showed up. The four of them cavorted dangerously near the over-their-heads level. At least when the waves came in.

Tiger Lily had just gotten up to drag them out when she noticed Cyril and Jock. They trotted to the cats and herded them away from the water's edge.

"Phew!" said Tiger Lily. *"I'm going to tell them to get back with Teresa or go find Mommy."*

Little Socks said, *"Why don't we try something else?"*

"What?"

"Why don't we call them over to the towel?"

"Why?"

"I don't know. Do you have a report? Can we make it a meeting and get them up to safety?"

"Good idea."

Simon Finnegan said, *"Maybe they'll respond better to us. It would be less like a summons and more like a fun thing."*

"Another good idea."

Tiger Lily and Little Socks walked to the towel, calling to Mo and Moriah as they walked. Soon, Teresa and Boone were witness to one of the largest detective gatherings Chelsea had seen. Five of Annie's, because Kali and Ko were still with Henrie, three from across The Avenue, Honey Bear and his precious Claire, and the small nanny kitties who lived in the same neighborhood as Honey Bear.

Tiger Lily asked if anyone had a report. Mo trilled several times. Sassy Pants was the only translator available.

"He sez we duzn't give reports cuz we knows all dat happened already."

Little Socks said, *"But we could have learned about new things."*

Moriah said, *"I think all the crime is done for now. Maybe until the Inn gets more guests."*

Tiger Lily and Little Socks drew tall at the same time. Mr. Bean said, *"You can't blame all the crime in town on the Inn. The worst one this month had nothing to do with us."*

"You're right. I'm sorry."

Tiger Lily said, *"That's okay. You're still new. I have something."*

"What?" asked Simon Finnegan.

"I saw pictures of the momma kitty and her baby. You know how she said her name was Scooter? Janet and Brian didn't understand her. They named her Spooky."

"Well, she is kind of spooky looking," said Little Socks.

Tiger Lily continued. *"She stays away from the house and winery, but she looks good. She's eating; she has several places to run and be safe."*

Mr. Bean asked, *"What about that boy kitty?"*

"His name is Marmalade."

"*Like the orange jelly?*"

"*Yes. And he looks good, too. Janet says he doesn't come to the house much, but the two girls do.*"

"*What are their names?*"

"*Bull's Eye and Half Track.*"

"*So the one with the black eye is Bull's Eye?*"

"*And the half black face one is Half Track?*"

"*Yes.*"

"*Great names. Does Simon like them?*"

"*Kinda not,*" said Tiger Lily, "*but that's okay. They won't come into the house.*"

"*But you said. . .*"

"*I'm sorry. I wasn't clear. They come to the deck, but they don't go in the house.*"

Daryll said, "*We have news?*" Daryll couldn't speak unless he said each sentence as a question.

"*Please tell us,*" said Tiger Lily.

"*You see Teresa here?*"

"*Of course,*" said Little Socks.

"*Well, this is good news? And bad?*"

"*What?*" asked Mr. Bean. "*Is she sick?*"

"*No,*" said Speckles. "*We're gonna come live with her.*"

The cats were speechless. Speckles had been the first nanny kitty – except for Kali and Ko – for Little Fred. Georgia, the head cook at Mo's, and a valued member of the team for other reasons, had come to town as a single mother.

Henrie, being Henrie, who never involved himself in the lives of others, found her a home, a job, and day care for Little Fred. He was also instrumental in the discovery that a cat's tail did wonders to calm the baby.

Since Kali and Ko could not move into her new home, Speckles was adopted from the shelter. Daryll was later rescued by the cats and Annie, and he became nanny kitty number two.

Tiger Lily finally asked, *"Why?"*

Speckles answered. *"Little Fred developed a lergy to us."*

"What?"

"A lergy?" said Daryll.

The cats pondered this a while. Finally, Sassy Pants said, *"A allergy?"*

"That's it!"

Tiger Lily was as amazed that Sassy Pants came up with the correct word as she was with the situation.

"What does that mean?" asked Mr. Bean.

"She sneezes all the time? And coughs?"

"And she can't breathe."

Little Socks asked, *"How's she going to get along without you?"*

Speckles looked at the sand. *"She hasn't held our tails for a long time. Georgia and Martha won't let her."*

"She still loves us? But she's used to not holding our tails?"

"Well," said Tiger Lily, *"you'll still have a fur-ever home, and you'll be on The Avenue."*

"Yeah," said Moriah. *"You'll be full-fledged detectives!"*

The cats continued, not noticing the humans. Boone had drawn his chair around so he could see what happened on the other side of Teresa. They looked at one another in wonder as the cats clearly held a corporate meeting.

Laila waved Annie to her circle of chairs. "Come on, Annie. The kids are with their friends and I'm just sitting here. Not that I need a tan."

Laila was Pakistani. She didn't need a tan.

Annie sat and opened her cooler. "I hoped I would find you. Want a glass?" She offered a bottle of chilled pinot Grigio.

"Absolutely. What's up?"

"Why does something have to be up?"

"You have 'that look.'"

"Am I so predictable?"

"You are, and you have had a harrowing experience. One you have not taken the time to confide in me. Not that I don't know all the details, of course."

"Of course."

"So, tell me. What's up? Nightmares? Trouble getting your head around it?"

"I've recovered. I'm pretty sure I've recovered. No. I've completely recovered. Tiger Lily has pronounced me one hundred percent emotionally healthy. She no longer follows me everywhere."

"But?"

"Neither I nor Tiger Lily have pronounced Chris one hundred percent. And if I am reading the signs correctly, neither has Sis."

"I hear he's beating himself up."

"There. That's what I need. No one is talking to me about what they hear or know about Chris. Tell me."

"He's blaming himself. If he hadn't left Jeff. If he had said the word 'boxes' to you and told you he was getting them. If he had predicted Hank's money was at the office. If he had been a man, had bigger round things."

"What?"

"That last part was me, extrapolating."

"Okay. So, I kind of understand, but why did he think he could mind-read all of that?"

"Because he, like you, believes he can mind-read you. And, I guess, by extension, that he should have done the same with Jeff. Or Hank. I don't understand those things. But you, I understand. Because I know you, I see that he thought he should know what was happening with you."

"That's just crazy."

"Yeah. What are you going to do about it?"

"I'm going to have to confront him."

"You. Mind-reading you. Silent you. You, the one that doesn't talk to him, because you both understand one another so well."

"Well...yeah. What else would I do?"

"Dance."

Chris carried a box filled with every sandwich, wrap, kabob and salad that could be had on the beach. Ian walked with him, a large vinyl cooler with bottles of water slung over his shoulder.

"Think we have enough food?" asked Chris.

"No. Have you ever fed teenagers?"

Ian was the community's ultimate volunteer. Employed at the local bank, he worked at least thirty hours a week coordinating community events and working with area teens.

He knew about teens and their eating habits.

Chris said, "Nope. Just cats and a dog. They don't eat this much."

"These kids had breakfast to eat their collective parents out of house and home, ran a half marathon, ate lunch, courtesy of the marathon committee, and more than you and I would eat in a day, have worked all afternoon on their volunteer project, and now it's time to eat again."

"I get the point. I'll drop the food off and head back for more."

"Good idea."

At the project tent, Chris put the box of food on a table and backed away as it was attacked by what must have been ninety teenagers. Or ten. It could have been ten.

He looked around. "So what's all this?"

Ian said, "We developed a survey. We put it online, administered it to teachers and staff at the school, sent it to church with all the teens in the group that go to one, and we've been walking around today, stopping every adult that will talk to us. These are the results so far."

Chris walked over to the displays. They held title cards. Under an over-arching title of "services needed" were cards that stated "shelter," "food," "jobs," "medical," and "mental/emotional." The same cards were under another section titled "willing to provide."

"So, what does this mean?"

"We've tabulated all of the surveys to date, and now we're adding today's results. These index cards move up with the number of people who say either they perceive a need and/or they are willing to provide something to meet that need."

"I see there are more perceived needs than there is a willingness to meet the needs. That isn't good."

"It isn't necessarily bad, either. As with all surveys, we need to take the results and put them into context."

"What context?"

"Well, for example, see how high the card is on a need for shelter? My guess is, if we take the town of Chelsea and count all active duty service members, veterans, and their families, we won't find enough people to equal the need that is identified. So, the willingness to meet the need may not be as low as it appears."

"And you'll do what with the information? Once it's in context, I mean."

"We'll publish it, make the circuit of local service clubs and organizations, government bodies. Hopefully shake loose a few people to do something."

"The kids will do this?"

"It's part of the deal. To participate in my training, be involved in a project. Involvement is from start to finish."

"You'll need adults at some point, right? Let me know what and when."

Chris turned around. "Box is empty. I'll be back with more."

Fiamma jumped to Ramon's chest and reached to give him a kiss. He was the best!

She trotted beside Jock and Ray, ecstatic. She would be out on the lake! On the boat! With Jock, Cyril and her new friend Sis. It would be great!

At The Escape, Ray let the dogs up and followed. "Chris, are we ready?"

"Ready. Everyone on board?"

"We are. Fiamma got Daddy's permission."

The sun was at least an hour away from setting. It was a beautiful end to a beautiful day. Chris engineered a gentle escape from the harbor while Annie, Janet and Cheryl arranged furniture on deck. Deck chairs, side tables, coolers with beer, chillers with wine, and a selection of crackers, cheese, kabobs and truffles were arranged to be within easy reach of the humans.

The canines were given a soft blanket, food and water on the foredeck. Sis joined Chris "up top," as Jock had taught her to say. She worried about Chris and wanted him to know she was there.

Chris brought the yacht to a halt. He dropped anchor and considered staying right where he was. Up top. Away from his friends. He looked at the foredeck and noticed three big dogs looking at up them.

"Get down there, Sis. Your friends are waiting for you."

Sis looked up, clearly not moving.

"I'm fine, girl. Get down there. Go on.

She left, not without a few looks back.

Chris stayed for a minute longer. Well, they were his friends, after all. They didn't blame him. In his heart, he knew he was the only one passing blame. But it was his fault. He should have known. He. Should. Have. Known.

Pete handed a bottle of water to Chris as he joined the group. Pete had a few personal bruises of his own. He should have known. He shouldn't have let Jeff go into that office alone. But Jeff was a big boy with many years of FBI experience.

He could cover it up better than Chris, though, because he had many years as a military police officer and several as Chief.

Bluster. That's what it took. He blustered a bit now.

"Hank had several identities in that bag, and lots of money. It's the only reason he came back. He was keeping almost everything in cash and bearer bonds. Nothing in banks. Nothing that could be tracked."

Cheryl asked, "What did the FBI find on those computer searches?"

"They figured out how he made most of his money. He was trafficking in defense security passwords and, as a sideline, selling secure data from our armed services."

"What?" asked Ray. "How could that nitwit figure out that stuff?"

"Had to do with connections he made in the Army. Apparently some higher-ups were pleased that he took care of that reporter. They've been paying him off and sending him business ever since."

"What in heaven's name. . ." started Cheryl. ". . .He's been doing this ever since he was in the Army? Wasn't he in the Gulf War?"

"Yes. He went there as a Reserve Officer. He served as regular Army before that. Came home to Chelsea, started his upward track as a scumbag, and, I don't know, was probably making money from his Army buddies all along."

"So did you ever find out, Annie, what he meant about your dad?"

Pete looked over at Annie, sitting next to Chris, her hand on top of his arm. Annie said, "Pete, why don't you tell them."

"Sure." He looked back toward Ray and Cheryl. "Part of it was political. Hank came back and expected to be a big fish in a small pond. Vic, Annie's dad, already held a lot of power. He didn't like Hank, and he continued to win every election. When business opportunities came up, people trusted Vic. They turned to Vic all the time, leaving Hank in the cold."

"But he always had money."

"Which is why I think he was getting money from his buddies before the Gulf War. The FBI is digging. It will be up to them to find it. The big thing is that we have him cold on the murders here in Chelsea, including a deathbed identification. The FBI can tie him to recent criminal activity. He'll never get out. He'll never be back."

"But if he had money already, why was he so angry with Annie?"

Annie spoke up at this. "Because he's crazy. He's a criminal, a sociopath, and a psychopath."

Cyril looked at Sis. *"He'll be okay. Really."*

Sis looked at the blanket. *"Are you sure? He's awfully sad."*

Cyril said, *"It wasn't his fault. Pete didn't know Hank was coming back to town until he was already back, and Pete was talking to all kinds of people about it."*

"I've heard them talking about it. He's heard it, too, but I don't think he believes it. Not yet."

"He will. Annie will help him."

Fiamma said, *"Tell me what happened."*

Sis looked at Fiamma. *"Let me tell you about Cyril and how brave he was."*

Jock snorted.

Fiamma said, *"Was he as brave as Jock? When he saved everyone on The Escape?"*

"He was! They made Chris and I go to the laundromat, but I saw everything."

"What did you see?" asked Fiamma.

"Well, it was Hank again, but this time, he was on dry land. He was at his office, and he had hurt Jeff Bennett. We didn't know it at the time. All we knew at the time was that he had Annie and was holding a gun to her head."

"No!"

Jock rolled over and played dead.

"Yes! Pete was there, helping Cyril, and Cyril got really low. He sneaked up on Hank, slow, and Hank didn't see him. When he got close enough, Cyril jumped and grabbed him. He got Annie free, got the gun out of his hand, and put him in handcuffs!"

Jock jumped up and went to help Ray drink a beer.

Cyril laughed. He would never have embellished the story, but hearing it told this way was priceless.

Fiamma and Sis shared a look. This was fun!

In the middle of the fireworks, Annie stood. She took Chris's hand and pulled, just a bit. He rose to follow her, not looking up. She led him to the galley, down the steps and inside.

She turned and faced him, placing herself in a dance stance. She placed his hands on her waist. She put both of hers on his shoulders. He didn't look up.

"Chris, look at me."

Finally, he looked up.

"The music is in our heads, remember? We do this all the time. I dance with you, you dance with me. We're one and the same."

Chris closed his eyes, wrapped his arms around her, leaned forward, put his forehead to hers, and they danced. Slowly. They wouldn't move around the room tonight. They wouldn't twirl. They would sway. Softly. Slowly. In rhythm to the music only they could hear.

The cats had already left the bed and were asleep in various places around the apartment. Sis slept on one side of Chris, one side of a triple spoon. Annie was the other side.

Tiger Lily crawled on Mommy's hip until she noticed a space that would work just fine. She pushed a little here, a little there, and snuggled in, curling into Annie's stomach and Chris's lower back.

She purred herself to sleep. In her dreams, she was a fire dragon, a nice one like Mommy, coming to protect her friends and family from all danger.

Thank You For Reading!

The family of cats and the author hope you enjoyed reading this book as much as we enjoyed writing it!

About The Author

Kathleen Thompson was raised on a small family farm in Indiana. She has an undergraduate degree in Sociology from Manchester College (now Manchester University) and an MBA from Indiana University South Bend.

In a variety of towns and circumstances, she served as a probation officer, parole agent and juvenile residential counselor before moving into administrative, marketing and fund raising positions in human service organizations. Ms. Thompson took a break from human services for seven years to own and operate a bar and restaurant. Let's be honest; that's another type of human service.

While making plans to return to her rural roots, Kathi and her mother discovered an injured kitten at the family farm. The kitten, whose face was a mass of injuries, decided to make Kathi her guardian. She wrapped herself around an ankle, purred like a V8 engine, and wouldn't let go.

Against the advice of her mother, Kathi took the kitten home and to a veterinarian. The vet diagnosed road burn serious enough to take all the fur from the left side of her face, and the kitten – Tiger Lily – eventually healed and took a huge piece of Kathi's heart.

Tiger Lily was joined by the rest, rescue kitties, all: Little Socks (thank you, Aunt Mary); Kali, Ko and Mo (thank you, Connie); Sassy Pants (thank you, Ant Sherwy); and Mr. Bean (thank you, Pulaski Animal Center). Recent arrivals Speckles (thank you, Tennille) and Moriah (thank you again, Pulaski Animal Center) have joined the cast but will not live at the Inn.

Tiger Lily's Café rattled around in Kathi's brain – there isn't much else up there – for all of the years since, sometimes as an actual café and sometimes as a book. It was less expensive to write the book.

Connect with Kathi and her family of cats at their website: www.tigerlilyscafe.com, or find them on Facebook: www.facebook.com/tigerlilyscafemysteries.

Find us on the web: www.tigerlilyscafe.com

Find us on Facebook: Tiger Lily's Café, A Mystery Series by Kathleen Thompson

Text to join: Emails are sent every two weeks. You can opt out at any time. LILYSCAFE to 22828 (You may also sign up for the emails from the website.)

Kathleen Thompson

www.ingramcontent.com/pod-product-compliance
Lightning Source LLC
Chambersburg PA
CBHW062010170626
46813CB00001B/95